"Nickel for your thoughts."

The Ferris wheel had moved, and suddenly Rachel and Lucas were way above the noise and clamor. Lucas put his arms around her and moved closer. Rachel's skin tingled with sensation, and she welcomed his strength by tucking her face against his chest. She listened to the strong, steady beat of his heart. He was solid and real, yet tender and caring.

"I was looking at the stars," she confessed. "We're so high I felt as if I could reach out and pluck one. I feel like I'm in heaven."

"The stars are so close I wish I could give you one to take home, so you'd have something to remember this night."

Rachel pulled away and looked into his earnest face. "I don't need a star to remember tonight," she assured him. "I'll always remember it."

Her heart seemed to leap into overdrive to pound against her chest. In one night, in one moment of desire, her defenses, so carefully erected during the past two years, were crumbling.

Christmas has always been one of my favorite holidays. I love the hustle and bustle of the season: decorating the tree, gathering with the family, shopping for those special gifts, anticipating my own presents, attending worship services at church. But Christmas became even more special for me in 1983. On December 14 that year, my husband entered the hospital for an arteriogram. This was not unexpected. Five years earlier Paul had suffered a massive heart attack; later he'd suffered cardiac arrest and gone into a coma while exercising at a health club. He fully recovered and we learned to live with heart disease. Still, we were not prepared for the results of the arteriogram. One of Paul's arteries was completely closed, the second was ninety-five percent closed, the third eighty-five percent. Surgery was scheduled immediately.

That Christmas I didn't give thought to decorating a tree or buying and exchanging gifts. My family had only one desire. My identical twin sons Michael and Malcolm wanted their father to live. I wanted my dearest friend and husband of twenty years to live. God granted our prayer. On Christmas Eve Paul was released from the hospital and on Christmas Day we celebrated the miracle of life.

—Emma Merritt

Wish Upon a Star
Emma Merritt

Harlequin Books

TORONTO • NEW YORK • LONDON
AMSTERDAM • PARIS • SYDNEY • HAMBURG
STOCKHOLM • ATHENS • TOKYO • MILAN

Published December 1988

First printing October 1988

ISBN 0-373-16276-6

Printed in U.S.A.

Chapter One

Rachel March stood beside the silver Tempo and gazed at the Texas hill country—rugged, rocky terrain that was harsh but also beautiful. Buffalo grass, cacti and wiry shrubs carpeted the valley; squat oaks and cedars clung to the rolling hills. Time and weather had gnarled the tree limbs and bent the trunks, yet the trees survived. They were as tenacious and enduring as the land itself.

The morning sun cast a warm, golden haze over the wilderness, and a gentle breeze, announcing the coming of autumn, rustled through the leaves and grass to brush against Rachel. As she unconsciously lifted a hand to tuck an errant strand of blond hair behind her ear, she heard a whinny and turned to spy a quarter horse tethered to a low-hanging limb of a nearby tree.

The bay was thick and stocky and powerful, as tough as the country around him. A shiny coat, the color of a dark copper penny, stretched over rippling muscles. As if aware of Rachel's presence, he lifted his face to stare at her. Sunlight burnished his muzzle to a high sheen. The round cheeks moved slowly as he chewed. Lazily, almost deceptively so, his bushy black tail flicked back and forth on his hindquarters. His curiosity satisfied, he snorted and tossed his head, then went back to eating.

Rachel didn't move from where she was standing the entire time the horse was looking at her. Again her eyes ran over the thick, muscled lines of the neck and square head. Totally masculine. Sheer power. Intuitively she knew this horse belonged to her client; he reflected Lucas Brand himself.

Rachel stood by the car for a moment longer, her gaze moving from the quarter horse to the barn that seemed to be an extension of the land itself. After hours of searching, she'd finally found Lucas Brand, but suddenly she was nervous; her palms were clammy. She had to make a good showing today. Her employer, Craig Maddocks, moved in the same social circle as Lucas and knew of him. So Craig had been surprised—not angry or upset, merely surprised—when he found Lucas had contacted her rather than himself about the property.

Rachel smiled. She had Rose Gerwood, a satisfied client, to thank. Ecstatic when Rachel sold her estate in Terrell Hills well above the price she had thought she would receive, the sixty-year-old widow became Rachel's friend for life. Rachel thought Rose was surely her guardian angel. Invited to a party Rose gave when she moved into her new town house, Rachel met Elaine Halston. Several weeks later Elaine contacted Rachel about selling her three-thousand-acre ranch in Kerrville. She could sell the property herself, the woman admitted to Rachel, but didn't want to be bothered. Her husband was terminally ill with cancer, and she had other things on her mind. When Rose learned about the listing, she called Lucas and gave him Rachel's phone number.

Rachel closed the door of the car and moved to the barn. Ducking under one of the weathered gray doors hanging precariously on rusted hinges, she stood in a ray of sunlight that beamed through a hole in the roof. Birds' nests covered the walls, and cobwebs shimmered like delicate lace in the breeze. On days like today Rachel was especially glad that she was a real estate agent and wasn't restricted to a desk. She loved the freedom her job allowed.

At the same time, she felt a sense of trepidation that was a contradiction to all she desired careerwise. Ever since she'd started working for the Greater Southwest Real Estate Brokers eighteen months ago, she had wanted to move into commercial sales. Now was her chance. Lucas Brand was in the market to buy thousands of acres of ranch land, and he had the wherewithal to do so.

Though Rachel earned her living by selling property, and had just the one Brand was interested in purchasing, she was at war with herself; she didn't want to sell it to him. She despised him and everything he represented: a wealthy attorney turned entrepreneur who earned his living by commercially exploiting the land, and who behind the scenes manipulated the politics and economics of the state.

For the past five years since the death of his wife, Lucas Brand had apparently vied for and won center stage on the social scene. His public appearances, always covered by local television and newspapers, were many, and always he was accompanied by a dazzling socialite. Rachel surmised that he was carefully building his reputation as Texas playboy of the decade! But she couldn't really fault him for that, could she? He dated women who were around his own age. Still . . .

During the hour's drive from San Antonio to the Lucky Brand Ranch outside New Braunfels, Rachel had rehearsed her introduction to Lucas time and time again, but so far nothing was going according to the mental script she had written. Rather than meeting her at his home at the most unusual hour of 6:00 a.m., as had been previously arranged at his insistence, he was riding the range in search of a wayward cow and its owner—a little girl of ten—so the housekeeper had said. Rachel sighed. Next time she'd have to make sure she wrote out the scenario and sent her client a copy. Then she wouldn't spend two hours waiting in a den for him and another hour driving across the wilderness he called his ranch.

A low, desperate moo echoed through the barn and was followed by a man's shout, gentle yet firm. "Don't stand there gaping. Get over here and help me."

The command galvanized Rachel into action. Glad of the walking shoes she had donned in anticipation of her jaunts through several of the ranch properties she had listed, she raced into the building, looking to the right and left.

"Well, get a move on!"

From the very back of the barn Rachel heard the swish and thud as a body landed in a pallet of thick straw; she heard the repeated lowing of a cow. Dust particles, dancing in the shaft of golden sunlight that poured into the room, served as a compass to guide Rachel to the voice.

"I'm moving as fast as I can, Lucas," a child answered. "And I'm not gaping. I'm watching."

Rachel's gait slowed to a walk, and her accelerated heartbeat returned to normal. She rounded the stall to see a small girl and her client crouching over a cow.

"Well, Mandy," he said, "I think Worthy has decided to have her calf. Leave it to her to choose this deserted old barn on the far end of the ranch."

"Oh, no!" Mandy turned her small head so quickly that the straw hat fell off and two thick, black braids flew through the air. "You don't mean it!"

"Yep, I reckon I do."

Rachel's gaze shifted from the jean-clad girl to the man. *So this is my prospective buyer,* she thought, her eyes carefully moving from the gray Stetson, western shirt and faded jeans to the worn boots. Rachel was taken aback. This wasn't the grasping, power-hungry entrepreneur whom she had expected to meet. This man was gentle and kind. He reminded her of the cowboy hero in the old B movies.

His attention concentrated on Worthy, Lucas said, "Don't worry, ole girl. Miss Amanda and I are going to take care of you."

Mandy laid her freckled face against the cow's neck and lovingly chided, "Silly cow! You should know better than to stray from the big barn." Then the child looked at Lucas, her brown eyes rounded with apprehension. "How are we going to get her back to the big barn?"

"We're not. Worthy's just going to have her calf out here in the wild blue yonder with me as her doctor and you as her nurse."

Lucas's confidence reassured Rachel, but not Mandy.

"You're not a vet, Lucas!" Panic caused Mandy's voice to rise.

"Well—" his tone was light, almost teasing, yet his manner was serious "—that's true, Mandy, so I guess Worthy will just have to settle for having a midwife. That's what she gets for wandering off."

Rachel's gaze was riveted to Lucas Brand. He looked exactly like the glossy color photograph she'd seen of him in the *Texas Monthly* in an interview done by Michelle Krier at the beginning of the oil crunch. Quiet, calm, and authoritative, the author had described him. A man accustomed to allaying fears and anxieties when emergencies and unexpected situations arose. Evidently he was a man to take the bull by the horns. Rachel grinned, her eyes returning to the cow. Well, Worthy wasn't a bull, but the sentiment was the same... wasn't it?

"Perhaps I can help you," she offered and pushed around the stall gate into full view.

In synchronized movement two heads swung in Rachel's direction, and two sets of eyes moved up and down her immaculate frame.

Lucas was so startled he couldn't speak. Rachel was a vision of loveliness. She was tall and slender. Shoulder-length blond hair framed a face that was one glorious smile and two sparkling green eyes. She looked to be in her mid-to-late thirties. Down went the curious gaze from the tailored white blouse to the black skirt. His perusal would have stopped there, but shapely legs compelled further review. His eyes slowly traveled their length to the practical loafers she wore.

When neither child nor man spoke, Rachel said, "I'd like to be of assistance if I may."

"Thanks for the offer," Lucas finally murmured, his eyes reluctantly returning up the shapely legs past the skirt and blouse to those gorgeous eyes. "But you hardly look like a midwife."

His gray eyes, warm and friendly, were the most beautiful that Rachel had ever seen. She couldn't have broken away from his gaze, even had she wanted to. "I'm not," she answered. "And I must say, you're not quite what I expected a midwife to be, either. Not meaning to be sexist, but somehow I always seem to associate a woman with the term.''

Lucas laughed softly, the sound deep and warm. "I've never heard of a midhusband. Reckon that's what I'd come nearer to being, ma'am?''

Rachel wasn't sure what Lucas would come nearer to being, but the images that flashed through her mind were at variance with what she'd heard and read about him. Her gaze slid past the sunlight-burnished blue-black hair that framed his rugged face to the sensuous lips...the nose that looked as if it had been broken...to the gentle, teasing gray eyes that seemed to know exactly what she was thinking.

Hiding her discomfort at such a thought, Rachel said, "You'll come nearer to knowing what you are than I. But I do know this: I have my car, and I could easily and quickly go for help.''

Lucas didn't get off his knees, but straightened up and pushed his hat farther back on his forehead. Then he dropped his hand, resting the palm lightly on his thigh. Gazing at her out of curious eyes, he said, "How come you're out here? This is a pretty deserted part of the ranch and definitely off the beaten path. You're not lost, are you?''

Rachel shook her head. "I'm Rachel March, your 6:00 a.m. appointment.''

Lucas mouthed a silent "Damn!'' and rubbed his arm across his forehead. In his anxiety to find Mandy and her gadabout cow he'd forgotten the meeting—the six o'clock appointment he'd insisted on because of other commitments. He turned his wrist and looked at his watch. Nine-thirty! Unable to believe that it was already midmorning, he jerked his head up and stared at Rachel. "I'm sorry. I had no idea it was this late.''

"When you asked me to meet you this early, I wondered what kind of commitments you had," Rachel said. "Now I know. However, I'll confess when I was sitting in your den waiting for you I didn't, and the longer I waited the more convinced I became that I'd made a mistake about the time I was to meet you. You know the grapevine syndrome: my secretary said that your secretary said that you said... I finally persuaded your housekeeper to give me directions out here."

Lucas shook his head and laughed apologetically. "No, Ms. March—" his eyes automatically sought her left hand, to find it ringless "—you didn't make a mistake. I set the meeting up for 6:00 a.m. because I wanted to see as much property today as I could, and at that time I assure you I had no idea that I'd be delivering a calf. I have a flight scheduled for departure early this afternoon, and this morning was the only time I had available. I'll admit I could have waited until I returned from New York, but I wanted to see the property before I left." Those beautiful gray eyes, filled with repentance, settled on her face. The laughter lines at the corner of his mouth and eyes softened into a smile. "I can fully understand how you felt. Appointments at six o'clock in the morning are unusual. I apologize for any inconvenience you've incurred."

As Rachel gazed into the mesmeric eyes, she realized she would be hard pressed to remain angry at Lucas Brand for long—no matter whether she had cause or not. Michelle Krier was right: Lucas Brand was charismatic. Rachel could well understand his success as a criminal attorney. With those eyes he could read the very soul of a person.

"When one has three children," she found herself saying, "who range in age from six to sixteen and who must be wakened, fed and gotten off to school, six o'clock appointments are more than inconvenient, Mr. Brand; they verge on insanity. It is Lucas Brand, is it not?''

"Of course!" Lucas dusted his hand down the side of his jeans, inadvertently bringing Rachel's attention to the stretch of faded denim across muscled thigh. He pushed up on his knees and extended his hand to catch hers in a firm clasp that was warm and friendly, that lasted longer than manners demanded. "I'm Lucas Brand, and I apologize for not meeting you at the appointed time and for not properly introducing myself." He released Rachel's hand and waved to the child. "This is Miss Amanda Taylor, whom we generally call Mandy, and this is her cow, Worthy. I'm not going to shoulder the responsibility for being late all by myself, Ms. March. These two have to share some of the blame."

"Hi, Ms. March." Mandy lifted her freckled face and gazed solemnly at Rachel. Her most outstanding features were two brilliant sapphire-blue eyes. "Please don't be mad at Lucas. He came to look for me and Worthy."

"Oh, I'm not mad," Rachel assured Mandy, "but I'm a little unsure of my ability as a salesperson. I've had clients be tardy or break appointments before. However, this is the first time I've been stood up for a cow."

Lucas's resonant laughter blended with Mandy's to echo through the barn and to settle warmly over Rachel. But the moment was short-lived. Worthy mooed as she tensed and jerked, then swished her tail through the air and tossed her head.

"Forgive me, Worthy," Rachel said. "I didn't mean to upset you, and I'll confess, if I'm going to be stood up I'd rather it was you than anyone or anything else I know."

Mandy laughed nervously, but Lucas only smiled. He crouched lower over Worthy, and Rachel knew without being told that Worthy was having a difficult time with her delivery. She saw the concern in Lucas's face, the anxiety in Mandy's.

"Worthy's a very jealous cow," Mandy finally said in an effort to talk away her fears. "She doesn't like being left out." Again she hunched over her pet to run loving hands over the distended belly.

"I can see that." Rachel knelt beside Mandy. "How do you think she's going to like having a baby? You know she's going to have to share the attention then."

"I've been sorta worried about that," Mandy replied, "but Lucas says it's natural for cows to have calves and for mothers to love their babies. He thinks she's gonna be all right." Mandy turned to Lucas. "She is, isn't she?"

"Yeah, baby," Lucas drawled without looking up, "this ole cow is going to be all right."

"I know she is," Mandy muttered. "Remember, Lucas, when we first brought her home?"

"I remember," Lucas said.

"Ms. March, you should have seen Worthy. Why, she was a sight for sore eyes," Mandy said.

Lucas chuckled. "I wouldn't go that far, Mandy."

"Well, Susie did."

"Sometimes I'm not too sure about Susie," Lucas teased.

"Oh, Lucas!" Childlike, Mandy momentarily forgot the seriousness of the situation and playfully jabbed her elbow into his side, but she looked at Rachel and explained, "Susie Lagustrum is my housemother. I live at the Lucky Brand Children's home. It's sorta like an orphanage. Only it's not."

"It's a small children's home." Lucas came to Mandy's rescue. "We never have more than ten or twelve in residence. Our primary purpose is to help deprived children stay out of trouble by teaching them to be responsible citizens. They don't necessarily have to be orphans, and the majority aren't. A few are."

"That's right," Mandy agreed, her head bobbing. "And each year Lucas lets us adopt one of his calves. Only this year he let us go on a buying trip with him. That's when I saw Worthy and knew I wanted her."

"At any rate," Lucas said, "she wanted you." He continued his examination of the cow but at the same time covertly studied Rachel, a habit he'd formed during his years as a criminal attorney. Not only was she beautiful, he decided, she was also a practical business-woman, appropriately dressed.

"Dugan said Worthy was born for the slaughter-house, but I couldn't let her go there."

Lucas said, "I think just maybe Ole Worthy knew how you felt 'cause she turned those doleful brown eyes on you, Mandy girl, and successfully pleaded her case. No amount of argument would dissuade you."

"None," Mandy agreed. "I didn't want a calf. I wanted Worthy."

Lucas pointed to the stall across the aisle from them and quietly said, "Mandy, get me that blanket over there."

Lucas's tone hadn't changed, but Rachel sensed the situation was approaching the crisis point. She asked, "What can I do to help?"

"Right now," he said, "just stay out of the way."

Taking the blanket from Mandy, he spread it over the straw and repositioned the cow, soothing the expectant mother with both hands and voice as he moved her.

"Looks like we won't be going anywhere today," Rachel said.

Lucas shook his head. "I doubt it."

"Do you think Worthy's going to be jealous of Ms. March?" Mandy asked anxiously.

Lucas raised his head and looked first at Worthy, then at Rachel. Understanding the child's anxiety and wanting to alleviate it as much as possible, he smiled. "I don't think so, Mandy. If you'd taken one good look at both of them, you'd know that Ms. March can't hold a candle to Worthy." When Rachel pretended to glare at him, he winked. "Why, Worthy's got four legs and Ms. March has only got two. Worthy has big ole brown eyes, and Ms. March has green ones that sparkle like spring grass coated with morning dew. And look at Worthy's ears. Why, all Ms. March's shiny gold hair covers her ears!"

Mandy giggled, and Rachel made a face at Lucas. As if Worthy understood Lucas, she turned her head, lowed, and nuzzled him. Her breathing accelerated and her body trembled.

"Mandy," Lucas said quietly, "I want you to go get some help. You were right. Worthy needs some professional care. We're going to be needing Doc Fred on this one."

Rachel correctly interpreted the seriousness in Lucas's tone, as did the child; her heart hurt when she saw Mandy's countenance fall. An animal lover and champion of the down-and-trodden, Rachel also felt Worthy tug at her heartstrings.

"I can go faster," she volunteered. "I have my car. Just tell me where—"

"It'll be quicker for Mandy to go," Lucas said. "You don't know your way around the ranch. Besides, she can

cut across country on the bay.'' He turned to the girl.
''Go to the big barn and tell Dugan what's happening.
He'll know what to do.''

''I don't want to go.'' Mandy's voice wobbled. ''Doc
Fred's in town at the fairgrounds, and by this time, Lucas, Dugan and the boys will be long gone.''

''Dugan won't be gone,'' Lucas said. ''You know as
well as I do that he's waiting for me to find you, so all of
us can go to the fairgrounds together. So scat.''

''Please, Lucas, let me stay,'' Mandy begged, tears
washing her eyes. ''I don't want to leave Worthy. She's
my cow, and she's old, Lucas, and she might die,
and—''

''I know she's your cow,'' Lucas answered in that
voice that was both firm and gentle, ''and I appreciate
your wanting to stay with her.'' He reached out and
lightly yanked one of Mandy's pigtails. ''But you'll be
helping her more if you go get Dugan. Ms. March will
help me with Worthy until you get back.''

''I'll help, Mandy,'' Rachel promised and reached out
to lay a reassuring hand on Mandy's shoulder.

Mandy, sniffling back her tears, turned her thin, ur-
chin face and stared at Rachel.

''Just tell me what to do, Mandy, and I'll do it until
you get back,'' Rachel said.

Mandy's face swiveled back to Lucas, two tears
tracking down her cheeks. ''Love her, Lucas. Talk to her
and let her know that you love her. And—'' Mandy
looked down at Worthy, her voice growing lower with
the intensity of her feeling ''—and don't leave her, Lucas. I don't want her to be by herself.'' Now Mandy
turned to Rachel. ''I don't want her to be lonesome.''

Rachel felt the sting of tears herself but blinked them
back and swallowed. Lucas enfolded the thin body in his

arms and hugged Mandy tightly. "I won't leave Worthy," he promised, a husky catch in his voice. "I'll stay with her until you get back."

Mandy pulled back and searched Lucas's face. Wiping the tears off her cheeks, she nodded, then jumped to her feet and ran through the barn to the horse that was tethered outside.

"Mandy's taking it hard, isn't she?" Rachel said.

"Yep," Lucas answered as he gently probed Worthy's belly. "Worthy's just about all she's got in the world that's really hers."

Rachel's heart was touched . . . by Mandy, by the pathetic creature that lay on the straw, and by Lucas's concern for both animal and child. She ran her hand down Worthy's neck, her fingers accidentally grazing his hands as they massaged the lowing cow's belly. She pulled away but couldn't take her eyes off his long, slender fingers with their short, clipped nails. Hands like that were powerfully reassuring.

Rachel was so caught up with looking at them that she barely heard him say, "Worthy is Mandy's entire world. As you can see, her world—the Lucky Brand Children's Ranch—is quite small."

Rachel's heart went out to this man who was so gentle and caring with both child and beast.

"Like Mandy told you earlier, I let the kids each adopt a calf because I believe in giving them something they can love and feel is their very own; also I give them the responsibility of taking care of it. If each passes muster, the calf becomes the child's own."

A sudden smile flitted across Lucas's lips to soften the gaunt hardness of his features. Sitting back, he took off his hat and ran his fingers through tousled black hair that brushed against the collar of his shirt.

"From the minute Mandy laid eyes on this cow she didn't want a calf; she wanted Worthy. Dugan kept saying, 'That cow ain't worth her salt.' Mandy kept replying, 'She is too worthy.'"

"Hence the name Worthy," Rachel murmured.

Lucas nodded. "And the critter's been nothing but trouble since then. She's just like Mandy, a free spirit, and a headstrong one at that. Haven't been able to keep her where she belongs. She's infatuated with Bernard, one of my bulls."

"Looks like she already spent some time with him," Rachel said.

"Quite a bit of time," Lucas agreed dryly.

Worthy lifted her head and snorted.

"Sorry," Lucas apologized. "I forget you understand English. I didn't mean to make you sound so free and easy."

Conversation ceased as Worthy moaned and her body began to tremble anew with the severity of her labor contractions.

Hunching a shoulder, Lucas wiped the perspiration from his forehead, then donned his hat again. "Patience, old girl," he soothed. "I'm here with you, and Dugan will be here soon to help us."

"Worthy might be willing to wait," Rachel said, "but I don't think the little one is."

Worthy dilated as the contractions hastened and deepened. Long, tense moments turned into an eternity as Rachel watched Lucas work with the cow, both man and animal perspiring and grunting from the effort.

"Come on, Worthy," Lucas coaxed. "Work with me. You can do it. I know you can. Think about Mandy."

Rachel looked up to see his brow furrow and his lips thin into a line of concentrated concern. "She's all right, isn't she?"

"Breech," he eventually muttered, lifting an arm to wipe his forehead again.

Unmindful of soiling her clothes, Rachel scooted closer and pulled Worthy's head into her lap, slobber and perspiration soaking into her skirt. "It's okay," she murmured, staring into those doleful brown eyes. "Lucas is going to take care of you."

Worthy's head lolled to one side; she was limp with fatigue and breathing heavily. She frothed at the mouth, too weak to work anymore.

"Help me, Worthy," Lucas grunted, reaching into her with both hands to turn the calf.

Bellowing in pain, Worthy jumped and knocked Lucas's hat off.

"I've...got...to...turn...it," he panted, his upper body covered with birthing fluids.

"I know it hurts," Rachel crooned, wrapping both arms around the cow's neck and pressing her face against Worthy's, "but it's going to be all right."

Long, anxious minutes later, Lucas stumbled back, his arms wrapped around a wet, slicked-down reddish-brown calf. Rachel watched as he worked, the movement of his hands smooth and fluid as they cleaned the calf. Finally he looked up and announced, "A boy. Worthy, you have a fine baby boy."

Tears of happiness streamed down Rachel's cheeks as she gazed at the newborn that was pushing itself up on spindly little legs. Worthy lowed and turned her head. She lurched, but couldn't make it to her feet and fell down again. Her stomach heaved as she dragged air into her lungs. After snorting a time or two she quieted, and her breathing seemed more relaxed. She closed her eyes.

As Lucas stripped off his shirt and wiped his hands and arms, Rachel continued to rub Worthy and croon to her. She laid her cheek on the cow's neck and talked to her; she felt the rise and fall of her body as she breathed. Then Worthy was still…too still. The stall was too quiet. Rachel knew.

"Lucas," she called. "Do something."

Lucas dropped the shirt and knelt beside the animal. A swift examination told him there was nothing more he could do. He turned to Rachel and caught her hands in his, but she jerked them away.

"Do something for Worthy," she cried. "We can't let her die. What's Mandy going to do?"

Lucas leaned over, clamped his hands on Rachel's shoulders and pulled her to her feet. "We can't do anything for her," he said gently. "She's dead."

"No!" All the life seemed to seep out of Rachel's body and she collapsed against Lucas. She wasn't that attached to the cow; she didn't know Mandy Taylor that well, but Rachel was haunted by those big, trusting blue eyes.

Sighing himself, also thinking of Mandy, Lucas caught Rachel in his arms and pressed her face against his chest. Although his purpose was to comfort and console Rachel, he was also aware of her as a woman. She was soft and felt good in his arms; her hair was silky against his flesh. Needing and wanting his comfort, Rachel slipped her arms around him and clung to him.

"Only Mandy thought the cow was worth her salt," he said quietly.

His words, though softly spoken, broke the spell that bound Rachel to him. She was suddenly aware that her body fitted perfectly against his. She became increasingly aware of a naked torso that was lean, solid muscle. Her hands gripped his shoulders, and her face rested on a mat of crisp, black chest hair. She heard the rhythmic beat of his heart; she felt the rise and fall of his chest.

Her hands slipped down his back as she pushed out of his arms to look at the calf. "At least, Mandy has a part of Worthy left to love."

Before Lucas could reply, brakes screeched and truck doors slammed.

"Lucas! We're here." Mandy's cry echoed through the quiet old building.

"Mandy and Dugan," Lucas said, gently setting Rachel aside. "I don't want her to see Worthy before I can talk to her. She's going to be pretty upset." Long strides carried him to the entrance, and he caught up Mandy in his arms as she ran through the door.

"Worthy," Mandy cried, fighting against his embrace. "How's Worthy?"

"Got here as soon as I could," Dugan MacAdams said as he followed Mandy into the barn.

His straw hat, the brim rolled up on both sides, the band stained with perspiration, was pulled low over his face. Like Lucas he wore a blue-and-gray checkered shirt, jeans and boots. A red bandanna was tied around his neck. He took off his hat and ran his fingers through thick, white hair.

"Had to git someone to take the kids to the fairgrounds before I could come," the ranch manager continued. "This counts as a school day for 'em. Gotta hold of Florence at Doc's office, but she said Fred was already gone. Said she'd keep on trying until we called back."

Lucas nodded, but Dugan could tell from his expression that the veterinarian was no longer needed.

Mandy looked from one man to the other. In a dull voice she said, "Worthy's dead."

"Yes," Lucas said, "Worthy's dead."

Chapter Two

"Why, Lucas?" Mandy whispered, her lips trembling, tears spilling down her cheeks. "Why did you let Worthy die?" In her grief the child unconsciously lashed out at the person whom she trusted and loved the most. "You said she was going to be all right. You promised me."

Lucas hugged the tiny body closer to his chest and swallowed his tears. At that moment he wished he had power over life and death, but he didn't. All he could do was love and console. "Remember when you begged me and Dugan so hard to buy her for you?" He felt Mandy's head move against his shoulder as she nodded. "How we explained to you that she was a sickly cow? She was too weak, baby, to give birth." He moved slightly so that he could look into Mandy's face. With a sad smile he said, "She should have known better than to get pregnant at her age."

"But I couldn't keep her away from Bernard." Mandy sobbed. "She just liked that old bull too much."

"You did the best you could," Lucas comforted her. "Worthy had a mind of her own, and she was determined to be with Bernard."

"I tried, Lucas. Honest, I tried." Fresh tears ran down Mandy's cheeks. Her crying turned into deep, heart-rending sobs. "Now she's left me all alone again. Just like my mama and daddy. I don't have no one to love me, Lucas. No one."

Unable to keep the tears at bay, Rachel turned her back to Lucas and Mandy and wiped her eyes; she felt as if her heart were breaking. She wanted to run to Mandy and throw her arms around her, to assure her that she wasn't alone, that someone did love her.

Although Rachel hadn't been an orphan she could understand Mandy's fear of being alone, her fear of having no one to love her and her fear of rejection. Rachel suspected it was akin to the desertion and loneliness she had felt when Jared had announced that he wanted a divorce, when he had so callously ended their seventeen-year marriage.

"I love you, Mandy," Lucas said thickly, "and Dugan and Mrs. Molly love you. None of us can take the place of your mama and daddy or Worthy, but we love you. You'll never be alone, because you have all the wonderful people at the children's ranch. All of us love you." He caught the bony shoulders in his powerful hands and held her away from him so he could look into her face. "Most of all, Mandy, Worthy loved you enough that she left you a part of herself. Something you can love for many years to come."

Rachel turned to look at the calf.

"I don't want it!" Mandy sobbed, pushing away from Lucas. "I want Worthy."

"All right." Lucas dropped his hands from her shoulders and rose to his feet. "I'll keep the calf."

Mandy wiped her face with her shirttail. "Can I go see Worthy?"

Lucas nodded. Hand in hand, he and the little girl walked down the aisle, and Dugan ambled along behind. When they reached the stall, Rachel stepped aside and watched Mandy as she leaned over the dead cow to run her hand down Worthy's neck and shoulders. Mandy deliberately avoided looking at the calf; then it bellowed, the sound nothing more than a pitiful wail. Mandy lifted her head and stared.

"Well—" Dugan brushed past Mandy and squatted beside the wobbly newborn "—here's one fine calf, Lucas. Guess we can let one of the children at the home adopt it. It's going to need a lot of special love."

"Yep, I reckon so." Lucas walked toward the stall, his hands hitched in his back pockets.

"It's an orphan, too," Mandy said dully.

"Yep." Lucas leaned against the gatepost, his soft, gray eyes resting on Mandy. "But we can't hold that against him. In fact, now that he has no mama he needs you more than ever. The little fellow is like us, Mandy. He needs someone to love and care for him."

Mandy squirmed around so that she was looking at the calf. "I guess it's my duty to take care of it."

"Nope." Lucas shoved himself away from the post. "Nobody adopts one of my orphan calves because it's their duty. We adopt them because we love and want them. Duty's a sad substitute for love, and I refuse to accept less than love." He knelt beside Mandy and dropped his arm around her small shoulders. "I can't let you offer any less than love, little girl."

Mandy jerked away from Lucas and leaped to her feet. Defiantly posed with a hand on each hip, she said, "I can too keep it if I want! Worthy was mine, and her calf is mine, too!"

Admiration for Lucas swelled in Rachel; she knew he loved the child; that was evident in all his actions. Also she wanted to applaud him for his superb ability in channeling Mandy's emotions. How deftly he swung her attention from personal grief to the calf's needs, from selfishness to giving. Rachel looked down in time to see Dugan quickly duck his head and begin an exploration of the calf. He was smiling.

"You're right," Lucas replied. "It's your calf, and you can keep it if you want to. But only if you love it."

Mandy raised her face to Lucas. "I do," she said. "I really do." Then she dropped her head and looked at the dead cow. Once again tears thickened her voice. "Only I'm going to miss Worthy so much."

"All of us are going to miss Worthy," Lucas said, moving behind her and placing a hand on her shoulder, "but we have to accept that dying is as much a part of life as living, little one. Worthy's dead, but in dying she gave us a wonderful gift. She gave us a new life."

"What are you going to do with Worthy?" Mandy asked.

"We'll bury her," Dugan answered.

"Can I have a funeral for her?"

"Well—" Dugan drawled, rising slowly "—reckon that'd be most appropriate. Reckon you can get Mrs. Molly to help you plan it."

"Do you think Mrs. Molly will, Dugan?"

"Of course she will," he replied, not in the least hesitant to answer for his wife. "Mrs. Molly's pretty good when it comes to planning and organizing people and things. Especially me." He gave Rachel a friendly grin and wink, stepped nearer and extended his hand. "In all the commotion we've sorta let manners slide, ma'am," he said. "I'm Dugan MacAdams, manager of The Lucky Brand Ranch."

Rachel liked Dugan; his handshake was firm, his gaze direct. "I'm glad to meet you, Mr. MacAdams—"

"Not Mr. MacAdams," Dugan interrupted amiably. "Call me Dugan."

Rachel smiled. "Dugan it is, and I'm Rachel March with Greater Southwest Real Estate Brokers."

Dugan grinned. "Lucas's six o'clock appointment."

"Dugan, you better remember who you work for!" Lucas exclaimed, his laughing eyes belying his threat.

"Yep," the older man agreed, his grin turning into soft laughter, "reckon I better. Sure don't want to do anything that would stop that paycheck."

From her world of grief, Mandy patted Dugan's chest and said, "When can we bury Worthy? Right now?"

"Nope," Dugan answered, turning toward the child, "not right now. Right now, Miss Amanda, we better git this calf over to the big barn or we're going to be burying two cows instead of one. This little feller needs a new mama quick." He leaned over and scooped the calf into his arms. "Run ahead and spread those blankets in the bed of the truck, and you can ride back with this thing. When we git home tonight, we'll talk to Mrs. Molly about a funeral for Worthy. How about that?"

Mandy clamped her hat onto her head and ran beside Dugan to keep up with his long strides as he moved toward the pickup. "You know what, Dugan," she said, "I already know what I'm going to name the calf."

"And what's that gonna be?"

"Worthmore." Mandy laughed. "You said Worthy wasn't worth her salt, but this little fellow—" she stood on tiptoe and brushed her hands against the velvety skin of the calf "—this one is worth more than his salt."

Dugan chuckled. "Well, Miss Amanda, let's me and you get Mr. Worthmore to the big barn."

"Oh, Dugan—" Mandy danced around and clapped her hands "—I really love him. From now on, his name is going to be Mr. Worthmore."

When Dugan had Mr. Worthmore and Mandy settled in the bed of the truck, he returned to the barn. "I'll send some of the boys over to bury Worthy," he said to Lucas. "You want to ride back to the big barn with me?"

Lucas looked at his watch; then he turned to Rachel. "Is it too late for us to go see the property?"

Rachel grinned. "Not for me. Remember six o'clock was your idea."

Lucas laughed with her. "Is there anyone else involved who could object to our being so late?"

"Someone else is involved," Rachel answered, "but Elaine doesn't object to our being late. Before I set out to find you, I called to let her know that you had been detained. She said we could come anytime. She just wanted us to call before we left, so she'd know when to expect us."

"If you don't mind then," Lucas said, "I'll let you drive me back to the house, and I'll make a few phone calls to see if I can reschedule my meeting. If not—" he turned to Dugan "—I'll meet you at the fairgrounds and give you a hand with the exhibits." His gaze moved to Rachel. "If I can reschedule, I'll bathe and change, and Rachel and I will head toward the wild blue yonder."

"So you can bathe and change!" Rachel exclaimed. "What about me? I look a mess."

A huge grin spanning his face, Lucas welcomed the invitation to inspect Rachel thoroughly. Her clothes were covered with perspiration, blood and afterbirth; her panty hose were one massive run. He finally lifted his face to encounter the expressive green eyes—eyes flecked with gold—eyes that were warm and full of laughter—eyes that he liked. They reminded him of the pasture in the spring when it was covered with a carpet of rich, tender grass.

"You look fine to me just like you are, Ms. March, but if it's a bath you're wanting, then it's a bath you'll be getting."

Lucas completely fascinated Rachel. His face softened when he smiled, and his eyes sparkled when he teased. She had a sudden desire to reach out and touch the shadow of beard on his cheeks. The thought served to bring her up sharply, and she said instead, "Thank you, Mr. Brand. You're so kind and chivalrous."

"Well," Dugan drawled, "if Ms. March is going to take you to the house, I guess I'll be on my way. See you later."

"Okay, Dugan," Lucas answered, his eyes never wavering from Rachel's face.

Mesmerized by his gaze, Rachel watched his large, callused hand as it moved toward her face, grazing her cheek when his fingers burrowed into her hair. Her heart skipped a beat, and the blood pumped through her body so fast she could hardly breathe. Reflexively she dodged his touch.

Lucas grinned as he reluctantly pulled back his hand and waved a piece of hay in her face. "Wouldn't do for you to have this in your hair when we reach the house, Ms. March. Our Mrs. Molly is a very old-fashioned lady with a highly suspicious mind. She's liable to think we've been tumbling in the hay."

He chuckled quietly when soft color seeped into Rachel's face. She appeared to be such an innocent. Her hair was like a golden halo, framing her face; it was textured like silk. He'd like to run his hands through it again...and again.

Lucas's humor was so infectious that Rachel laughed with him. "In fact, she wouldn't be incorrect, Mr. Brand." It had been a long time—nearly two years—since she had verbally sparred with a man, and it felt good.

"But so far wrong indeed, Ms. March." Then as if he were dismissing the intimacy such bantering introduced, Lucas casually placed his hand on Rachel's back and said, "But I guess it's high time for us to be on our way."

His closeness was unnerving to Rachel; it emphasized his masculinity. She wanted to move away, but she couldn't do that. His gesture was friendly, with absolutely no overtones of sexuality. Yet his very proximity stirred her. She felt the heat of his flesh through her silk blouse; she smelled the tangy after-shave that reminded her of the Texas wilderness, of which he was such an integral part. Drawing a deep breath to still the thundering of her heart, she walked beside him.

Rachel was glad for the brilliant blast of sunlight when they left the barn. Coupled with the breeze, it served to clear her head. She walked to the driver's side of the Tempo and stood for a moment, again gazing at the hill country. "Everything seems different, doesn't it?"

Lucas nodded as his eyes caught and held hers. "You noticed it."

"Although it's the first day of autumn," Rachel said, "the day suddenly seems brighter, the sun more golden, the trees a little bit greener. Almost like it's spring again. April rather than September."

"I guess you can say it's spring," Lucas returned, a certain wistfulness in his voice. "Spring is the rebirth of the earth, and what you saw today was a rebirth of life. That universal breath channeled into a new creature." His gray eyes caught and held Rachel's. "To me nothing is more beautiful than a mother giving birth. I only wish—" Abruptly Lucas stopped speaking. "Sorry, enough of my philosophizing." He opened the door and slid into the leather seat on the passenger's side before Rachel had time to reply.

Rachel didn't understand the full significance of Lucas's confession, but she knew he had begun to share something so intimate and precious with her that it left him wide open and vulnerable; therefore, she waited a moment to give him time to collect himself before she climbed into the car. She was also puzzled by the man. He was wealthy; he was an entrepreneur and attorney but seemed to be so down-to-earth and caring, so human...a characteristic totally unknown to Jared March.

"How on earth do you move this?" Lucas asked.

Surprised at the sharpness of his voice, Rachel ducked into the car and looked across the seat; then she started laughing. His knees were pressed against the dashboard, his chin resting on top of them, and he was searching for the lever to adjust the seat.

"It's not funny," he said, scowling at her.

"It is too," she retorted; then as she added, "It's on the—" the seat whooshed backward.

"That better?" Rachel asked.

"Much better, and no thanks to you." Lucas's grin took the bite out of his words. "Don't tell me that you have a misplaced sense of humor." He sighed as he stretched his legs.

"No, it's not misplaced," Rachel said. "It's where it belongs." Suddenly she smiled; her answer was self-revelation. During the past eighteen months since her divorce from Jared, she had often wondered if she had a sense of humor left. Now she knew: she did. She looked at Lucas and said, "I'm sorry for the inconvenience. Normally I would have been in my town car, but it's in the shop today for a tune-up. I had to borrow my daughter's Tempo."

Still grinning, Lucas said, "I thought maybe you were repaying me for having you come out here at six o'clock."

"No—" Rachel laughed and her eyes twinkled "—I'm not a vindictive person. Especially when that person happens to be a prospective buyer."

"From the moment I first laid eyes on you, Ms. March, I knew you were an astute businesswoman," Lucas murmured, liking the way Rachel's soft, husky laughter wrapped itself around him to make him feel warm and good all over.

"Although I started later in life than most, I strive to be," Rachel replied.

"Why later in life than most?" Lucas asked casually as Rachel turned the key and revved the motor.

"A divorce eighteen months ago," Rachel answered. "For the first time in my adult life, I was in need of a salary-earning job."

"And voilà, real estate," Lucas said, settling in the seat so that he could look at Rachel.

She laughed. "Not quite as easy and quick as that, Mr. Brand."

"Call me Lucas."

"All right," Rachel agreed, "if you'll call me Rachel."

"Done, Rachel. Now tell me about your getting into real estate."

"I received an educational allowance as part of the divorce settlement," Rachel said easily, not at all uncomfortable discussing this aspect of her life with Lucas, "but I needed an immediate career with an income substantial enough to provide for me, three children and a cat. Also I wanted a job that I would enjoy doing. Real estate was my choice. After I graduated from real estate school, I began to work for a firm in Dallas. Several months later at a national convention, I met Craig and Nancy Maddocks, and Craig offered me a position with Greater Southwest Real Estate Brokers. With his and Nancy's help I moved from Dallas to San Antonio and have been there ever since."

"I've known Craig and Nancy for years. They're nice folks," Lucas said. "You couldn't work for a greater guy."

"No, I couldn't," Rachel replied. "He's the perfect boss."

Lucas grinned. "He may be the perfect boss, but I seem to remember his one glaring fault. He has a lead foot when it comes to driving. Of course, now, I haven't been around him in about five or six years. That could have changed."

Rachel laughed and shook her head. "No, he's in court today because of his excessive speeding tickets."

"Same old Craig," Lucas murmured. After a pause, he asked, "How does San Antonio compare to Dallas?"

"I love it," Rachel replied. "It's so comfortable and laid-back in comparison to Dallas. Living is slower and easier."

They lapsed into a comfortable silence. Rachel concentrated on her driving, and Lucas, noticing again her badly stained blouse and skirt, thought about her. She was warm and caring. How quickly she had come to Mandy's and Worthy's rescue...perhaps his own...with no thought of herself. None of the women with whom he'd been associating since Debra's death would have so quickly volunteered aid to a birthing cow. His soft chuckle caught Rachel's attention, and she turned her head to look at him. Her brows were raised in question.

"Since you started selling real estate, I don't suppose you've had a day like this."

"Not quite," Rachel conceded as she negotiated a curve in the dirt road. She brushed a hand through her hair and grinned. "This is a day I'll remember and cherish the rest of my life."

"I know," Lucas softly agreed. "A new life always affects me like this."

"Not only Mr. Worthmore's birth," Rachel said, giving Lucas a quick glance, "but the wonderful way you interacted with Mandy. You must be an extraordinary father."

Lucas was quiet for a few minutes before he answered, "No, I'm not an extraordinary anything. I'm sure my daughter would agree that I'm a good father, but even she would draw the line at extraordinary."

"You were extraordinary with Mandy," Rachel insisted.

"I love her," was Lucas's explanation. "Her parents were employees of mine. Their trailer burned up a year ago. They...were killed."

"I'm sorry," Rachel murmured, the words totally inadequate to express her feelings.

"Mandy escaped because she was spending the night at a friend's house. After the fire she went from aunt to cousin and back again. Finally she ended up at the home, and we've had her for the past six months."

"Her relatives didn't want her?" Rachel asked, aghast at the idea.

"They aren't close kin," Lucas explained. "A great-aunt, and cousins so far removed you can't count them on one hand. They were as surprised to learn about Mandy as she was about them. But they are her family."

"Was she hurt because they didn't want her?"

"No, she wants to stay here with me." Lucas stopped talking and leaned forward to point. "Look at the deer."

Rachel glanced out her window at the small herd of deer that was loping into a cluster of trees. Then her gaze returned to the road. She slowed the car, eased out of the ruts and went around a large mud hole in the road. Lucas was quiet, but she didn't prompt him to talk. She thought perhaps he was preoccupied with thoughts of Mandy.

Eventually he stirred and said, "It was really nice of your daughter to let you borrow her car today."

Rachel laughed. "Don't get too free with the compliments. Jae's a wonderful daughter whom I love dearly, but she's a mere mortal like the rest of us, and sixteen years old at that. I had to sign in blood to get her car this morning. I threw all her plans out of joint. The cheerleaders had a special meeting today, and this was her Friday to drive."

Lucas laughed. "Oh, Lord, I can remember those days only too well. Cheryl, my daughter, thought she had to be involved in everything. After her mother's death, I tried to be mother and father to her."

"I understand," Rachel said. "Jared's not dead, but since the divorce—" she hesitated only fractionally before she rushed on "—he...hasn't had much time to spend with the children, and I've had to be both parents."

Thinking perhaps the atmosphere was growing a little too heavy with personal confessions, Rachel tilted her head back, her golden-brown hair brushing against her shoulders. "The hill country is lovely. No matter how many times I've seen it, I'm never quite prepared for its beauty. It's like I'm always seeing it for the first time."

"I feel that way about it, too," Lucas confessed. "That's why I moved out here. That's one of the reasons why I'm so interested in the Halston Ranch. Three thousand acres or so on the Frio River. Craig thinks it might be exactly what I'm looking for."

"Yes," Rachel said with a twinge of regret, "he's right. It might be." *Probably was, with all those historic old buildings still intact!* Another beautiful wilderness to be converted into a summer vacationland for thousands of *cityites*. Condos! Hotels! Cabins! Bait stores! Commercialism! Selling beautiful undeveloped land to commercial investors was the biggest drawback to Rachel's job.

"I have several other listings," Rachel said, "that I'd like to show you. They have an even greater potential for development than the Storch-Halston place. Tommy Deltron has some property for sale out of Castroville— about fifteen hundred acres. Comanche Creek runs right through it. Emilio Esparza has a little over two thousand acres for sale south of Poteet. A river runs through that, also. I have photographs of it in my briefcase if you'd care to see them."

"No, thanks," Lucas replied. "I'd rather see the real thing, and I'll know it when I see it. I want just the perfect spot for my Lucky Brand Lodge."

"The Lucky Brand," she murmured. "Ranch, supermarkets, an orphanage. And now you're contemplating a lodge. Many would count you a very lucky man, Mr. Brand. Your name as well as your reputation are spread all over the state."

"The name's Lucas," he reminded her, then drawled without conceit, "Yeah, I guess they are."

"Is Lucky your nickname?"

"Was when I was growing up."

"And are you?" She turned her head to look at him. "Lucky, that is?"

Lucas gave her a lazy grin. "Most folks think I am because I always get what I want out of life, but I don't think of myself as being lucky." He paused, then said, "I've always known what I wanted, I've known how to get it, and I've worked to get it. I planned to found a financial empire, and I have. Now I'm ready for the Lucky Brand Lodge."

Words from the article in *Texas Monthly* danced in front of Rachel's eyes: Born and reared in poverty, Lucas Brand determined as a child to go from rags to riches; by the time he was forty he was a multimillionaire. Rachel respected Lucas's business acumen. She was a businesswoman herself; she'd spent the eighteen months since her divorce from Jared learning to be one. In the beginning the single-parent scene and the road to independence had been long, hard rows to hoe, but Rachel had hoed them, inch by inch. She had learned that she possessed more strength and integrity than she had ever imagined. She also discovered—or cultivated—patience along the way.

"What's the agenda like?" Lucas asked.

"I had originally planned for us to start with Poteet, swing over to Castroville and drive back this way, our last piece of property being the Halston Ranch."

"If I hadn't been so late that would have been good," Lucas answered. "As it is, I think I'd better see the closest today. If it's not what I want, then we'll make plans to see the others. Okay?"

"Okay." Rachel swallowed her disappointment with a nod of her head. His plans made perfect sense.

"Have you seen the Halston place yet?" Lucas asked.

"Mmm-hmm," Rachel murmured.

"Craig said it was beautiful with the Frio River running through it."

"It is," Rachel agreed.

"Are the buildings still intact?"

"Yes," Rachel answered. "However, they're desperately in need of repair. Mrs. Halston thinks one or two of them will need to be torn down."

"If the structures aren't sound, they'll come down," Lucas replied noncommittally.

Rachel couldn't stand the thought of all the old buildings on the ranch being torn down. This was another drawback to being in real estate. She couldn't dictate the purpose for which her clients bought the property, nor could she make stipulations.

"What kind of lodge are you planning?" she asked. "Personal or some kind of commercial venture?" She glanced at him and added, "If I know what you want the property for, I can better serve your needs. Perhaps we have other land parcels that would fit your requirements more satisfactorily. You know, property that has no buildings intact that need to be demolished."

"Personal and commercial venture," Lucas said, "and I don't mind if there are buildings. I just want to make sure I get the property I want." He waved his hand in the air and said, "Turn here. We'll take the shortcut back to the house."

As Rachel whipped the Tempo around and headed up the road he indicated, he said, "Part of the grounds are to be converted into a game preserve and vacation area for the children."

"The children?" she asked.

"Orphanage," he answered.

Lucas's confession touched Rachel, but deep down she wondered if Lucas was playing a game. Her experience with the Marches—an old money family in Dallas—and her subsequent divorce from Jared had left its scars on her life. Whereas before the divorce she had been trusting, she was now skeptical and cynical. "It's really wonderful of you to do all this for them."

Rachel understood the wealthy and their compulsion to help the underprivileged. Noblesse oblige, it was called. The obligation of honorable, generous, and responsible behavior was associated with high rank or great wealth. The Marches had seen to it that Rachel was well indoctrinated and trained to perform good works.

Her own idealism had soon vanished in the wake of discovery. Their concern wasn't for the needy and underprivileged or for the ill, but rather that their name always be associated with care and sacrifice. They liked to be portrayed as social martyrs. Rachel had soon learned that working with volunteer organizations was merely an obligation, like everything else in the lives of the Marches—something one did without any emotion.

"In addition to the cabins," she heard Lucas say, "the lodge will serve as the site for several historic company buildings. Leighton sold me the first building his company used as a warehouse, an old train depot in the Rio Grande Valley. He's also letting me have some of the first counters they used in their stores at the turn of the century. When I buy the property, I want to have all those buildings restored—if it's possible—so the Halston and Leighton heritage can be shared by all.''

Rachel was so surprised she could say nothing. Lucas was altogether different from the man she had imagined him to be. She thought of his gentleness and patience with Worthy and Mandy. Now she was touched by his concern for Morris Leighton.

"What's wrong?" Lucas asked, peering across the seat at her. "You don't like my idea."

"Oh, no," Rachel stammered. "I'm...just... surprised.''

"Why?" he asked. Public opinion didn't bother him; Rachel's did.

"I would think that he wouldn't be so generous, considering that you bought his food store chain," Rachel answered.

In an involuntary response, Lucas reached out and laid his hand lightly on Rachel's arm, as if his touch could dispel her doubts. "Leighton was bankrupt when I came along. I think we've been a great help to each other. He's grateful that I cherish the Leighton heritage and want to perpetuate it at the lodge. He's also glad for a chance to help the Lucky Brand Children's Ranch.''

Rachel's eyes darted to the fingers that clasped her arm. They were firm and callused from work.

"Wealthy people are no more ogres than any others," Lucas continued. "It's just that the public seems to think the rich have only vices, while the poverty-stricken have only virtues.''

Rachel withdrew her arm from his disconcerting touch. "I wasn't implying criticism."

"No...I'm sure you weren't," Lucas said, then added softly, "I've learned to deal with public opinion, but it matters what you think of me."

His magnetic gaze caught and mesmerized her.

A devilish twinkle in his eyes, he finally said, "I think you'd better look where you're going, Rachel. If not, we're going to go—"

The spell broken, Rachel jerked her head back to the road and uttered a squeal.

"—into the field," he finished.

"How could you?" Rachel fumed as she twisted the wheel and swung the car back onto the road.

"How could I?" Lucas exclaimed, laughing. "You're the one who is driving, not me. Don't blame me for your carelessness."

Her carelessness! she thought, both irritated and surprised at herself. How right he was. She was being careless. She was out here on business, and that was all. Lucas Brand was a client, nothing more. And she would do well to remember that. She needed to keep her errant emotions under rigid control. She needed to curb her wild and fanciful imagination.

"Here it is," Lucas said as they drove through the double gate. The name Lucky Brand was embossed on a huge wrought iron horseshoe. In the distance, sitting on a hill, was the ranch house, a two-story white stone structure, as austere and commanding as the countryside.

Although Rachel had seen the house earlier when she arrived, its majesty commanded reaction now. "It's so beautiful, Lucas."

"Yes," he answered, his eyes clouding with unhappy memories, "it is. I bought the ranch about fifteen years ago when Debra and I decided we wanted to get away. I was unhappy living in San Antonio and wanted to move back to the country." His features hardened, and he paused only fractionally before he said, "The original house is sitting to the back of the property. We had the interior totally renovated. That's where Dugan and Molly live. Debra wasn't quite cut out for the rustic life, so I had the new house built for her."

As they drove up the tree-lined gravel road, Lucas talked about the house, describing it in detail. Although Rachel had already seen the den, she was curious to see the rest. She could tell that Lucas was proud of it but also detected a hint of detachment. It was one of many possessions. That characteristic reminded her of Jared.

Rachel parked the car in the shade of the oaks that were clustered in front of the house. Lucas slid out and walked to Rachel's side of the car. When he opened her door, his lips curled in that lazy grin Rachel was coming to associate with him. "Shall we go inside and take our bath?"

The question was so innocent that Rachel could hardly take exception to it. Yet the look he gave her was so intimate, the eyes were so soft, the words so sensual that she felt she should take immediate flight. But she had nothing to protest about but her own overactive imagination, her own errant feelings. His hand closed around hers, and he gently pulled her from the car.

Chapter Three

"I guess we'd better go in through the back," Lucas said, a smile playing across his lips. "No telling what Mrs. Molly'll do if we come sauntering through the front door. Fact of the matter, no telling what she'll do when we come in the back one, looking the way we do." With a chuckle he added, "You know the old adage: you're damned if you do; you're damned if you don't. That's us right now."

"In that case," Rachel said with a flourish of her hand, "you lead on, sir, and I'll follow. I'll readily admit to being a coward."

"Mrs. Molly is sixty-five if she's a day," Lucas replied in a conspiratorial whisper, "but she makes cowards of us all, Dugan included."

Rachel grinned and followed Lucas. Although she knew he was teasing, she figured from what she'd seen earlier of the housekeeper that Mrs. Molly could hold her own with anybody and was quite adept at tongue-lashing, especially when it came to her domain: the house.

In the triple garage Lucas opened a door and they walked down a wide hallway and through a sunshine-filled utility room. Lucas, ahead of Rachel, had taken only a few steps into the large and homey kitchen, decorated in country gingham, when a familiar, feminine voice boomed out.

"For land's sake, Lucas Brand! What on earth has happened to you? How come you're going through my kitchen when you're such a mess? Get a hose and wash off in the backyard."

Over Lucas's shoulder Rachel saw the large, buxom housekeeper standing in the doorway, her arms folded across her breasts. It was the same woman who had reluctantly directed Rachel to the barn earlier in the morning.

"Looks like you been rooting in the pigsty," the woman said to Lucas; then he stepped aside and Molly's blue eyes shifted to Rachel. Slowly they went up, down, and up again. Her lips twitched at the sight. "And the lady does too, for that matter. Now this, Ms. March, is what I call dealing in real estate at the dirt level." She smiled at the pair of them.

"Not exactly rooting in a pigsty," Lucas answered. "More like helping Worthy give birth in a stall in the old barn."

Molly bobbed her head so vigorously that her white curls danced around her face. "I figured that's where you'd find 'em," she declared. "Told Ms. March that this morning. I don't know why, but all the kids and animals seem to love that place. Reckon you're gonna have to fix it up, Lucas. Too dangerous for 'em like it is." Molly pushed away from the door and walked to the counter where she lifted the clear Pyrex pot off the coffee maker. "How about a cup of coffee when you get cleaned up?" She moved to the sink and turned on the spigot to rinse out the pot.

"I could do with that," Lucas said, "and some hot biscuits and butter if you don't mind making them."

Molly beamed. "You know I don't, Lucas Brand. Cooking is my talent and I love to do it." She turned to Rachel. "How about you, Ms. March? Just biscuits and butter? Or would you like to have a full-fledged breakfast?"

"Just coffee," Rachel answered. "I don't think I could eat a bite. I've already had breakfast."

"We'll see about that," Molly answered with another emphatic bob of her head.

Rachel turned a questioning face to Lucas who said, "No one can turn Molly's biscuits down. They're the kind that melt in your mouth."

"Don't know if they melt in your mouth or not," Molly declared, "but I do know my Dugan loves 'em." As she poured the water into the reservoir of the coffee maker, she said, "So Worthy's finally calved. A boy or girl?"

"A boy," Lucas answered.

"I'll bet the ole hellion isn't kicking so high now, is she?" Molly said fondly.

"She's not kicking at all," Lucas returned. "She died, Molly."

Crestfallen, Molly spun around, her apron fluttering through the air. For a long moment she stared at Lucas, the empty Pyrex container suspended in the air and a sparkle of tears in her eyes; then she said in a gruff voice, "Always said that cow was too sickly to live, much less carry a calf. How's Mandy taking it?"

"Pretty bad," Lucas replied. "Right now Dugan's helping her get the calf settled into the big barn with a wet nurse. And speaking of getting settled, Ms. March and I need to take a bath and change clothes."

"I'll say you do," Molly replied, setting the pot on the warmer. "Look at me just rattling off. If I don't hush, we won't get a thing done." With a brush of her hand, she said, "Since you know where to go and what to do, Lucas, do it. I'll take care of the lady." Molly turned to Rachel. "Follow me, Ms. March. You can take off them clothes, and while you're taking a shower, I'll wash and dry them."

Lucas grinned at Rachel and winked as he walked out of the kitchen and left her in Molly's keeping. Rachel followed the housekeeper, retracing her steps into the utility room where Molly opened the door to the half bath.

"Strip down in here, and I'll give you one of Lucas's robes to wear up to the guest room where you'll be bathing. This way I can get your things in the washer that much quicker. And if y'all are still planning on going to Kerrville, you'll need to save all the time you can."

Rachel accepted the white terry-cloth robe Molly handed her and eased into the small room to shed her soiled garments and hand them out to the housekeeper. Gratefully Rachel slipped into the soft, clean robe but was unprepared for the sensations that inundated her. As she smelled the elusive scent of Lucas's after-shave, she shivered to think of him naked in the robe. She felt as if the man himself were wrapped around her.

"I'll wait out here for you, Ms. March."

Molly's shout jarred Rachel out of her daydreams, and Rachel was thankful to be rescued. But she realized how susceptible she was; eighteen months without a man in her life had made her vulnerable. She must be careful. Lucas Brand was a client, nothing more. She had to remember that. Resolving to control her thoughts about

the man, she hastily opened the door and stepped out of
the room to follow Molly through the house up the stairs
to the guest bath.

"You'll find everything you need," Molly said as she
opened the cabinets and pulled on drawers. "All kinds
of perfumed bath oils over there." She pointed. "Hair
dryers over here. Curling iron. Hot rollers." Doors
continued to open and bang. "If you need it, hunt for
it. We're bound to have it, and I'm sure it's here somewhere."

"Thank you," Rachel said, feeling an instant famil-
iarity with the room because it looked so much like her
own. "I'm sure I'll find all I need. The larder seems to
be well stocked. You can always tell when there are
women in the house."

"Singular, Ms. March," Molly said, instantly on the
defensive where Lucas was concerned. "We have only
one woman in the house and that's Lucas's daughter,
Cheryl." Molly closed the door to the linen closet, laid
the towels on the tiled vanity, and turned to look directly at Rachel. "This is the guest room, Ms. March,
but when Cheryl is home for the holidays, she brings her
friends."

The housekeeper's explanation was clipped and
pointed; she resented anyone making an assumption that
Lucas Brand was the kind of man to furnish all this for
his women friends, though in the last couple of years
there had been many of them. Molly liked Lucas and
didn't judge him; she didn't want others to do so, either.
"I'll take care of your clothes for you," she said and
walked into the bedroom.

"Mrs. MacAdams—" Rachel rushed after Molly.
"I'm not a person who jumps to conclusions, and I cer-

tainly didn't mean that as a criticism of Lucas. Because
I have a teenage daughter myself, I—"

"I'm sorry too, Ms. March." Molly stopped at the
door and turned. "I'm a little testy and protective when
it comes to Lucas. Might say I'm an old mother hen. The
press hasn't been too kind to him since his wife died;
they've tried to make out like he's a high-flying playboy, and he's not." Having had her say, Molly smiled.
"I'll be back later with some clean underwear."

When the door closed behind Molly, Rachel emitted
a sigh of relief and walked into the bath. She would have
to be careful what she said around Molly MacAdams;
the woman was a living, breathing dragon when it came
to Lucas Brand. Shedding the robe, Rachel stepped into
the ivory-tiled shower and turned on the spigots. She
welcomed the warm, peppering spray and washed herself thoroughly from head to foot.

Half an hour later when she emerged from the bathroom, she found fluffs of nylon underwear lying on the
bed. She picked up the bra and looked at the label. Expensive. The kind she had worn when she was married
to Jared. But no more; she found the less expensive
brands just as good. And she didn't mind the econo-
mizing. Having to adjust to a smaller yearly income after the divorce hadn't bothered Rachel. Her only concern
was the way it was affecting the children, her daughter
in particular.

Jae had been the one who was visibly hurt most by the
divorce. Public school, a frugal budget, a working mom,
occasional baby-sitting and housekeeping chores did not
fit into the sixteen-year-old's picture of life. Rachel knew
that Jae loved her and wanted to be with her and the
boys, but Rachel also knew—and it was this knowledge
that hurt her so deeply—that Jae wanted the luxurious

life that Jared and his family guaranteed and that they had often used to entice her to return to them.

Unconsciously Rachel balled her hand into a fist and crushed the delicate fabric of the bra as she walked to the window to stare unseeingly at the panoramic view below. Jared was doing everything he could possibly think of to modify visiting rights now. His driving ambition was to see more of the children he hadn't wanted when he had announced his intention of getting a divorce.

Rachel knew the entire issue of visiting rights was a ploy of Jared's to get a reaction from her, and it angered her to know that he would stoop so low as to use his own children in this personal battle between the two of them. As usual Jared had turned to money. His philosophy was that buying affection was quicker and easier than earning it; thus, money was the carrot that he continually dangled in front of the children, and of all three Jae was the most susceptible. The boys, Neal and Sammy at ten and six, were too young to be affected yet, but Rachel knew the time would arrive when they, too, would become players in the game.

Rachel would never forget the day Jared announced he wanted a divorce. A bleak December day. Midafternoon, a week before Christmas. How surprised she had been when she pulled into the driveway of their estate home in Highland Park and saw Jared's red Jaguar. How shocked she had been when she ran up the stairs and found him in their bedroom, packing his suitcase.

His statement of intent was simple: "I want a divorce." As he moved back and forth between bed and dresser, he had gone on to say, "You'll have custody of the children. They need to be with their mother."

But that wasn't his reason for letting her have them at all. He didn't want to be bothered with them. He wanted no encumbrances to hamper his new freedom and life-style.

"I'll pay you child support, so you'll have no cause to contest the divorce. I'll—" With no thought for Rachel's feelings, Jared callously outlined his divorce plans. The word "I" continued to figure prominently.

"Why?" Rachel had asked. "Why a divorce, Jared?" As she stared at him, she wondered how she had ever thought him handsome and appealing. His features were closed and drawn. Not a strand of his graying brown hair was out of place. His eyes were hard and glassy like blue cat-eye marbles. He was immaculately clothed as always, dark suit and white shirt. "Is it another woman?"

He turned from the dresser and looked at her. "No, Rachel—" he had sighed impatiently, angrily "—it's not another woman. I'm just tired of being married to a paragon of perfection. You're the perfect mother, the perfect hostess, the perfect socialite. The perfect organizer for those damned charities. All your time goes to them and to the children. You've never had time for me."

"I am what you wanted me to be," Rachel replied. "What you and your family trained me to be."

"You've turned into a parasitical clinging vine," Jared charged, "suffocating and drawing out my lifeblood."

Feeling as if her life had ended, Rachel crumpled onto the bed. Dazed, she had listened to the accusations Jared kept hurling at her, heaping them on top of her until she didn't think she'd ever crawl out from under the rubble. She had been too numbed, too frightened to challenge him.

Jared was right. For seventeen years she had worked unceasingly to be the perfect wife, to be the perfect Mrs.

Jared Jaeson March. She had thought that was what he wanted. After two years of college she had given up her education to marry Jared, and from that time on she had become the private property of the Marches. At the time she hadn't minded. She loved Jared and wanted to do everything within her power to please him.

The Marches had insisted that Rachel stay home. They didn't want her to work, because she had a certain image to maintain. Rachel hadn't argued with that. Readily she complied with the wishes of this great, old money family into which she was marrying.

Rachel Ruel Randolph was forgotten as the Marches sculpted the girl their son had married into the woman they wanted. Rachel in turn worked until she became the perfect wife and daughter-in-law, the perfect mother and charity organization chairwoman. She had given her life to that damned family, and they hadn't cared!

Oh, yes! She crushed the panties in her fist. She fully understood noblesse oblige. *Only too well!* If Rachel had learned anything during her thirty-nine years, it was that money meant power and that it made arrogant fools out of weak, gutless men. Money made people manipulative—people like Jared.

He had thought she would fall flat on her face after the divorce, but she hadn't. She had stumbled and fallen, but she hadn't stayed down. Painfully, slowly she learned she could stand on her own two feet. She proved Jared's analogy wrong: She was no clinging vine; she was an oak tree. Now established in her career, Rachel directed all her drive and energy to it and to the rearing of her children. She had no time in her life for men, and even if she were to have the time, she wasn't sure that she wanted a man. She was doing quite well without one, and the thought of returning to the dating scene frightened her. She was afraid of being hurt again, and at all costs she wanted to avoid heartache and disappointment.

A knock at the door brought her back to the present. "Yes," she called.

"It's Molly, Ms. March. May I come in?"

"Certainly."

Opening the door, Molly walked into the room. Draped over one arm was a red skirt and an ecru blouse; in the other hand were Rachel's loafers, now clean and shiny. "The shoes will do, Ms. March, but I'm afraid your clothes were ruined. The stains wouldn't come out. I looked at the labels and decided that you and Cheryl are about the same size. Lucas suggested you wear one of her outfits."

"I really don't have much choice, do I?" Rachel said.

From down the hall she heard Lucas laugh and say, "Not at all." Booted feet moved to her door and stopped. "Are you decent?"

"Of course I am. What kind of question is that?"

He jiggled the doorknob and said, "Then...ready or not, here I come." He waited a moment, in case she wasn't dressed and didn't want him barging in on her.

"Come on in," Rachel invited, wishing she could laugh and joke as easily as Lucas did. She admired his free and relaxed manner. "I'm dressed as well as decent."

A grin tilted the corners of Lucas's mouth. As old-fashioned and full of worn-out clichés as they were, these verbal games he and Rachel played were enjoyable. He pushed open the door to see her standing there bundled up in his robe. The sight was so alluring that he sucked in his breath. When he realized that both Rachel and Molly were staring at him, he cleared his throat and said, "If you don't wear Cheryl's clothes, what do you propose to do? Spend the day in your soiled skirt and blouse or in my robe?"

Rachel was as spellbound with him as he with her and couldn't formulate an answer to his question. In fact, she didn't even hear the question. As when she had first seen him, he was dressed in western attire—a blue shirt, jeans and gray eelskin boots. Was he always so calm and composed? she wondered. Was he always in command of any given situation? She had thought he dwarfed the car because it was so small, but she realized that Lucas was a compelling presence who would dwarf any room where he was. Right now he seemed to fill the entire doorway.

"Please accept the loan of the clothes," he added, his eyes as warm as his voice. "I owe it to you. It's my fault we met at the barn and you had to become my nurse."

"We could drive to town," Rachel suggested, shying away from any kind of intimacy with this man, "and I could buy me a new dress."

Lucas shook his head. "You could, but that would take a lot of unnecessary time. I want to see the property today, and I need to be home by nine."

Rachel burst into a smile. "You were able to change your meeting and your flight?"

Lucas loved the way she radiated happiness. He nodded his head. "I don't have to fly out until eleven. Now hurry up and put on Cheryl's clothes. I readily take the blame for not being here on time and for causing the delay, but please don't make both of us suffer the consequences."

"No, I won't," Rachel promised, her answer almost a whisper.

She had no time to lose. She had promised Jae that she could go to the football game with Kirk Wilder tonight. Now that meant Rachel would have to call Cindy, her next-door neighbor and friend, and ask if she would keep an eye on Neal and Sammy until Rachel arrived home.

"Thank you, Lucas," she conceded with a smile. "As much as I hate to say it, this does seem to be the best solution."

"When you get to know me better, Rachel March, you'll find that I generally do know best."

Lucas's teasing grin took the boast out of his words, but Rachel wondered how much truth there was to his claim.

Molly rolled her eyes in exaggerated irritation and marched across the room. When she reached the door, she placed both hands on Lucas's chest and shoved him away from the jamb. "Let's get out of here, O Mighty One, while you're still alive."

"If you don't mind," Rachel said, before Molly closed the door, "I need to use the phone to make a couple of long-distance calls. I want to arrange for a baby-sitter in case I don't get home in time, and I need to call Elaine Halston to let her know that we'll be there." Reaching for her purse, she added, "I have my card."

"You're welcome to use the phone, and you don't have to put it on your card," Lucas said, peering around Molly's shoulders. "You wouldn't be having to make these calls if it weren't for me." Just before Molly shut the door, Lucas called from down the hallway, "We'll be waiting for you in the kitchen."

Rachel quickly made her calls, the first one to Cindy, who was really more than a neighbor. Within months of being the same age as Rachel, Cindy Zaldivar was a friend, confidante, counselor—and an at-the-last-minute baby-sitter.

"Don't worry," Cindy said as soon as Rachel explained her predicament. "I'll keep an eye on the boys. If you're not home by bedtime, I'll tuck them in over here. You know Ethan and Cody will love that."

Rachel laughed as she envisioned the four boys together for the night. "How about you and Robert?"

"We'll spend the night thinking of ways we can get even," Cindy teased.

After Rachel completed her call to Elaine Halston in Kerrville, she returned to the kitchen to join Lucas, who was already seated at the oak table. Molly was busy at the counter.

"Everything okay?" Lucas asked, standing to pull out a chair for Rachel. His eyes ran appreciatively over her figure. She modeled the skirt and blouse to perfection. He liked it on her.... He liked her.

"Fine," Rachel replied. "If I'm not home, Cindy will keep an eye on the boys, and Elaine is expecting us within the next three or four hours."

Lucas chuckled. "You were going to give us plenty of time."

"After this morning I'm not sure what might happen."

"That's sorta the way life goes with Lucas," Molly said. Coffeepot in hand, she moved to the table and filled Rachel's cup. "Never a dull moment." She pointed to the lazy Susan. "Your preference. Butter. Jams and jellies. Syrup and honey."

"Really, I shouldn't," Rachel began.

"Really, you should," Lucas insisted, spinning the tray so that the biscuits, aromatic and golden brown, were right in front of her nose and eyes. "You've never tasted food like this before. The jams and jellies are homemade. And the honey comes from Mrs. Molly's apiary."

"And the butter comes from the local Lucky Brand Supermarket," Molly added dryly as she dragged a chair from the table and sat down.

"I've never been able to pass up temptation," Rachel confessed, her mouth already watering, "especially when it comes to raiding the cookie jar."

"Then you're at the right house," Lucas said. "Molly actually encourages us to become cookie thieves; she always keeps the jar full of goodies."

While they laughed and talked so easily and effortlessly, Rachel drank two cups of coffee, ate two biscuits, and sampled all the jams and jellies and the honey.

"Have another," Lucas said.

Rachel shook her head and laid her napkin on the table. "No more for me." She looked at Molly. "Everything was so delicious that I stuffed myself. I won't be hungry for a week."

"Sure you will," Molly said. "That's just enough to keep you a couple of hours."

"I hate to eat and run," Lucas said, the chair grating against the floor as he stood, "but it's time we left if we intend to get to Kerrville today. How about our taking my car?"

"We'll go in mine," Rachel returned. Time in the car was too valuable for getting to know the client for her to give it up voluntarily. "All of my things are in it."

"I insist," Lucas said, then grinned. "More legroom."

As if the matter were settled, Molly said, "I guess that means you're going to come back by the house before you leave tonight?"

Fifteen minutes later Lucas guided the black Mercedes out of the garage, down the driveway, and through the double gates of the Lucky Brand Ranch as he and Rachel headed toward Kerrville. Rachel always enjoyed traveling through the hill country, but today the trip was special. The autumn weather was sunny and mild, just right for a drive in the country, and Lucas's company was enjoyable. All too soon they were parking in front of Elaine Storch Halston's two-story Victorian mansion situated on the banks of the river in downtown Kerrville.

As soon as they stepped onto the veranda, the door opened and a woman in her early sixties came out. Her short white hair was brushed away from her face in waves, and she wore a beige lightweight sweater and dark brown skirt that complemented her slender frame. Gold earrings and chains were her only jewelry.

"Hello, Rachel," Elaine Halston said with a friendly smile. "It's so nice to see you again."

"I'm glad to see you," Rachel said, then added, "Mrs. Halston, I'd like you to meet Lucas Brand."

"Call me Elaine, please," the older woman instructed as she extended her hand in greeting. Her eyes twinkled. "I'm so glad to meet you, young man. I've heard a lot about you from Rose Gerwood."

Lucas smiled. "Rose is quite a woman."

With a nod of acknowledgement, Elaine continued, "And I shop regularly at our new Lucky Brand Supermarket. Quite a store. It's giving the competition a run for the money."

"Thank you," Lucas said. "That's my intention."

"But enough of compliments and shoptalk," Elaine said. "I know you're eager to see the ranch." When Lucas nodded, she stated, "I'm going to drive my car, and the two of you can follow in yours."

Immediately Rachel and Lucas protested, but Elaine silenced them with a wave of her hand. "This will be better for all of us," she said. She fished through her purse for her keys. "If you want to stay longer at the property than I want to, you can remain and I can leave. Also I'm going to show you a shorter route to San Antonio, one that doesn't come back through town. Save you some time in getting home."

An hour later, Lucas parked his Mercedes next to Elaine's Cadillac in front of the two-story native stone building. Small outbuildings were clustered around the main house.

"Been in the family over one hundred years," Elaine said, a catch in her voice.

"Why are you selling?" Lucas asked as he turned to study the woman standing next to him.

Elaine didn't answer immediately; instead she took several steps, stopping when she was in front of her car. Her back to Rachel and Lucas, she said, "My husband has terminal cancer, and the medical costs are piling up on us. I'm sixty-three. Phil's seventy. I've...decided that I want to have peace of mind during his last years. The land means a lot to me, but Phil means more."

Both Rachel and Lucas were moved by Elaine's confession, but Lucas spoke first.

"Surely you have other alternatives. You don't have to sell the land."

Elaine turned. "It's true I have other alternatives, and I've carefully considered all of them. This is the one that suits me the best. With the money I get from the ranch,

I can save the house in town. As it is, I run a risk of losing everything. I would rather have the house than the ranch." She paused for a second, then said brightly, "That's that. Now, let's look around. Ask me what you will, and I'll answer to the best of my ability."

"Do you have any children?" Lucas asked, sinking his hands into his back hip pockets as he and Elaine walked toward the house and Rachel followed.

"A daughter," Elaine replied.

"How does she feel about your selling the ranch?"

"To be frank," Elaine said, turning to look directly into Lucas's face, "Roberta's feelings don't really come into consideration. This is my property to do with as I see fit, but as a courtesy to you I'll tell you. She understands that we must sell and basically agrees with me. She would rather have the property and town house than the ranch."

"So if we start negotiating, you won't abruptly change your mind because of sentimentality?"

"I shelved sentimentality and nostalgia a long time ago, Lucas," Elaine confessed. "I'm a modern woman who lives in the present, I move with the times. Now is the time for me to sell Storch-Halston Ranch."

Elaine deliberately led the way so Rachel and Lucas could walk together through the house and all the buildings that surrounded it. They listened raptly as Elaine told them colorful anecdotes about her pioneering family.

"If you buy the ranch, what do you intend to do with it?" Elaine asked curiously as they returned to the cars.

"I want to turn it into a game preserve and lodge," Lucas answered.

"Commercial?" Elaine asked softly.

Lucas nodded.

Elaine, holding her hand above her eyes to shield them from the sun, looked out over the green, rolling hills she'd known since she was a young woman. Soon they would put on their winter coat of golden brown. Finally she said, a small catch in her voice, "It would work out well. You know we have the Frio River running through the property."

"That's what I want to see," Lucas said.

By the time the three of them had returned from a tour of the property and said goodbye, the sun was setting low in the west. Again Rachel was glad that she was with Lucas; he could do the driving and she could curl up in the passenger's seat and relax . . . and watch him.

Chapter Four

"Tell you what," Lucas said when they came to the Interstate 35 access road, "it'll be just as quick if not quicker if I drive you home and have one of the boys bring your car to you tomorrow."

"I wish I could," Rachel answered, "but tomorrow's a full day, and we have to have a car. Since I can't get the Lincoln until Monday, Jae's is it."

"No problem," Lucas said. "I'll stop at a filling station along the way and call Dugan to have him bring yours—" Suddenly he stopped and said, "Well, now, there is one little problem. What about a key?"

"No problem," Rachel said and grinned. "I have one under the right fender, attached by a magnet."

"Good. Dugan can meet us at your house. That way I'll kill two birds with one stone. You'll have your car, and Dugan can take me to the airport and drive home in mine." His head moved in her direction, and he gave her a warm smile. "Is that okay with you?"

"Yes," Rachel murmured, pleased with the turn of events. For the moment she conveniently forgot she was a realtor and Lucas a client.

Glad that he was concentrating on his driving, she studied him. He was a handsome man, not beautiful like

Jared but rugged and enduring like the hill country whence he came, like the bay he rode. He had a self-confidence and strength of character that Rachel admired. When she remembered him this morning with Worthy and Mandy, she readily admitted that he was also gentle and caring.

She looked at the wavy black hair that blended so well with the sun-browned skin, which softened the gaunt angles of his face and brushed against the collar of his shirt. She smiled at the errant lock that fell across his forehead. His dark brows were thick, his lashes long and curling. Laughter lines fanned from the corners of his eyes.

Sensing Rachel observing him, Lucas glanced at her in a questioning manner. Embarrassed that he had found her staring, Rachel quickly dropped her gaze, but not before she saw the small acknowledging smile flit across his lips as he returned his attention to the interstate highway. She wondered if he knew she was admiring him.

"What do you think about the property?" she asked to cover her embarrassment.

"Not bad," he answered, "but she's asking way too much for it, considering that most of the buildings are going to require a lot of money and attention if they're to be salvaged. I want some time, say a week, to consider a counteroffer. Since she was amenable to my suggestion to bring in my own appraisers, that's exactly what I'm going to do. I want to see how the figures compare. Besides, you said you had several more pieces of property to show me. I'd like to see them before I make a final decision. Now," he said, "what do you think about my stopping at a restaurant instead of a filling station? That way—"

"—we can kill two birds with one stone," Rachel interjected. "You can make your phone call to Dugan and we can get something to eat at the same time." She laughed when Lucas teasingly glowered at her.

"Well, Miss Priss," he asked, "do you want to stop and eat or must you rush home?"

"As much as it hurts me to admit it," Rachel confessed, "I am hungry. After all those biscuits this morning, I didn't think I'd ever be hungry again."

"All those biscuits," Lucas exclaimed. "All of two biscuits, Rachel March. No wonder your stomach is complaining."

"To answer your second question, no, I don't need to rush home. Cindy said she would feed the boys, and if I'm not home by bedtime, she'll put them up for the night."

"She's more than just a neighbor," Lucas said.

Rachel nodded. "She's my closest friend. We take turns baby-sitting for each other. Tomorrow I take care of the entire crew. They have basketball practice."

"Tit for tat."

"Mmm-hmm. Works out great for us to swap off baby-sitting, especially with me being in real estate and with Jae's extracurricular activities. I never know when Jae will be home to keep tabs on the boys or how long I'll take with a client."

Lucas glanced at her and raised a brow. "Talking about me, Ms. March!"

Rachel grinned. "I never know what kind of appointment I'll be keeping. This is the first time that I've been a midwife's assistant."

"You didn't do too bad, tenderfoot. I wouldn't mind having you assist me again. Now back to the matter at hand. What kind of food shall we get?"

Such a simple question, yet to Rachel it was one of the most important she'd been asked in a long time. How long had it been since a man asked her out to dinner? Jared had never asked her opinion of anything.

"Steak," she murmured, closing her eyes and squirming to lean her head against the backrest.

Lucas glanced over in time to see the silk material of her blouse pull across her breasts to reveal their supple firmness.

When he didn't answer, her eyes flew open and she rolled her head toward him. "You don't like the suggestion?"

"Love it," he replied, reluctantly returning his gaze to the road.

When he heard Rachel's soft laughter, he turned his head again. Hiking his brows, he said, "I admit to having a wonderful sense of humor, but generally I know what I've done or said to elicit laughter. I haven't said anything funny in the last two minutes. So give? What's funny?"

Rachel's eyes danced with laughter. "I was thinking of Sammy."

"Sammy?"

"My younger son."

Lucas raised a brow and said dryly, "Don't tell me I remind you of your younger son!"

Rachel laughed some more—now she laughed freely—and shook her head, silken strands of hair shimmering around her face. "When it comes to choosing restaurants, he's one of the most decisive people whom I know. When the kids and I go out to eat, we never ask Sammy where he wants to go."

"Must be pretty bad."

"Not bad, just redundant, especially when Sammy requests to eat there seven days a week."

"I'm almost afraid to ask where," he drawled.

"Sombrero Rosa."

"Fast food, Mexican style." He laughed with her. "There is one of those big pink hats over here somewhere, but it's a little out of the way. I take it you'll settle for Miss Julie's Country Kitchen?"

"Sounds good to me," Rachel answered.

Later, after Lucas had called Dugan, had given him directions to Rachel's house and told him what time to meet him, the two of them sat in one of the booths, eating their dinner.

"Tell me about yourself, Rachel," Lucas said, leaning back to study her as he drank his iced tea.

"What a dull story," she said in between bites. "I'm a thirty-nine year old divorcée with three children."

"Your sixteen-year-old cheerleader and Sammy I already know about. What about the other boy?"

"Neal is ten," Rachel answered. "Sammy is six."

"You're fortunate," Lucas said, a sad wistfulness in his voice and eyes. "I always wanted a large family...four or five children...but we...only had the one."

"Cheryl?" Rachel said.

He nodded and moved. In an innocent gesture he caught her hand in his and squeezed reassuringly, much as he would have done had Rachel been a child. "While I'm glad to learn about your family, Rachel, I'd like to know something about you."

Startlingly aware of Lucas, of his lean, hard body sitting across from her, of his legs brushing against hers as he shifted restlessly in the chair, Rachel was unable to look into the gentle gray eyes; she lowered her head and stared at their hands.

"Please tell me something about yourself, Rachel."

Slowly Rachel lifted her head, her eyes moving up the line of mother-of-pearl snaps on the front of his shirt to the opened neckline. Her heartbeat accelerated when she saw the V of dark crisp hair and the corded lines of his throat. When finally her gaze reached his lips, she saw a smile that was both sweet and tender.

"I don't—I haven't—" Talking about herself was a subject Rachel deliberately avoided. The wound of the divorce had healed, but the scar tissue was still sensitive and painful. When she thought about her life with Jared, she hurt all over.

"Rachel." Lucas's voice was soft. "It'll help to talk about it. I haven't been through a divorce, but the woman I was married to for twenty-five years died of cancer. So in a way we've been in a similar situation. I learned the hard way that talking seems to dissipate some of the hurt and loneliness." His eyes held Rachel captive while his thumb traced designs on the back of her hand. "Let me be your friend."

How easily she allowed Lucas to persuade and guide her. Before she quite knew what was happening, she was telling Lucas all about her early years in east Texas as the only child of older parents; she told him of their death; she told him about her seventeen-year-marriage to Jared and her life with the Marches. She glossed over the divorce and spoke of the children.

"They're a handful, but a wonderful handful," she finished.

"If they're anything like their mother, I'm sure they are," he agreed. "And now, Rachel March, you'd better finish your steak before it gets cold."

"Yes, sir," she answered jauntily as she dipped her fork into her baked potato.

Lucas was intrigued by the woman who sat across
from him. She totally captivated him. According to the
intensity of her feelings, the color of her eyes varied
from a brilliant emerald to a forest green. He enjoyed
listening to her talk. Everything she said or did interested him.

He wished he could call and cancel his meeting in
Dallas. He'd love to spend the rest of the evening with
Rachel. He wanted to find out everything he could about
her. Most of all, he wanted to erase that haunted look
from her eyes, take away the hollow wanting sound that
sometimes floated into her voice. He understood loneliness and vulnerability. He'd had his share of it during
his life and saw it every day in the children at the home.

"Lucas—" Rachel swallowed her last bite of food and
leaned back to sip her iced tea "—now tell me something about yourself."

Lucas hesitated. He had a special talent for getting
people to open up and discuss themselves and their
problems; that was one reason for his great success as a
criminal attorney. But he was a quiet, inward person
who didn't like to discuss himself, especially with
women. They seemed to think any conversational ref-
erence to self was an open door to intimacy that would
ultimately lead to marriage, something that he had so far
avoided.

His reluctance to answer disappointed Rachel, although she said nothing. She should have known better
than to let her guard down. Evidently he wasn't going to
do the same. As usual, friendship seemed to be a one-
way street, and the traffic never seemed to go in her
direction. She wiped her hands on the napkin and tossed
it onto the table; then she reached for her purse and
smiled. "I guess it's time for us to go."

Lucas leaned across the table and laid his hand over hers again. "No," he said, "I don't have to go yet, and I'm not ready to take you home."

"Then talk," Rachel said softly. "I'm interested in learning about you."

"What do you want to know?"

Lucas sat up straight and pushed a hand through his dark, wavy hair. "I was the son of a small rancher, and I worked long and hard hours and had little money. My father died when I was fifteen, and I had to quit school to take care of my mother and two younger brothers. At eighteen—"

Lucas paused as the waitress picked up his plate. "Would you like to see our dessert tray?" she asked.

"Not for me," he answered and looked at Rachel, who shook her head.

"At eighteen," she said when the woman departed.

Lucas grinned. "You're determined to hear this to the bloody end, aren't you?"

"I am."

"At eighteen I married Debra Singleton and soon afterward joined the army. By the time my enlistment was over, I was stationed in San Antonio and had gotten my high school equivalency diploma. I enrolled at St. Mary's University, where I completed both my undergraduate and law studies."

Lucas had sounded as if he were giving Rachel an interview. He had given only dry facts, careful to reveal nothing about the man inside, the man she wanted to know more about.

"You've become a criminal attorney of such renown that you handle cases all over the United States."

"Not quite true," he said. "I've never handled one in Hawaii or Alaska yet."

Rachel smiled, then asked, "But that's not saying you won't. Your career as an attorney isn't over yet, is it?"

"I'm slowly working out of the firm," he said, then surprised Rachel by adding, "At times I feel guilty because I'd rather be doing something else besides practicing law."

"Why?" Rachel asked. This was the first time she'd seen a crack in his outer wall of defense. Now she was seeing the man inside.

He shrugged and took a swallow of tea. "Debra worked the entire time I was at the university and afterward until the practice became self-supporting." His eyes grew cloudy with a faraway look. The last of his defenses were down. "We lived from payday to payday. Our big treat was to go to McDonald's for a Big Mac. We certainly couldn't afford children. We waited until I had my degree. When I was twenty-six, she got pregnant, and we had Cheryl."

A sad smile curving his lips, he stopped talking and drank some more of his iced tea. Then he said, "I wanted more children, but Debra didn't. Yet she finally consented to another pregnancy, which resulted in a painful miscarriage. After that she refused to get pregnant, and she never wanted to consider adopting a child."

"Did this bother you?"

"I was hurt," he admitted, making light of the deep scars on his soul, "but I could understand Debra's feelings and I had to accept them."

Now Rachel knew why Lucas had founded the Lucky Brand orphanage. "Through the years you've channeled your love into other children."

"I guess I have," he admitted warily. Revealing his soul to another person, especially to a woman, was a new experience for him.

"How does your daughter feel about it?" Rachel asked.

Lucas's brow furrowed with thought. "She used to love the orphanage, but I don't know anymore, Raye," he finally said, unconsciously giving her a nickname. "At times I'm not sure I understand Cheryl at all. She changed so much after her mother died, but that was to be expected." He shrugged. "It was bound to have changed her."

Lucas thought about the heated argument between Cheryl and himself when she announced that she and her boyfriend were going to live together. Believing that Cheryl was moving in with Duanne because she was trying to prove something to herself rather than because she loved the young man, Lucas had asked her to wait. In a fit of anger Cheryl had accused Lucas of being possessive and overly protective; he was suffocating her. Lucas still bristled with resentment when he thought of her accusations.

"How old is Cheryl?" Rachel asked.

"Twenty."

"Going to college?"

"Mmm-hmm," he said, finishing off his glass of tea. "She's getting her degree in marketing, and she's a highly successful model."

"You're proud of her."

"Yes," Lucas admitted, "I am."

Rachel looked at her watch and sighed. "It's time."

"I wish it weren't. I've enjoyed being with you, Rachel."

"Thank you. This has been a wonderful day for me also."

They didn't do much talking as he drove her home. Both were reluctant to see such a beautiful afternoon come to an end. When Lucas pulled up in front of Rachel's brick two-story house, it was a little after five and the sun was quickly sinking in the west. Her car was parked in the driveway. His arms folded across his chest, Dugan leaned against the trunk of the large pecan tree that shaded the entire front lawn. Lucas pulled the Mercedes into the driveway next to the Tempo and cut off the motor.

"Thanks for such an enjoyable day," he said. "And I'm really sorry for any inconvenience I've cause you."

"None," Rachel said. "And I thank you for an equally wonderful day. Keep me posted on Mr. Worthmore. I feel like he's part mine."

"I will," Lucas promised. He reached into the back seat for her briefcase. Then he opened the door, slid out, and called to Dugan. "Give me a few minutes, and I'll be ready to go."

Dugan nodded his acknowledgement as he looked at Rachel and smiled. "Howdy, Rachel. You're looking a fine sight better than you did the last time I saw you."

Rachel laughed. "Thank you, Dugan. Won't you come in?"

"No, thanks," he said. "I'll wait out here. It's cool and peaceful this time of evening."

When Lucas and Rachel stood in front of the white brick house, he took the key from her and unlocked and opened the door.

"Would you and Dugan like a cup of coffee before you leave?" she asked, taking her briefcase.

"No, thanks. If I'm going to catch my flight, I need to be leaving." Yet Lucas didn't want to leave.

"Are you still interested in seeing the other property?" When he nodded, she asked, "Shall we set up another appointment?"

"I'll call you as soon as I return from Dallas. If you need to reach me while I'm gone, leave a message with my secretary."

Rachel nodded, and the two stared at each other for a full minute before he smiled and backed away. When he reached the Mercedes, he waved goodbye.

Rachel remained in the driveway until the car was out of sight; then she turned and walked into the house. She laid her briefcase on a table in the den as she moved to the kitchen, where she called next door to let the boys know she was home. When Cindy insisted they stay for supper, Rachel agreed. Then she heated a kettle of water and prepared herself a cup of Sanka. Walking into the living room, she stood in front of the window and stared into the street.

She wondered what Lucas thought of her as a person. Did he find her attractive? She certainly hoped so, because she found him to be one of the most stimulating men she'd met in a long time. His touch, the simple gesture of his laying his hand over hers, had awakened dormant emotions in her and had made her totally aware of his masculinity.

Hardly the thought a real estate agent should harbor for her client. She lifted the cup to her lips and took a swallow of the coffee, but it tasted bitter. She set the cup down and folded her arms over her breasts.

Lucas hadn't been gone more than thirty minutes, and already she felt lonely. In one short day he had caused her to remember what it was like to have a man in her

life. Poignantly he served to remind her of her loneliness and vulnerability, of the hurt that could come with
caring too much about a person. She didn't want to feel
as strongly about any other man as she had about Jared;
she didn't want to give anyone the ability to hurt her as
he had.

The back door opened and was slammed shut again,
and a child's shout jarred Rachel out of her ruminations. "Mama! Are you home?"

"In the living room, Sammy," Rachel answered.
When the towheaded six-year-old ran into the room,
Rachel turned.

"Hi, Mama." Sammy gave his mother a big snaggle-
toothed grin and reached up to swat golden-brown hair
out of his blue eyes. "We're gonna eat hamburgers with
Cody and Ethan, and we need the potato chips and the
ketchup and some ice, Cindy says. And we need it real
quick." He darted back into the kitchen to open the
pantry door. "Cindy says you can come over if you
want."

"Tell her thanks," Rachel said, "but I've already
eaten." Standing behind Sammy at the pantry door, she
reached for a plastic grocery bag into which she put the
potato chips and an unopened bottle of ketchup. "Did
Jae get off to the game all right?"

"Yeah," Sammy drawled disgustedly. "She was in
pain, Mama, 'cause Kirk couldn't come by and pick her
up and she had to ride with Mary Jane 'cause you had
her car and she couldn't pick up Kirk."

Rachel grinned at Sammy's disjointed explanation
and asked, "How come Kirk couldn't come to pick her
up?" She opened the freezer door and dumped ice into
a second plastic bag.

"Reckless driving," Sammy mumbled as he rummaged through the refrigerator. "You don't have to be too smart to figure that one out. Have you ever seen him on a skateboard?" Finally Sammy straightened. In one hand he held a jar of olives, and in the other pickles. Without stopping to draw a breath he said, "Kirk wrecked his mom's new car, and his dad wouldn't loan him his. Jae said to tell you you didn't have to come meet the bus tonight at school when the game is over. She'll ride home with Mary Jane, and if they decide to go out to get something to eat, she'll call." He turned and with one expert swing of his leg closed the refrigerator door.

After Sammy left with his bag of groceries, Rachel walked to her office and listened to her messages, but the only one of importance was from Craig, who wanted her to call as soon as she could. Picking up the receiver, she quickly tapped the buttons and listened to the intermittent rings until she heard his resonant voice.

"Hi, Craig. Rachel. What can I do for you?"

"How'd it go?" Craig asked.

How did it go? Rachel repeated mentally, thinking more about Lucas as a man than a prospective buyer. She grinned at her wayward thoughts and tucked a lock of hair behind her ear.

"Very well," she heard herself answer. "Lucas is very much interested in the ranch but thinks Elaine's asking too much for it, so he's going to have his own appraisers evaluate it." For the next thirty minutes, Rachel told him about Lucas's plans for renovating the buildings and creating a lodge.

"Sounds great," Craig answered.

"Yes," Rachel reluctantly admitted, "it does sound great the way Lucas describes it. A three-thousand-acre wilderness resort."

Craig's loud, good-natured laughter flowed through the line. "Has Lucas already converted you, Rachel?"

She felt the heat suffuse her cheeks and was glad Craig couldn't see her face. "Not really, but he's not as bad as I thought he was going to be." Before her employer could retort, she asked, "How did your day in court go?"

Craig groaned. "No sympathy from the judge at all. My record didn't exactly vouch for my having been an innocent victim. Six speeding tickets in the past nine months. I had to enroll in safety driving classes."

After Rachel hung up, she went to her bedroom and undressed. She carefully folded Cheryl's clothes and placed them in a plastic bag. She would have the skirt and blouse dry-cleaned before she returned them to Lucas. She took a long, leisurely shower, donned her nightgown and robe, and curled up in bed to read *Magnolia Nights*. Although the historical novel was highly praised by the critics, it didn't hold her interest tonight. Lucas's face kept haunting Rachel. She missed his quiet laughter and gentle teasing. She remembered his tender ministrations to Worthy and his love for Mandy.

Abruptly Rachel slammed the book shut. She was irritated because she was allowing herself to get carried away by her imagination. She was acting more immaturely than her daughter over a virtual stranger. She picked up the remote control to the television set and flicked from channel to channel. Finally she found an old Western movie, which she watched. At least it kept her from thinking...about Lucas.

As the credits flashed across the screen, Rachel heard the boys calling and knocking on the back door. Quickly she made her way through the kitchen to the utility room. She switched on the light, turned the bolt and unfastened the chain.

"It's about time you came home," she said. "I was about to call to see if you were making a night of it."

Neal raked golden-blond hair out of his eyes. "Nope. Not tonight. I want to finish painting my Revolutionary War soldiers. My project is due on Monday."

"Can I help, Neal?" Sammy begged. "Please."

"No, you can't," Neal exclaimed, brushing past his mother. "You don't make anything but a mess. In fact, kid, you're nothing but a mess looking for a place to litter."

"Neal," rebuked Rachel sharply, "don't talk to Sammy like that."

"I'm not neither," Sammy declared indignantly as he danced around his mother and swung at his older brother. "I don't make messes, do I, Mama?" Without stopping to let Rachel answer, he said, "Make him let me help him, Mama. Make him."

"Not his Revolutionary War soldiers, Sammy," Rachel said quietly, relocking the door. "Since that's part of his project for Social Studies and American Freedom Day, he must do it himself. Besides, those are exclusively Neal's, and you have to respect his right to them."

"I share my toys with him," Sammy grumbled as he pulled his T-shirt over his head and dropped it into the utility hamper.

"Well, don't do it anymore," Neal shouted from the hallway. "That way you won't feel like I should share with you." The bang of his closing door punctuated his sentence.

"That's not fair," Sammy complained, pouting.

"Life is life," Rachel pointed out, "and you just have to learn to deal with it. Now get into the bathroom and take your bath. Then it's to bed, little man."

"Aw, Mama, do I have to go to bed so early? It's Friday night. Why can't I stay up late like Neal?"

Rachel sighed. "You have to go to bed earlier because you're younger than Neal and you need the extra rest. Now off and no more grumbling."

When Rachel passed Neal's room, she knocked and waited for him to answer before she opened the door. She walked to the large conference desk on which he was reconstructing one of the battles of the Revolutionary War.

"You were a little sharp to Sammy a few minutes ago, Neal. I think you owe him an apology."

"I know, Mom." Neal sighed. "I didn't really mean it, he just gets on my nerves sometimes."

"I know," Rachel agreed softly. "He's little and he's learning, but we have to be patient with him."

"I guess I could let him paint some of my soldiers," Neal said, relenting.

"No," Rachel replied quickly. "These are exclusively yours, and Sammy must learn that each of you has toys that are individually yours, but sharing is wonderful and I want you and Sammy to do so willingly."

Neal grinned suddenly. "Sure, Mom, and I know just what to do. I'll get Sammy to find me the rocks and trees I need for my diorama."

Rachel was so proud of her son that she thought her heart might explode. "It's really looking good," she said as she inspected it closely.

"Thanks, Mom," Neal said, his tongue protruding from the corner of his mouth as he touched the tiny metal figure with the tip of the brush. "I just have one more group to paint and glue down, and I'm finished with the soldiers." He set the figurine down. "But I'm gonna need some more rocks—" he pointed "—'cause I'm gonna need a boulder over here and some trees over here. That's what I'll get Sammy to help me with."

For a long time Rachel listened as Neal described all the details of his project. At his request she read his written report. "This is excellent," she said when she was finished, "but you really need to do some editing. You have quite a few grammatical mistakes in there."

Neal grimaced. "This is a history report, not an English composition."

Rachel laid down his paper and stood. "The assignment is a history report, but there's no way you can make a written report without writing a composition. Matter closed. Now reread your paper and make your corrections. I'll look at it again tomorrow."

"Okay, Mom," Neal said, but the report was quickly forgotten. Brush in one hand, soldier in the other, he was painting again.

"Don't forget to take a bath before you go to bed."

"Okay, Mom."

"Good night, Neal."

Neal looked up and grinned. "Good night, Mom."

Rachel closed the door and walked toward her bedroom. Outside the bathroom door, she stopped and listened to Sammy's tuneless serenade. She smiled; her boys were precocious, but they were also precious. She loved them dearly.

An hour later Sammy was in bed fast asleep, Neal was painting in his room, and Rachel was in bed, watching television again and waiting for Jae. She couldn't rest until all her brood was safely in the house. She heard a car pull up in the driveway, a door slam, then the key in the front lock. She breathed a sigh of relief. Jae was home.

When Rachel heard the soft knock on the door, she knew it was Jae coming to give her a blow-by-blow description of the game. "Come in."

Wearing her red, white and blue cheerleading costume, Jae bounced into the room, her long blond hair shimmering around her face. Her eyes, the same color as her mother's, sparkled. "Did you hear the news?"

Rachel grinned and nodded. "Won over Judson by a field goal."

"We beat Judson!" Jae danced around the room. "We beat Judson!"

Taking off her shoes, she curled up on the end of Rachel's bed to share the entire night's happenings with her mother. "And we decided not to go out because Kirk is on restriction. Really bad." She pulled a long face. "And Jeff hurt himself during the game and had to be taken to the emergency room."

"That's enough to ruin your night," Rachel sympathized.

"But, Mom—" Jae's face brightened visibly. "All isn't gloom and doom. Remember Alicia's birthday party that I told you about? The formal dance at the San Antonio Country Club? It's going to be big, Mom. I mean *real big*. And Kirk has asked me to go with him."

"That's wonderful, Jae," Rachel said. "We'll have to go shopping for a dress."

"I've already found the one I want, Mom. We just have to go buy it."

"That was a quick shopping trip," Rachel quipped.

"I went with Mary Jane today after school to pick up her gown, and I found mine." Jae's eyes sparkled with anticipation. "Mom, it's so beautiful."

Jae was so eloquently descriptive that Rachel could easily visualize the creation in emerald-green silk and lace.

"I've never wanted anything as badly as I want this one, Mom," Jae pleaded.

"I'll get it if I can," Rachel promised. "I have three days off next weekend, Saturday, Sunday and Monday. Saturday is American Freedom Day, which I've promised to spend with Neal, and Sunday's is Sammy's and the zoo's, but Monday is free. And if I remember correctly Monday is a student holiday for the high school. If it's okay with you, that'll be our day."

"If that's okay with me!" Jae exclaimed and scooted up the bed to hug her mother. "We'll make a day of it," she planned. "Just you and me. We'll get the dress at Saks, and Leon's has just the shoes to match it."

"Saks! Leon's!" Rachel exclaimed.

"It only sounds expensive, Mom," Jae hastened to explain. "Both the dress and shoes are on sale."

"I don't know," Rachel said.

"Please, Mom," Jae begged. "Don't say no without seeing them first."

Rachel sighed, then said, "We'll look, but I'm making no promises."

Jae clapped her hands together and grinned. "Afterward we'll eat lunch at Luby's and get home before Neal and Sammy are back from school."

"I have a feeling that I'm being taken for a ride," Rachel murmured as she ran her fingers through Jae's golden hair.

Jae laughed and pulled back to look into her mother's face. "Do you mind?"

"No," Rachel said, lifting her hand to cup Jae's cheeks, "I don't mind. Not in the least. I trust your ability to drive."

"Thanks, Mom," Jae whispered and leaned closer to press a kiss on her mother's forehead. "You're the world's greatest."

Chapter Five

Tears running down her cheeks, Rachel backed to the wall behind her and reached for the phone. She sniffed and hunched her shoulder to wipe her cheeks as she laid the receiver against her ear. "Hello."

"Rachel?" Lucas said anxiously.

Rachel was so surprised to hear his voice that she almost dropped the receiver. She did drop the paring knife and circled the counter to slide onto a bar stool. "Lucas."

"What's wrong?"

"Nothing." Rachel laughed, dabbing at her eyes with a paper towel.

"You sound like you're crying."

"I am." She sniffed and laughed again. "I'm dicing onions for the tuna salad," she explained and almost melted when she heard his deep, resonant laughter.

"I wanted to let you know that my appraisers, John Wesson and Company, have come up with figures that contradict Elaine Halston's. Before I even consider an offer, I want to look at those other two sites you told me about, and I want to talk with you. I'm flying in tomorrow evening, and I wondered if we could get together...say Saturday morning."

Rachel knew what she wanted to say, but couldn't. She'd promised the children for the past two weeks that this was their weekend, and they were counting on it. She could see the disappointment on Neal's face if she failed to show at his Freedom Day program—another broken promise because of work, one of many since the divorce. Yet she desperately needed this sale. She needed the money.

Her hesitancy prompted Lucas to say, "Saturday isn't a good time?"

"No," Rachel replied, "it isn't. Neal is a finalist in the American Freedom Day Contest at the Thousand Oaks Library, and I promised that I'd attend the program. I hate to disappoint him, since I don't get to go to many of them with him, but—"

"No," Lucas said, "I can understand his wanting you to be there, and I'm sure you have to turn him down too many times because of work."

"How about Saturday afternoon?" Rachel suggested. "Say four or five."

"Can't," Lucas answered flatly. "I promised Mandy that I'd—" He stopped in midsentence, then exclaimed, "I've got an idea! I promised Mandy that I'd come to the rodeo and see her racing around the barrels. Why don't you join me...and the kids, too? I'll pick you up as soon as the program is over, and we'll spend the afternoon and evening here."

"A rodeo," Rachel reminisced, running her left hand beneath the faucet.

"And a carnival and the midway," Lucas said, laughter in his voice again. "Livestock exhibits and rodeos. I know it doesn't sound too exciting, but..."

"I haven't been to a fair in so many years."

"Then go with me," Lucas said. "What time shall I pick you up?"

"The awards will be presented at eleven."

"Rachel," Lucas said tentatively, "would you mind if I joined you for the program?"

Rachel was so pleased that Lucas would want to that she couldn't immediately answer.

Wondering if maybe she thought he was being presumptuous, he added, "I'd like to see Neal's project myself, and also I'm interested in the program. It might be one we could use at the Children's Ranch."

"I'd love for you to come," Rachel finally said.

"Good!" Lucas was glad. "What time does Neal have to be there?"

"Nine," Rachel replied. "Everything's already set up. The projects have been on display for the past week."

"I'll pick you up at eight-thirty. Okay?"

"You're sure?"

"I'm sure," Lucas replied. "The morning belongs to you and yours, but the afternoon is for me and mine. Pact?"

"Pact," Rachel replied, laughing.

Long after she'd hung up the receiver, Rachel stood by the phone, smiling.

"Hi, Mama." Sammy hooked his baseball cap onto the back of the bar stool as he walked into the kitchen and opened the refrigerator door to extract his personal water jar. "How come you're leaning against the wall and grinning so silly like?"

"Am I?" Rachel asked, hastily moving back to the counter to resume her tearful job.

"Mmm-hmm," he droned as he unscrewed the lid. "What are we having for supper? I'm starved."

"Tuna and noodle salad."

"Yummy," Sammy squealed and slammed the door as he climbed atop a bar stool. "Boy, Mom, I like it when you cook supper for us."

Grinning at her younger son, Rachel leaned over and kissed the tip of his dirty little nose. Pulling back, she traced her fingertip over the splattering of freckles that ran across his nose and cheeks. "It takes so little to please you. Call Neal and Jae, and wash—"

"My hands," Sammy said, holding out two grimy palms.

"More than your hands," Rachel said. "Everything from your waist up."

Sammy gave her a toothless grin and drank his water. "Mama," he asked seriously, "do you think it's possible to wash your body away from too many baths? You know, like one day you'll send me to take a bath, and I'll disappear down the drain and you'll never see me again."

"Nope." Rachel cast Sammy a glance and said dryly. "You hardly stay in the water long enough to get the dirt off, much less skin. Now scoot."

"Who was that on the phone, Mom?" Jae asked when she walked into the kitchen and leaned over the counter to dip a spoon into the salad.

"Lucas Brand," Rachel answered.

"Who's he?"

"The man who's interested in buying the Halston Ranch. You know, the one I met last week." Rachel reached out and tapped Jae's hand as she swooped for the second spoonful of salad. "Wait until supper."

"Mmm. Good," Jae mumbled, her mouth full.

"What?" Rachel teased. "Lucas or the supper?"

Jae dropped the spoon into the sink and spun around. "Is there something you're not telling me, Mom?"

Hearing the disapproval in Jae's voice, Rachel smiled self-consciously and wiped her hands down her slacks. "Well . . . Lucas wants to join us for the American Freedom Day ceremonies and afterward he wants to take all of us to a fair in New Braunfels."

Jae stared at her mother with solemn eyes. "Is that a wise decision, Mom? Going out with your client?"

Having to answer to her own daughter was a new and not too pleasant experience for Rachel. "This is more business than pleasure," she explained.

"I know I'm only sixteen," Jae drawled skeptically, "but even I know business from pleasure, Mom. This man wants to meet your three kids! Give me some credit." Quickly she turned her attention to the olive jar. She tilted it and fished around for the last two olives.

"Well?" Rachel asked. "What do you think?"

"I think you ought to be careful, Mom," Jae replied, popping an olive into her mouth and munching. "You may be nearly forty, but you're an innocent."

"Thanks," Rachel drawled, mimicking her daughter, "but I wasn't asking for advice. I wanted to know if you were going with us or not."

"Can't," Jae answered. "The National Honor Society is meeting Saturday afternoon to plan our annual fund-raiser, and I have to be there since I'm one of the officers."

"Can't you change your plans?"

Jae shook her head. "Think of it this way, Mom. You're down one kid, only two to go."

Rachel laughed. "Set the table, then go get your brothers. Supper's ready."

"YOU LOOK LOVELY, Rachel." A slow smile curled Lucas's lips. "In fact, I've been wanting to tell you all evening, but this is the first time that we've been alone."

As he talked the noise of the midway slowly receded, and the throng of people seemed to dissipate. Rachel's world consisted of Lucas and herself. He didn't touch her physically, but she felt the warm, tingling touch of his expressive gray eyes as they slowly moved from her green western shirt to the formfitting jeans and western boots. When he lifted his face and his eyes again met hers, she saw appreciation. Moreover she saw admiration.

Rachel returned his smile. "Jae insisted that I buy an outfit suitable for the rodeo," she explained. "This is the first time that I've been a cowgirl."

Staring into each other's eyes, Lucas and Rachel were totally oblivious to the hustle and bustle around them. Lucas tucked a stray wisp of hair behind her ear, then laid his hand on her face. Rachel quivered when she felt the gentle yet abrasive touch of his callused palm on her cheek. Unconsciously she moistened her lips with the tip of her tongue—the gesture purely innocent, utterly provocative. This moment marked a subtle change in their relationship, which each recognized and accepted.

"I'm a first for you in many ways, aren't I?"

The question was loaded with meaning, of which both were aware. "Yes," Rachel answered, a breathless excitement running in her veins, "you are."

Attuned to her feelings, Lucas asked, "Do you mind that the children went home with the MacAdams and Mandy?"

His fingertips gently caressed her temple, sending shivers of anticipation speeding down her body to remind her that she and Lucas were by themselves.

"No," Rachel finally answered, "they'll enjoy being with the other children, especially Mandy. Thank you for today, Lucas. I really appreciated your being there to see Neal win first prize. And the rodeo and carnival were—" Rachel didn't have words to express the gratitude she felt for the kindness and attention he had shown her children all day.

"Neal's a swell kid, and I was happy to be there. In fact, Ms. March, both are special children—even Sammy, the hat man." Lucas's eyes twinkled. "I figure he needs a good cowboy hat, so he can change once in a while. Think I'll buy him one."

"Then you'll have a friend for life," Rachel promised.

"A person can't have too many of them," Lucas said. "And I think Sammy's the kind of friend everyone needs at least one of." Again they laughed, and Lucas unconsciously twined a strand of Rachel's hair around his fingers. "I wish Jae could have joined us. I wanted to meet her."

"I wanted you to meet her, too," Rachel said.

"Neal told me she looked just like you."

"Most people think so."

"Then she's bound to be beautiful."

"Is that a left-handed compliment?" Rachel smiled shyly.

"Right-handed." A warm smile played at the corners of Lucas's mouth. "I can hardly wait for you to meet my daughter."

"If she's anything like her father, I know I'll like her."

"You think so?" The warm, husky tones washed over Rachel.

She nodded her head, inadvertently rubbing her cheek against Lucas's hand. The sensation was headier than a caress. She shivered, a little from the autumn chill, more from Lucas.

Immediately solicitous, Lucas said, "You're cold."

"Chilly," Rachel admitted. "I should have worn a sweater or light jacket."

Lucas shrugged out of his jacket. "Here," he said, slinging it over her shoulders, "try this on for size." He laughed when it swallowed her. "At least it will ward off the chill."

Rachel slipped her arms into the sleeves of the jacket and submissively allowed Lucas to zip it up. They looked into each other's eyes again and smiled. Rachel slid her hands into the pockets and gratefully snuggled into the warmth. She inhaled deeply, drinking in Lucas's intoxicating scent. His after-shave reminded her of the fragrance of the hill country in spring. Outdoorsy. Primitive. Sexy.

A strangling tightness cramped Rachel's heart, and she lowered her head. She could no longer look Lucas in the eyes for fear he'd read her inner thoughts. She was much too aware of him as a man, and she wasn't ready for a man in her personal life yet. Especially not Lucas.

His hand touched her chin and gently raised her head. "Rachel, do you like me?"

"Yes," she whispered.

"You're very special to me." Sensing Rachel's fears and doubts, he dropped his hand. "Now, Rachel March, you and I are going to enjoy this carnival. We're going to do whatever your heart desires."

Rachel thoroughly enjoyed the evening. She and Lucas laughed with the abandon of children. They enjoyed the sideshows; they tossed coins at dishes; they ringed bottles; and Lucas tossed baseballs at wooden milk cans to win her a huge red teddy bear.

"If it's a bear, it's just barely," Lucas said when he took the brightly colored stuffed animal. "Haven't figured out what it looks like but when I do, I'll let you know."

They laughed; they ate a candied apple and cotton candy.

"Did you have a good time?" Lucas asked as they sat at a knee-knocking table and shared a soft drink with two straws.

Rachel stared into the earnest gray eyes and quivered with excitement when she felt his legs brush against hers in the confined space. "I don't know when I've enjoyed an evening more, Lucas."

"Me neither." Lucas reached out and caught her hand in his. "The enjoyment comes not so much from what you're doing as whom you're doing it with. Thank you, Rachel March, for an enjoyable day."

"Is it about time for us to pick up the children?"

Lucas nodded, and both of them stood. When they reached the exit, Rachel stopped and turned around. For some reason she wasn't ready to leave yet. Strange as it seemed, this world of merry-go-rounds and carousels was a special realm for Lucas and herself. Although neither of them had been there for many years, each seemed to belong. How quickly and easily they shed the trappings and demands of society!

Holding the teddy bear in front of her with both arms, she gazed down the aisle of bright lights at the carnival. As if it were a magnet, the double Ferris wheel caught her attention.

"Lucas," she said with the wistfulness of a child, "let's ride the Ferris wheel one more time before we leave." She turned to him. "Please."

Lucas was as loath to leave this magical world as Rachel. His lips slowly curved into that deep, warm smile that was his alone. He gazed intently into her eyes as he took the teddy bear from her unresisting fingers, caught one of her hands in his and raised it. "Your wish is my command," he murmured, brushing his lips against her knuckles, his breath seductively caressing her skin. "To the Ferris wheel we will go." Her hand still captured in his, he drew her nearer.

As they walked the length of the midway, Rachel was truly lost in the spell Lucas had woven around her. She didn't notice the jostling crowd; she didn't hear the music and noise. She was aware only of Lucas.

They didn't talk, but they held hands and smiled at each other as they waited their turn; then they were racing up the boardwalk to their chair. Rachel flopped Barely Bear between them.

"No, ma'am," Lucas said, picking up the teddy bear and settling in next to Rachel. "I've shared you with cows and children, but I'm not sharing you with a stuffed animal." He lowered his voice. "I'm certainly not letting him come between us."

Rachel wasn't quite sure when the Ferris wheel moved, but suddenly she and Lucas were way above the noise and clamor. When Lucas put his arms around her and moved closer, Rachel's skin tingled with new sensations, and she welcomed his embrace by tucking her face against his chest. She listened to the strong, steady beat of his heart. He was solid and real. Yet he was tender and caring.

Lucas laid his cheek on the top of her head and whispered, "Nickel for your thoughts."

"I was looking at the stars," she confessed. "We're so high I felt as if I could reach out and pluck one. I feel like I'm in heaven." Rachel waited a moment to see if he was going to laugh at her, but he didn't.

"The stars are close," he eventually replied, "and I wish I could give you one to take home with you so you'd have something to remember this night by."

Rachel pulled away and looked into his earnest face. "I don't need a star to remember tonight," she assured him. "Nor the teddy bear. I'll always remember it."

"I will, too," he promised. "Always I shall remember Carnival Night. A special time and place for you and me." He lowered his face to hers, but Rachel shook her head.

Her heart seemed to leap into overdrive as it pounded against her chest. Her body yearned for Lucas with a fierceness that terrified her. In one night, in one moment of desire her defenses, so carefully erected during the past two years, were crumbling. The revelation was so awesome that Rachel turned her head for fear Lucas might read her thoughts.

"No," she murmured, "it's much too soon."

When Lucas felt her withdrawal, he wanted to hug her tightly and console her. But he didn't. Instead he said, "I understand. I don't want to rush you. May I see you tomorrow?"

"I already have a date."

Lucas was disappointed.

Before he could say anything, Rachel laughed. "I'm taking Sammy to the zoo."

"Oh, Lord," Lucas groaned good-naturedly, relieved that she wasn't going with another man. "I see we have another exciting day ahead of us."

"We?" Rachel angled her head so that she was looking at him.

"May I tag along?" A lopsided grin tugged at one corner of his lips. "I promise I won't be any trouble, and I think all of us could have a fun time together."

"Yes," Rachel assured him.

His eyes moved to hers, and he said, "I especially want to prove to you that I'm a wonderful person to be with."

"You already have," she answered.

Rachel and Lucas laughed as the Ferris wheel bounced to a halt and the adventurers departed. The two of them, holding hands, walked down the midway and through the exit gate. They talked quietly as they drove the short distance from New Braunfels to the Lucky Brand, where they picked up two exhausted and sleepy boys. By the time they reached Rachel's house, both boys were asleep in the back seat.

Rachel succeeded in waking Neal and he stumbled to the front door, but Sammy was fast asleep. Lucas picked him up. "Which room?" he asked, as he strode quickly down the hallway.

"Second on the right," Rachel called out as she ran ahead to turn on lights and open doors. "Neal," she said, "into your pajamas and off to bed." Then she looked in on Jae, lightly touched her daughter's face and kissed her. "Good night, darling girl."

After she walked out and closed the door, she checked to see that Neal had indeed changed his clothes and was in bed. She tucked the cover under his chin and gave him a quick kiss on the cheek. "Good night, little man," she murmured. She switched off his light and joined Lucas in Sammy's room.

Lucas, pulling open drawers, looked up when she entered and grinned. "I'm having a time finding his pajamas. Most of his drawers are filled with books and toys and junk. Where does he keep his clothes?''

Rachel laughed. ''That's the way he cleans his room.'' She moved to the dresser. ''This one is for clothes.'' She pulled out Sammy's pajamas and quickly undressed and redressed her younger son. After she'd tucked him under the covers, she kissed him good-night.

She and Lucas stood at the door for a moment, looking and smiling at Sammy. Then Lucas switched off the light and draped an arm over her shoulder. They walked into the den, the only light a small wedge shining in from the hallway. When they stopped, Rachel turned into Lucas's arms.

''Would you like to have a cup of coffee?'' she asked.

He shook his head. ''No, I need to get back and get some sleep. We have a big day ahead of us tomorrow, and I want to be rested.''

''Lucas, you don't have to,'' Rachel began.

''I want to because I want to be with you—'' he lifted a hand and caught her chin ''—but I promise you that we'll have some time for each other. Selfish time that we don't have to share with the children. The opera. The ballet. The symphony. A play at the Majestic Theater.''

''I would love that,'' Rachel murmured, trying to remember the last time she'd had an evening planned totally for her enjoyment. It was so long ago, she didn't want to waste precious time with Lucas thinking about it.

Lucas cupped Rachel's face in his hands. ''Rachel March, you're one of the most beautiful women I've ever seen, and your green eyes with the golden flecks are the most beautiful I have ever beheld.''

Pleasure gushed through Rachel. ''And you're a flatterer, Mr. Brand.''

"Innocent of that charge," Lucas said. "I've always dealt with the truth or held my peace. Now it's time for me to leave. Good night." He brushed a light kiss onto her forehead. "What time shall I pick you up?"

"Ten," Rachel said.

Reluctantly Lucas dropped his arms and caught her hands in his. He squeezed gently. "Until ten."

After Lucas was gone, Rachel dressed for bed, but she was too excited to sleep. Putting on her robe and slippers, she went to the kitchen and quietly warmed some milk for a cup of hot chocolate.

"Couldn't sleep?" Jae asked, shattering the quietness.

Rachel was momentarily startled and spilled milk onto the counter. When she set down the boiler, she smiled and said, "Too much excitement today. I need something to settle me down. How about you?" She filled the remainder of the cup with thick marshmallow crème and lifted it to her lips.

"I was sleeping all right," Jae returned, her voice rather sharp. "You and Lucas awakened me."

Rachel jerked up her head in surprise and swallowed too much of the hot liquid too quickly. "I'm sorry," she apologized. "I didn't realize we were that noisy."

"Did you enjoy it?" Jae asked.

"Enjoy what?" Rachel asked coolly, although she knew.

"His holding and kissing you," Jae said. "Did you compare him to Daddy? Or did you even think of Daddy?"

Rachel resented Jae's inquisition and accusations, though she did feel a tad uncomfortable on learning that her daughter had witnessed such an intimate scene between Lucas and herself. She was so angry that she took several deep breaths and walked into the den where she set her cup on the end table and switched on a lamp. Having to answer to parents when you were a minor was one thing, but having to answer to a minor when you were a parent was quite another!

While Rachel understood her daughter's feelings and knew she couldn't ignore them, she wanted Jae to understand her own needs as an adult. She and Jae must face the issue honestly and openly; communication between them was a must.

Rachel turned to face Jae. "I enjoyed being with Lucas tonight. He's a wonderful man whom I want to get to know much better. And, no, I didn't find myself comparing him with your father."

Jae laughed bitterly. "So much for love, huh?"

"I am not going to lay a guilt trip on myself, nor will I allow you to," Rachel said, then added softly, "You must realize, Jae, I'm a grown woman. I have a life to live just like you."

"Grown woman!" Jae explained. "You were making a fool of yourself with that man! Why, you don't even know him, yet you were letting him kiss and fondle you!"

"That's enough," Rachel said. "I will not stand here and listen to your accusations. Lucas was not kissing and fondling me."

"No? What would you call it?" She laughed bitterly. "Maybe if you had allowed Daddy the same liberties, you would be married to him today."

"I married your father because I loved him, and more than likely I would still be married to him today if he had not initiated the divorce. But we are divorced, Jae, and that's a fact you're going to have to face. I faced it and I'm through with my bitterness and disillusionment."

Rachel's voice softened. "And you must also understand that just because I'm divorced from Jared doesn't mean that I'm divorced from my emotions or needs or desires. I'm simply a woman, no more, no less, and it's time I moved on with my life."

Jae didn't reply; she turned and walked into the kitchen to open the cabinet for a cup. Using the remainder of the warmed milk, she made another cup of chocolate. Her back to her mother, she said, "You're my mother, so it's hard for me to think of you as anything but Daddy's wife and my mother." She ran her hand around the rim of the cup. "You're going to see Lucas again?"

"Yes," Rachel replied, "I am."

Jae picked up the cup and took a swallow of the chocolate.

"If you knew Lucas, you'd like him," Rachel said.

Jae shrugged. "Maybe. But even then, I'm not sure I'd like him for you."

Rachel smiled wearily. "Would you like any man except your father for me?"

Again Jae shrugged.

Rachel walked up behind Jae to lay her hands on her shoulders. "I loved your father at one time, but we're divorced now. While I could live in a vacuum for the rest of my life, I'm not going to. I love you and Neal and Sammy very much, nothing or no one will ever rob you of that love. But I also want to be loved...and to love a man."

"Is Lucas that man?"

"I don't know, but I'd like the chance to find out."

Jae spun around. "Does it matter what I think?"

"It matters, but it's not going to stop me," Rachel said, staring directly into Jae's eyes.

"Then there's nothing else to say, is there?" Jae's eyes sparkled with tears.

"Are you going to the zoo with us tomorrow?"

"No." She turned and walked to her room, calling over her shoulder, "Some of us are meeting tomorrow to make our posters for the pep rally next week. Like you, I have my life to live."

"So be it. Good night, Jae."

"Good night."

Her heart heavy, Rachel left the cup of tepid chocolate on the table. She understood Jae's reservations about her being with a man other than Jared. Rachel wanted to help Jae come to grips with her dilemma, but Jae would have to work this out by herself. All Rachel could do was be there and love her.

Besides, Rachel had her own ghosts to fight. Tonight's events had resurrected old fears to haunt her. She was just beginning to get over the anguish of Jared's walking out on her, just beginning to make a new life for herself. She was afraid to open herself to another man, perhaps to another hurt. Her newly found independence meant too much to her. She also understood that Lucas had been playing the field romantically for the past five years, and she had no assurance that she would be anything but one of many conquests for him. She was leery of rushing into a relationship. Jared had swept her off her feet—and look where she'd landed. That wouldn't happen to her again! Never again!

Chapter Six

"I'm ready to go home. I've had about as much of the zoo as I can take." Cindy Zaldivar raised both hands and pushed them through a mass of short black curls. Dark brown eyes were hidden by large-rimmed sunglasses. "Since the kids don't have school tomorrow, Rachel, why not let the boys come home with me? They can watch videos tonight, and you and Lucas can spend the evening together. We have two new *Star Trek* movies."

"Yeah, Mom, say yes," Neal said. "I want to go home with Cindy."

"Yeah, Mom, me, too." Sammy shouted and clapped his hands. Looking up, he saw Lucas and Ethan walking out of the Aquatic Museum. "You, too, Lucas?" he called.

"Me, too, what?"

"You want to go with me to Cindy's to watch *Star Trek*?"

"Aw, Sammy," Neal scoffed. "I'll bet Lucas doesn't even watch *Star Trek*."

Lucas made a solemn face and lifted his left hand to make the sign of the Vulcan. "I'd have you know, Neal March, I am a devoted Trekkie."

"Goody!" Sammy danced around Lucas. "You can come with us. First, we're—"

"First, we're going to eat supper, then take a bath," Cindy said.

"Ugh!" Sammy's exuberance died. "Mother's are all alike. Always wanting to give their kids a bath. Where's Cody?"

"Over there." Neal pointed his finger and moved in the direction of the monkey cages. "Come on, Ethan. Let's see what the brat's up to."

"Neal, don't be calling people brats," Rachel called.

Neal looked over his shoulder and grinned. "I won't, Mom. I promise."

Rachel grimaced and sighed her irritation; Lucas chuckled.

"See that you treat your brother and Cody with the same respect you give other people, Neal," she called out.

Neal nodded his head but didn't look back.

"Well," Cindy said, once the children had wandered off, "how about it, Rachel? Can the boys spend the night at my house?"

Before Rachel could answer, Cody called and waved, "Mama! Come see the baby giraffe."

Cindy grinned. "Think on it while I look at the giraffe."

When they were alone, Lucas caught Rachel's hands in his. "If you don't mind the boys spending the night with Cindy, I'd certainly like us to have this time together by ourselves. I'd like to get better acquainted." He paused, then added with a disarming grin, "I'd like to think you wanted it, too."

I do, she thought, but was still unsure of herself. She felt very much like a young girl being asked out on her first date. Breathless and excited. Suddenly aware of her womanhood. But she wasn't a young girl; she was no longer innocent and didn't look at the world through rose-colored glasses. She was suddenly wary.

"But if you want the boys with you," Lucas continued, wondering if he was pushing her too fast, "I'd like for the four of us to spend the evening together doing whatever you or they want." The gray eyes were frank and direct. Lucas's clasp tightened over her fingers. "I just want to be with you, Rachel. I enjoy your company."

Rachel nodded and looked down at the big hand closed about hers. His grip was strong and reassuring, the warmth of his touch spreading through her body.

"We're going," Cindy called. "Have you made up your mind?"

"Please, Mom," Neal called, "say yes."

"All right," Rachel replied, smiling at the boys. "Be sure to make them mind, Cindy. Don't take any guff from them."

"I won't," Cindy called over her shoulder and led the boys to the entrance.

"You hungry?" Lucas asked.

"Come to think of it—" Rachel grinned "—I am."

The gray eyes twinkled and a crooked grin touched the firm mouth. "Sammy's not here, so we're not going to Sombrero Rosa tonight."

The grin turned into soft laughter. "Taco Cabana," she ventured.

"How about the Tower?"

Rachel looked at her denim skirt and sweater. "Dressed like this?"

"That's the wonderful thing about living in tourist country," he returned. "No one notices how you're dressed."

"How about a compromise, Counselor?"

Pure devilment glinted in the recesses of the gray eyes. "Only if the conditions are right."

Excitement skittered through Rachel's body. "How about our eating on the river," she suggested.

"The river it is."

"But first—" her eyes followed the brightly colored cable cars that swung through the air and glided over the rock quarry that had been turned into an exotic botanical wonder "—let's go to Sunken Gardens."

"Shall I drive around?" he asked.

"No, let's take the sky ride."

Hand in hand Lucas and Rachel strolled across the street, up the hill to the ticket office. Soon they were settled in a bright red gondola. The western sky was ribboned in orange and purple, and the setting sun cast San Antonio in its brilliant evening glow.

Rachel looked over the side of the cable car into the silvery pool and gardens below. "I love Sunken Gardens," she breathed. "Even in autumn."

"You sure can't tell that was once a rock quarry, can you?"

"The last time I was here," Rachel said, "in May, they were having a wedding. Over there beside that century plant." Without thinking, she leaned across Lucas and pointed to one of the brick paths that wound down the side of the quarry. Not until she realized her breasts were pressed against his chest did she remove herself and say quickly, "The...uh...the minister was standing about three steps above them, and the bride and groom—"

Lucas concealed his grin and listened attentively as Rachel described the ceremony. His thoughts, however, weren't on the wedding or the garden. They, like his eyes, were on Rachel herself. Her hair, spun gold by the afternoon sun, formed a nimbus around her face. Her eyes sparkled with life; her voice was animated and happy. He enjoyed being with her. She infused him with her enthusiasm for life.

"Lucas?"

Jarred from his ruminations, Lucas blinked.

Rachel laughed softly. "Where were you?"

"Not where," Lucas countered, a slight huskiness giving his voice sexual overtones, "but with whom?"

Thinking of the beautiful women he'd often been pictured with, Rachel's eyes darkened. "Oh," she whispered through numbed lips.

"With you," he answered and reached out to lay his palm against her cheek. "You're a beautiful woman, Rachel."

"Thank you," she murmured. Uneasy with the compliment, she turned her face away from him.

Reluctantly Lucas moved his hand and dropped his arm behind her, slipping his fingers over her shoulder. He had to be careful; she was as skittish as a colt. "You haven't gone out with many men since your divorce, have you?"

"No," she murmured, "You're the first."

Gentle fingers traced designs on her shoulder. "Rather traumatic, isn't it?"

She turned her head, her hair gently swinging around her cheeks, and looked at him in surprise.

"I remember my first date about a year after Debra died." He grimaced and laughed. "When you're twenty-one, you're so full of confidence and youth, your only concern is when to do something. You think you're eternal. When you're forty-one, you know beyond any shadow of a doubt that you're a mere mortal, and your primary concern is what to do.''

Rachel relaxed and laughed with him. "And you find yourself answering to your children rather than to your parents.''

"I think that's when we really begin to appreciate our parents,'' Lucas answered dryly, "and realize they weren't nearly as hard on us as we thought. Children can be most demanding.''

Thinking about Jae's outburst last night, Rachel sighed.

"Care to talk about it?'' he asked.

"I don't want to bore you.''

"I wouldn't have asked if I hadn't wanted to know.''

"It's Jae,'' she began. "She's taking the divorce pretty hard. In fact, she won't accept it. She believes deep down that one day her father and I will get back together.''

"Will you?'' Lucas asked, keeping his tone light.

"No.''

"For my sake, I'm glad.'' Relief surged through him, and for a moment, they stared into each other's eyes. "Tell me about the divorce,'' he said softly.

As Rachel stared into the depths of those dove-gray eyes, she was compelled to talk. Quietly she recounted the events leading up to and following her divorce from Jared. Again she was surprised. The retelling didn't bring the usual hurt and grief. Rather than being an integral part of her story, she was merely the narrator now.

"Do you still love him?''

Rachel paused fractionally, then said, "No.''

The hesitation disappointed Lucas. Rachel thought she was over Jared, said she was, but he wondered what she had stored away deep down in the coffers of her heart.

"I've begun to think that I never loved him," Rachel confessed. "He swept me off my feet when we first met. I was so young and my parents had just died. I was living with an aunt who really didn't want me. We were...married before I realized what had happened. Then for seventeen years I starred in the role of Mrs. Jared Jaeson March."

"Jared Jaeson," he repeated. "Jae's named after her father."

"Jae Ruella after Jared and me," Rachel answered. "Ruel was my middle name."

"Why didn't she come with you today?" Lucas asked, deliberately shifting the topic from the divorce. His questions had been answered; now he wanted to move the conversation in a happier direction. He didn't want to share Rachel with Jared. She was his right now, and he wanted her to be aware of him.

"She and the other cheerleaders are making posters for next week's pep rally."

"Perhaps I'll get to meet her when I take you home tonight."

"I'm not sure that this is the right time for you to meet her," Rachel said. "Last night was the first time she's seen me with...another man. Our coming in awakened her. She got up in time to see you...*tell* me good-night."

"She's upset about my kissing you good-night."

Rachel nodded.

"She'll get over it. The first time they see their parent with a date is the hardest on them. Believe me, I know. I've been through this with Cheryl."

The gondola jostled over the connecting joint and lurched into the station. The attendant caught the door and brought it to a swaying halt. "Round trip?" he asked.

"No, we're getting out here." Lucas caught Rachel's hand in his as they disembarked and ran to join the group moving down the winding path to the stone pagoda.

"The Japanese Tea Gardens," Rachel said. "Isn't it lovely?"

"Beautiful," Lucas agreed, "but not as beautiful as you, Rachel."

Rachel didn't blush but she felt pleasure warm her cheeks. "Thank you," she murmured.

Lucas was touched by Rachel's innocence and her vulnerability. He wanted to hold her in his arms and to protect her; he wanted to slay all the dragons lying in wait for her. Yet he sensed that Rachel wasn't a woman who would want a man, or anyone for that matter, to fight her battles. He admired her for her strength of character.

He squeezed her hand and they continued down the path to the stone building. They walked to the edge of the upper terrace and stood, staring into the quarry below. The garden was ablaze with autumn's colors.

Lucas slipped his hands into the back pockets of his jeans. Rocking back on the heels of his boots, he said, "Time changes all things. Seasons and reasons."

"You're talking about Jae's reaction to my going out?" Rachel asked.

Lucas nodded and caught Rachel's hand once more, guiding her to the steep and winding stone stairs that led below. "Cheryl was fifteen when Debra died. For a while we clung together, afraid of losing each other as we'd lost Debra. Slowly, however, we began to make new lives for ourselves. At first she didn't like the idea of my dating, but came to accept it. Jae'll come around. Give her time.''

"How long?" Rachel asked, not really expecting an answer. They walked farther, stopping when they reached the bridge in the middle of the garden. She leaned over the railing to look at the huge goldfish swimming in the crystal-clear water. Behind them a waterfall splashed down the side of the quarry. "How long does it take before you really feel like living again, Lucas?"

He shrugged. "Two years maybe."

"I guess it's different for you, isn't it?"

"Perhaps it's easier when the person you love dies. At least you know they returned your love and wouldn't have left you had they had any choice in the matter. Look!" he exclaimed and pointed to a large catfish. "I wish Mandy could see this."

"How is Mandy?"

"She's doing just fine."

"And Mr. Worthmore?"

Lucas's eyes crinkled at the corners when he smiled, and his face softened. "The two are inseparable. She's going to have a spoiled calf on her hands."

"The way you handled her was wonderful, Lucas. I think about it frequently."

"I love her," he said simply. "I want to adopt her."

Rachel had seen him show his love for the child, so the announcement didn't take her by surprise. She turned to look at him. "Have you heard anything from her relatives?"

Lucas leaned against the railing and folded his arms across his chest. "Nothing new. As I told you the other day, the cousin, Oscar Maynard, and his wife can't make up their minds what they want to do with Mandy. One minute they want her to come live with them, the next they don't know how they'll manage with one more mouth to feed. But at least until they make up their minds, I have temporary custody of her."

"How does Cheryl feel about your adopting Mandy?"

"She's all for it. She always did want brothers and sisters."

"I would have thought she'd be rather possessive of you."

"It's the other way around," Lucas returned. "That's probably one of the reasons why Cheryl wants me to adopt Mandy. After Debra died, I was so afraid of losing Cheryl that I became possessive and overly protective of her. I didn't realize it, but I was suffocating her with love."

"I know," Rachel agreed, "I think all single parents have that tendency."

"As a result, the minute Cheryl entered Southern Methodist U, she rebelled." His voice hardened. "She moved in with a boy she had known for only a few months, not because she loved him but because she was proving something to herself...to me...I don't know."

"Perhaps she's searching for the love that was snatched from her so rudely and prematurely," Rachel suggested.

"Moving in with a stranger!" Lucas laughed without humor and pushed away from the railing, throwing up his arms.

"She may flounder for a little while," Rachel assured him, "but you've taught her responsibility and values. You've taught her to make choices. She'll learn to stand on her own feet."

The green eyes were so earnest, Lucas caught Rachel's shoulders and stared deeply into her face. "Thank you."

Knowing that he was going to kiss her, reading the question in his eyes, Rachel gently pulled away from him. "Not now," she whispered, her voice caught and carried away by the gentle evening breeze. "Give me time."

"All right."

He adroitly hid his disappointment as he stepped away and dropped his hands. Slowly they began to walk up the steep and meandering paths. By the time the sun dipped behind the western horizon, they stood on the upper terrace of the tea gardens.

"Are you ready for the river?"

"And for dinner," she added. Lucas nodded, and hand in hand, they ran down the steps on the other side of the pagoda to the parking lot.

When they stood beside the Mercedes, Lucas opened her door. The wind, blowing more strongly now, picked up a strand of hair and swirled it across Rachel's face. Lucas's hand rose, and his fingers brushed against her cheeks as he removed the recalcitrant lock.

"Are you having a good time?" he asked.

"Yes," she whispered, gazing into the startling gray eyes that were focused so intently on her.

Lucas stood there fighting a battle within himself. He wondered why he had insisted on spending the weekend with her. He had known from the first time he saw her that Rachel was different from the women he usually dated. Those he selected carefully. While he admired and respected them, he chose women with whom he could enjoy a casual relationship—no strings attached for either of them. Rachel was different. Nothing about her was casual.

"Time to go." Lucas caught her shoulders and eased her into the car, then closed the door.

Although Rachel was disappointed, she was relieved deep down. She enjoyed being with Lucas; this had been one of the happiest days in her entire life. But she wasn't ready for more than the friendship they already shared. By the time he slid under the wheel, she had fastened the seat belt and was looking out the windshield. For different reasons both of them retreated from the intimacy they had shared a moment ago. While enjoyable, their conversation was light. Lucas parked the Mercedes off Market Street, and they walked down the steps to the river.

"I love it down here," Rachel breathed. "It's an entirely different world, so far removed from the hustle and bustle of the city. I always feel as if I've stepped back in time."

"Yet the river area is one of the most modern parts of the city," Lucas commented, his gaze sweeping over the new River Center Mall.

Rachel smiled and added, "It's the heartbeat of San Antonio. I love to come down here in the spring; it's absolutely beautiful."

"Let's come together then," Lucas said softly. "I want to see it with you."

Rachel stared into the mesmeric depths of his gray eyes and drew in a deep breath. "I'd love to," she whispered.

"And we'll come again at Christmas," he said. "Together we'll enjoy the millions of lights twinkling in the trees and reflecting in the water."

Rachel was quiet. Lucas was so different from what she had first imagined and so different from Jared. Despite his wealth, he was not materialistic. He was down-to-earth and friendly and was quickly insinuating himself into her life.

"I've never been to the river at Christmas," she finally said.

"Why?" Lucas asked softly.

Rachel drew in a deep breath and said, "Jared left me two weeks before Christmas. I haven't had much Yuletide spirit the past two years."

"If you'll let me, Rachel," Lucas said, "I want to change that for you."

Rachel smiled tremulously. "How about our working on it together?"

He nodded, his hand tightening warmly over hers. "And we'll begin right now. Come right this way."

Rachel glowed with happiness; she hadn't felt so special since she and Jared first started dating. How wonderful the feeling was! Irish songs from the pub next to the Hilton Palacio del Río followed them down the river as they made their way to the Little Rhine Steak House. They stopped at the bottom of a narrow, stone staircase that spiraled through the restaurant's outdoor terraces. Lucas caught both her hands in his, and they stared at each other. Slowly they smiled.

"Wait here," he said. "I'll be right back. Let me get us a table."

"I'll wait," Rachel promised.

Reluctant to leave her for even a moment, Lucas loosened his clasp, turned and climbed several steps to the first terrace. In low tones he spoke with the maître d'. After several nods, the man withdrew and Lucas returned.

He grinned and his gray eyes danced with secret merriment. "It'll be a few minutes before we can get a table. Shall we go to the bar and get something to drink while we wait?''

Both ascended the steps and threaded their way through the crowd to find a small table for two in a dimly lit corner of the building. After the waitress departed with their order, he leaned his arms on the table.

"Ms. March—" a smile shimmered in the depths of those silvery-gray eyes "—when are you going to be able to show me those other pieces of property?"

For a minute Rachel stared at Lucas blankly and wondered what he was talking about. Then, just as quickly, she remembered. "Uh . . . whenever it's convenient for you," she stammered.

"How about Tuesday?" he asked.

"Tuesday's fine."

"How about Thursday evening for Rachel and Lucas?"

"Thursday for Rachel and Lucas?" She was confused.

He smiled and nodded. "I'd like to take you out Thursday night."

Her face brightened and she exclaimed, "I'd love to go out—" her animation died and her voice trailed off "—with you . . . but I can't. The cheerleaders are having a special party for their parents, and I promised Jae that I'd go with her."

"I know I'm not her parent, but I'd like to go with you."

Remembering Jae's strong reaction to Lucas, Rachel said, "I don't think so."

Lucas was disappointed. "Am I reading more into our relationship than you want?"

"No," was her soft reply.

"Would you rather I didn't meet Jae?"

"No. I want you to meet her, but Thursday night isn't the right time. She's already prejudged you, and I need time to prepare her for the meeting."

The waitress approached their table. "Here you are. Two glasses of wine?"

"That's us," Lucas answered. After she left, he said, "I got to be a successful criminal attorney because I made my chances, Rachel. Don't sell me short."

Rachel picked up the wineglass and held it to her lips, looking at Lucas over the rim. When she set the glass down, she said, "I won't."

"The next time Cheryl comes home from school, I want you to meet her." Glancing over her shoulder, Lucas saw the maître d' motion to him. "Time to go," he said.

Rachel looked surprised but stood to follow him through the crowd. They walked out of the restaurant down the steps that connected the flagstone terraces to the water's edge. Waiting for them was a riverboat, on its deck a long table spread with white linen and bedecked with succulent food.

"Lucas," Rachel breathed, "this is wonderful."

"I thought you'd like it," he said as they moved down the narrow aisle to their seats.

The waiter lighted the candles as soon as the boat was moving up the river and began to serve dinner. At the stern the mariachis began to strum their instruments and sing hauntingly beautiful Mexican tunes.

HER FACE RADIATING her happiness, Rachel locked the door and stood in the foyer for a moment, remembering every detail of her evening with Lucas.

"I wondered if you were going to come home tonight." Illuminated by a small wedge of light, Jae stood in the doorway of the den. "The next time you go out, we're going to set a curfew."

Rachel laughed and walked into the den, setting her purse on the corner table. "I've been away so many nights, you really had a reason to be concerned."

"It's not the number of nights you've been out—" Jae picked up the crumpled foil, the only remains of her TV dinner "—it's your age. I just didn't figure a woman your age—"

Rachel playfully swatted Jae's posterior. "What do you mean, a woman my age? What I lack in youth, my dear Jae Ruella, I make up for in experience."

Jae squealed and jumped away from her mother to dart into the kitchen. Rachel followed.

"Wow," she exclaimed. "Who cleaned up?"

"I got home earlier than I figured," Jae answered, rinsing the fork and dropping it into the dishwasher, "so I thought I'd straighten up for you."

"That much less for us to do tomorrow." Remembering a load of clothes in the dryer, Rachel walked to the utility room.

As her hand closed over the knob, Jae said, "I folded them, too, Mom."

"Making sure I'm in a good mood tomorrow?" Rachel teased.

"Every little bit helps." Jae grinned.

"I think I'll go take a shower and get ready for bed then," Rachel said. "You and I have a big day ahead of us."

The phone rang and Jae leaped for it. "It's for me."

"Always is," Rachel murmured, walking to her bedroom.

As she showered, she relived every moment of her day with Lucas and enjoyed anew all the pleasures they had shared. Afterward she slipped into her gown and house-coat and was sitting on the edge of the bed, towel drying her hair when Jae entered.

"I rented a video, Mom. Do you want to watch it with me?"

Not really! "What's the name of it?" Rachel asked.

"Robocop."

Rachel's head came up. "Haven't we seen that about four times already?"

"Three," Jae answered, moving to the television set on the corner of the dresser. "This will make four."

"I don't get a choice?"

Jae giggled and flipped through the tapes. "From Neal's or Sammy's library of movies? Here's some they taped from *Star Trek, The Next Generation*."

"Let's watch that," Rachel decided, then lay back on the bed to think about Lucas earlier today when he'd confessed to being a Trekkie. His face had been so solemn, but the silvery eyes were dancing with laughter. Then she thought about the sparkle in them, the secret smile when he'd made arrangements to take her to dinner on the riverboat.

"What'cha grinning about, Mom?"

Rachel rolled over onto her side. "Nothing."

"You and Lucas?"

"Sort of," Rachel answered, a bit embarrassed that her feelings had been so evident.

Jae flopped onto the bed beside her mother and raised a brow. "Sort of?" she said skeptically. "Tell me about your day, and I'll make my own decision."

"Well—" Rachel pretended to be solemn "—after you left for school, I walked down the hall and woke Neal up. He was—"

Giggling, Jae picked up a pillow and bopped her mother on the head. "Not every little detail, silly. I know all about Neal and Sammy. I want to know about you and Lucas."

"There's nothing to know about me and Lucas."

"If there's nothing," Jae answered, narrowing her eyes, "you won't mind telling me, will you?"

"Are you mimicking me, Jae Ruella?"

"Mmm-hmm." She grinned. "Now tell me what happened."

To the accompaniment of *Star Trek, The Next Generation*, Rachel described her afternoon and evening with Lucas. She concluded with, "He wanted to go to Parents' Night with us."

"You're not bringing him!" Jae bolted upright to glare at her mother.

"No."

"It figures he'd want to come," Jae said, lying down again, returning her attention to the television screen. "He knows if he's going to get you, he's got to get my approval."

Rachel cocked an eye. "What makes you think that?"

"Donna told me. Her mother's been divorced three times. She said every time her mother starts dating a new man, she has to go through the same routine. She told me all about it. Boring. Boring." Jae flopped over, propped herself on an elbow and cupped her chin with one hand. "But it does give one a sense of power. Maybe we'll invite him over one evening."

Rachel smiled and reached out to ruffle Jae's hair. Suddenly her world seemed brighter than it had for a long time. "You'll like him," she promised. "I know you will."

"I CAN'T BELIEVE you'd do this to me!" Jae shouted as she slammed the door of the silver town car and stamped across the lawn. Her voice quavered and tears weren't far off. "If I don't have that dress, I'll be too humiliated to go to the dance. If I go to the dance in anything else, I'll be a laughingstock. Humiliated in front of the whole world. My life will be nothing without that dress."

"I haven't humiliated you," Rachel replied calmly, following her into the house, "and I certainly hope your life is predicated on more than a few yards of silk and satin. And remember, I only promised to look at Saks. I didn't promise to buy you the dress."

Jae whirled around and glared at Rachel. "Mom, can't you understand? Donna's mother bought her dress at Frost Brothers. Nina's came from the Menger Smart Shop. Linda has her own credit card for Saks. Sharon's came from Lord and Taylor. And you expect me to shop for my clothes at Loehmann's!"

Shifting a few parcels under her left arm, Rachel slid the key into the lock and opened the door. "I expect you to understand that I don't have the money to buy the dress you want at Saks. And I see nothing wrong with shopping at Loehmann's."

"Well, I do. They get the clothes that Frost Brothers no longer wants. I'll be wearing rejects." She padded down the hall in pale blue tennis shoes. "Daddy would have a fit if he knew you wanted me to dress out of a discount house."

"I don't think Loehmann's qualifies as a discount house," Rachel called out. *And I think your father really doesn't care from where or how you're dressed, as long as he isn't bothered and doesn't have to foot the bill.*

"I'm going to call Daddy," Jae shouted from her bedroom. "He'll buy me the dress."

Rachel flew down the hall to stand framed in the door. "Jae Ruella March," she exclaimed, "you will not call your father!"

"You can't stop me," Jae cried, stamping her foot for emphasis. "He's my father."

"Right, he's your father," Rachel returned, her voice firm with resolve. "Wrong, I can stop you. In case you've forgotten, I'm the mother. You're the child. You're in my custody and will obey me."

"You better be careful how you treat me." The defiant words were accompanied by a toss of head and swirl of golden-blond hair, but her lips trembled with unshed tears when she said, "I'll go live with Daddy."

Not for the first time, Rachel felt helpless and ineffective. She was bitter and angry that Jae was beginning to show some of Jared's worst characteristics. What was more, she was hurt. Her lovely daughter was turning into a spoiled brat. Rachel wanted to buy Jae the dress she had selected; she wanted to fulfill all Jae's desires. But she couldn't.

"Mom, please," came the plaintive cry. Now Jae was changing tactics. "You have some money in savings."

"I do," Rachel returned quietly, "and that's where it's staying. I'm not going to be blackmailed into buying you a gown that costs more than five hundred dollars for you to wear on one occasion, Jae."

Jae and Rachel stared at each other for immeasurable seconds.

"Don't call your father and ask for money, Jae."

With a nonchalant shrug Jae turned and moved to the stereo in the corner of the room. She picked up a cassette tape and slid it into the slot.

"Do you hear me?" Rachel asked.

"I heard." Her back to her mother, Jae pressed a switch and a blast of loud, discordant music filled the room.

Chapter Seven

"Aren't you forgetting something?" Rachel called as she rinsed breakfast dishes.

Clad in fresh T-shirt and jeans, Sammy stopped short of the front door and turned. From beneath the brim of his baseball cap, he gave his mother a curious look. Then he dropped his head and silently took inventory. Shoes. Jeans. T-shirt. A worn, leather glove hooked over the end of a bat was slung over one shoulder; he carried his hardball in the other hand.

"Nope," he announced.

"Your books." Rachel pointed to the satchel lying on the edge of the sofa in the den.

"Oh, yeah," he mumbled and ambled back down the hall. "Them. I thought you meant something important."

"Mom," Neal called, rushing out of the bathroom into the den, wiping his mouth with a hand towel, "I'm going to be a little late today. Mrs. Jeffers is going to help me set my diorama up in the library for open house at school next week." The hand towel landed on the breakfast counter as he slid onto a stool and picked up his glass of milk.

Rachel nodded at the same time Sammy yelled, "Bye, Mom. I'm going to get Cody."

"All right. See you this afternoon."

Neal quietly attacked his breakfast of bacon, eggs, grits and toast. When he was through eating, he looked around and asked, "Where's Jae? I haven't seen her all morning."

"I'm right here," came Jae's petulant answer.

"Are we in a bad mood this a.m.?" Neal mocked, sliding off the stool and scooping his books into the crook of his arm. "What happened, big Sis? You didn't get your way yesterday when you and Mom went shopping?"

"Shut up, Neal!" Jae shouted. "Make him shut up, Mom."

"Leave her alone, Neal," Rachel said, then asked, "Eggs, bacon, and toast?"

"Toast and a half glass of milk," Jae answered. "I'm not very hungry."

Grinning, Neal struck an effeminate pose and lifted his hand to his cheek, his gaze moving slowly from Jae's striped cotton blouse to the short denim skirt to the socks and tennis shoes. "Are we on another diet?"

"Neal!" Jae exploded. "Leave me alone."

"Neal," Rachel said quietly.

He laughed. "Okay, Mom. I was only joking."

"She's not in the mood this morning," Rachel pointed out, careful not to pay too much attention to Jae's petulance. "Now scoot or you're going to be late."

While Jae sat down at the breakfast table to munch her toast, Rachel loaded the dishwasher. The telephone rang, and Jae jumped up, the chair grating over the tile floor as she pushed it back. Hurriedly she wiped her hands on the napkin and swallowed her last bite of food.

She rested the ivory-colored receiver against her ear and said, "Hello." In the pause that followed her eyes darted furtively to her mother. "Daddy!"

Rachel slowly straightened up and closed the dishwasher door. She dreaded Jared's calls to the children, and considering Jae's present frame of mind, his timing on this one was horrid. Inwardly Rachel was shaking, and she hated herself for allowing Jared to upset her like this. He had never physically abused her; he hadn't needed to. Emotional abuse was much more effective.

"Mom, it's for you!"

Staring at the receiver lying on the counter, Rachel flipped the dishwasher dial and wiped her hand on a towel. Slowly her hand closed around the ivory plastic and she raised it to her ear. Her palms were sweaty; her heart drummed erratically; and anxiety gnawed at the pit of her stomach. To this day Jared still intimidated her.

"Hello," she said, immediately hating herself again because she allowed him to have such control over her.

"Rachel, for God's sake quit mumbling!" Jared's deep voice barked the command. After a minute's silence he said, "This is Rachel, isn't it?"

"Of course it's me," she said, her voice louder and firmer. Automatically she straightened her back and squared her shoulders. "Who did you expect?"

Silence greeted her response; then Jared said a little more quietly, "I'm sending Jae a thousand dollars through Western Union."

"You're what?" Rachel was livid; undiluted anger surged through her body. She glanced at Jae, who squirmed uncomfortably in the chair and refused to look at her.

"You heard me, Rachel. I'm sending Jae a thousand dollars, and I want you to make sure the child gets it. Get that gown she wants."

"Are you insinuating something?" Rachel asked.

"Yes, I am, damn it. If you were careful with the child support money and managed it better, you wouldn't have to deny the children so much."

"Have you heard of inflation, Jared?"

"Don't try to weasel out of it, Rachel."

Before Rachel had quaked with fear; now she shook with anger. "You can send Jae the money, Jared, and I'll see that she puts it into her savings account, but she won't buy the gown because I've already told her she can't have it."

"I'm telling her she can."

Rachel's green eyes pinned Jae to the wall. "I can't stop you from sending the money. I may not be able to stop Jae from buying it, but I guarantee you, Jared Jaeson March, that Jae won't wear the gown to the dance. I will not let her defy me. I love her too much for that."

"My God, Rachel, I can't understand the commotion over one gown. You've always had a talent for creating mountains out of molehills."

"The commotion isn't over one gown," Rachel said, slumping against the counter. "The commotion is over the wrong kind of attitude, Jared, but you wouldn't understand."

"No, I don't. Let me speak to Jae."

"Not right now, Jared. It's time for her to go to school."

"You can't keep her away from me indefinitely, Rachel." He laughed mockingly. "You know I'm going to end up with all three of the children, and don't think the incident over the gown is over. Next weekend is my weekend with the kids. I'll see that Jae gets exactly the gown she wants. And I'm warning you, if you want to keep Jae's love, you won't deny her the gown or the dance."

When Rachel recradled the receiver, she turned to Jae. "You called your father after I told you not to?"

Unable to look her mother in the eye, Jae stood and picked up her saucer and empty glass. Walking to the sink, she said, "Yes, I did. I didn't feel that you had the right to keep me from him."

"Jae," Rachel said, "you've disappointed and angered me with your actions. You'll be grounded for the next month. I'll let you attend the football games because you're a cheerleader, but you'll come directly home afterward rather than going out with your friends. You won't go out on the weekends. Your father may buy you the dress, but you won't wear it. In fact, you may not go to the dance at all, Jae. I have a lot of thinking to do."

Jae's eyes opened wide. "Mom, you can't mean that!"

"Yes," Rachel said calmly, "I most definitely mean it. I don't like your sneaking behind my back and playing your father and me against each other. I love you and want you to live with me, but I won't be manipulated, Jae. Not by you or your father."

Her heart breaking, Rachel watched Jae pick up her books from the sofa and walk out of the house. For a long time she stood leaning against the counter. Angry, bitter tears ran down her cheeks. She rushed from the kitchen into the bathroom and jerked several tissues from the dispenser, balling them against her eyes. By the time her crying was spent, she was lying facedown on the bed.

The soft chime of the doorbell abruptly reminded her that Lucas was coming. In the commotion over Jared's call she had forgotten. Slipping off the bed, she walked into her bathroom and splashed her face with cold water. After she had blotted her eyes dry, she straightened the collar of her white blouse and retied the paisley print scarf. Then she walked down the hall to unlock the door.

Not wanting him to see her tear-stained face, she said, "I'm not quite ready. Give me a few minutes, then come on in and wait for me in the den. There's a fresh pot of coffee if you want a cup."

Rachel hadn't shut the door to her bedroom, when Lucas called, "Want to join me?"

"Yes...yes, I will. Pour me half a cup with a teaspoon of sugar."

"Cream?"

"No."

It didn't take Rachel long to repair her makeup and comb her hair. When she returned to the den, she saw Lucas's hat on the arm of the sofa. Lucas himself was standing behind the counter pouring the coffee. He looked up and smiled. Today she was the professional saleswoman, clad in her black straight skirt and yellow blazer. His smile quickly gave way to concern when he saw her swollen eyes, but he said nothing. He would wait for her to tell him.

"Have you already eaten?" he asked.

"Mmm-hmm," Rachel answered, picking up her coffee cup. "How about you?"

He grinned and moved from behind the bar, the gray lizard boots moving silently over the Mexican tile. "Mrs. Molly wouldn't think of letting me out of the house without my breakfast."

Inadvertently Rachel's gaze swept over Lucas's frame, the blue and gray western shirt, several snaps open to expose a V of dark brown hair; the jeans that hugged his hips and legs to accentuate their lean muscularity; the boots.

"She thinks I'm a growing boy who needs three balanced meals a day," he said, his voice trailing away into silence as Rachel lifted her face and their gazes locked. He set his cup down, crossed the room to stand in front of Rachel and took hers from limp fingers. Catching her hands in his, he pulled her to the sofa and gently pushed her down. "What's wrong?"

"What—what makes you think something is wrong?" she asked.

He lifted a hand and brushed a bent finger under her eye. Then he held it out, a tear glistening on the knuckle.

"Oh, Lucas," she exclaimed, gladly letting him gather her into his arms and spilling out her grief to him.

Lucas held her against his chest and listened as she told him about her argument with Jae. At some point he leaned toward the end table and yanked several tissues from the dispenser, tucking them into her hand. Long after the torrent of words had died down, long after the tears ceased falling, he cradled her against him.

"You can understand Jae's reaction. She's only a child," he told her.

"I can't understand Jared's attitude," Rachel said. "He's an adult." After a moment she added, "I never fully realized what he was like until we separated."

"But now you do," Lucas said.

Rachel liked the warmth and protection Lucas's embrace provided; she enjoyed the feel of his hand on her back—strong and present. Instinctively she snuggled closer, rubbing her cheek against his chest. But the slight movement brought her breasts more firmly against his chest, too. Suddenly self-conscious, she insinuated her hands between them and pushed away.

Her lips curled into a tremulous smile. "Thanks," she whispered. Then when his eyes roamed her face, she added, "I must look a sight."

Lucas chuckled. "You do, Rachel March. Even with red, swollen eyes you're lovely."

He moved, the movement so slight that neither was aware he had done so. His hands covered her cheeks and guided her face to him. This time she didn't withdraw. She knew their kiss was inevitable. Their lips met, the tentative caress touching Rachel to the depth of her heart. How many times Jared had kissed her, she didn't care to remember, but what they shared was physical. Lucas reached a part of Rachel Ruel March that Jared had never reached. She felt innocent, virginal.

When she sighed and parted her lips beneath his, Lucas wanted to let the kiss deepen. He wanted to take what she was offering to him, but he couldn't take advantage of her vulnerability. While one part of her was seeking reassurance of her womanhood, the greater part was seeking only comfort and strength.

Exerting self-control, he acted accordingly. He slid his hands from her face to her shoulders; he lifted his lips from hers. Gray eyes, darkened with desire, gazed into rounded green ones. Rachel slipped her hand between them, resting her palm on Lucas's chest. She felt the steady cadence of his heart.

She gave him another shaky smile and rose. Now that the intimate moment was over, she was unsure of herself, even uncomfortable. Picking up the cups of tepid coffee, she moved into the kitchen. When she realized

Lucas had followed, she asked rather nervously, "Would you like to have another cup of coffee before we—"

"Rachel, I'm sorry about your disagreement with Jae," he said, catching her by the shoulders and turning her around, "and I'm sorry that it was Jared's illtreatment of you that drove you into my arms, but I'm glad that I was here to hold you. I'm not going to apologize for kissing you. I wanted to, and I enjoyed it very much."

"I did, too," she whispered.

"Now—" Lucas dropped his hands and stepped back; although he wanted to prolong the moment, although he wanted more from Rachel than consolation kisses, now was not the time "—let's get on the road. We have a lot of miles to cover today."

THE DAY WAS one of the most beautiful Rachel had ever spent. Easily and quickly she left her troubles behind and concentrated on showing Lucas several ranches between San Antonio and Del Rio, Texas.

"Well, what do you think?" Rachel asked when they were headed back home.

"It's definitely the Storch-Halston Ranch," he said, "but I can't see her price. She's way above the appraised value of the land. Did you look at the figures I sent you?"

"I did," answered Rachel, "and I agree."

"Let me tell you what I intend to do, and see what you think about it."

Rachel listened as he outlined his plan, asking questions here and there to make sure she understood his terms.

When he was through, he said, "Well?"

NO COST! NO OBLIGATION TO BUY!
NO PURCHASE NECESSARY!

PLAY "LUCKY 7"
AND GET AS MANY AS SIX FREE GIFTS . .

HOW TO PLAY:

1. With a coin, carefully scratch off the silver box at the right. This makes you eligible to receive one or more free books, and possibly other gifts, depending on what is revealed beneath the scatch-off area.

2. You'll receive brand-new American Romance® novels. When you return this card, we'll send you the books and gifts you qualify for absolutely free!

3. Unless you tell us otherwise, every month we'll send you 4 additional novels to read and enjoy. If you decide to keep them, you'll pay only $2.49 per book*, a savings of 26¢ per book. There is no extra charge for postage and handling. There are no hidden extras.

4. When you join Harlequin Reader Service, we'll send you additional free gifts from time to time, as well as our newsletter.

5. You must be completely satisfied. You may cancel at any time just by dropping us a line or returning a shipment of books at our cost.

* Terms and prices subject to change.

"It's a fair offer," she said, "but I'm not the one who has to be convinced, and I'm not sure how Elaine will react. She seems rather set on her price." She turned her head and smiled. "We can't lose anything by trying, can we?"

"Nothing," he murmured, his eyes moving across her face. He had thought she was beautiful the first time he saw her, but every time she smiled he saw a miracle. Her face was transformed from simple beauty to absolute loveliness. It glowed; her eyes danced; she radiated happiness. "I'm flying out to Dallas tonight."

"Oh." Rachel swallowed her disappointment.

"I'll be back Friday afternoon. Are you free that evening?"

"Oh, yes," she exclaimed, then added on a doleful wail, "Oh, no, Lucas, I'm not. It's Roosevelt's homecoming game, and I promised Jae. Oh, Lucas, there's always something—"

Lucas laid his hand over hers on the steering wheel. "I asked you once before, Rachel, and you turned me down, but I'm asking again: How about my joining you?"

Rachel's head swung in his direction, her eyes rounded in surprise. "You really want to, Lucas?"

"I do. This will be my opportunity to meet Jae." A slow smile curled his lips. "But you've got to promise to schedule me into your busy agenda. I want us to have some time for ourselves, Rachel. Prime time. Okay?"

"Okay," she murmured, aware that her heart was thudding erratically.

CASUALLY DRESSED in black slacks and a white blouse, Rachel edged the town car into the parking slot at the airport garage. Neal and Sammy sat in the back seat, Jae in the front. As soon as the car stopped, Jae flung open the door and flounced out.

Bending over and peering into the interior of the car, she said, "Don't you think it's rather ironic that Lucas couldn't make it back to town last night for the game, but manages to get home in time for you and the boys to spend the day at his ranch with him and his daughter? I think it's quite evident that he doesn't really want to get to know me better. He's avoiding me."

"He's not avoiding you. He was detained because of business, Jae." Rachel neglected to remind Jae of the little tantrum she'd pulled when she learned that Lucas planned to attend the game. She sighed and pressed the switch that unlocked the trunk, then opened her door and slid out.

"Even so," Jae maintained indignantly, following her mother to the trunk, "that proves that he's more interested in work than you. Had he wanted to be here badly enough, he could have."

"No one was more disappointed that he didn't come than I," Rachel said, "but these occasions do arise."

"Let's just wait to see how frequently they do," Jae said with an arrogant toss of her head. She swung her suitcase through the air and moved toward the staircase that led into the airport terminal.

As Rachel lowered the trunk lid, she knew Jae was merely lashing out, yet the accusations hurt. She wondered if Lucas really had time in his life for a personal commitment, for the kind of commitment that she wanted.

Standing at the head of the stairs, tugging on the brim of his cap, Sammy yelled, "Hurry, Mom, or we're gonna be late."

"We have plenty of time," Rachel called out. "Neal, carry your sister's suitcase."

Grumbling under his breath, Neal reached out and took Jae's luggage. Long strides carried him to his brother's side and the two of them disappeared down the stairs.

"Southwest," Rachel called out.

"I know," Neal flung the response over his shoulder. "Are you checking the suitcase or carrying it, Jae?"

"Carrying it," she answered.

Neal nodded. "We'll meet you at the gate."

"Oh, Mom!" Jae exclaimed, her hand flying to her cheek. "You've got to call Donna when you get home. I forgot to tell her I loaned her chemistry notebook to Sharon. Maybe you'd better call Sharon and remind her to bring it to Donna Monday morning. We have notebook check, and it would be horrid if she forgot. Donna would crucify me."

"Anything else you'd like for me to do?" Rachel asked dryly.

"Yes, there is." Jae snapped her fingers. "You'd better call Nina. I didn't know that you and the boys would be gone today, and I told her she could return my tennis racket this afternoon. Also if you have time, I'd like for you to go by Mrs. Spencer's and get my project paper. She's made corrections and wants me to retype it for the Science Fair. I'll need it when I get home Sunday afternoon."

Lucas was forgotten as Jae gave her mother last-minute instructions. When they reached the departure area, Jae checked in and Rachel walked to the window to watch the air traffic. Holding her boarding pass in hand, Jae moved to where her mother stood.

"Mom, why don't you come home with me?"

"How many times have we been through this, Jae?" Rachel began.

"Daddy would love to see you. I know he would." She reached out and laid a hand on Rachel's arm. "Please, Mom. Let's all go home together. Let's be a family again."

Sammy scooted up in time to overhear Jae's request. "We can't go to Daddy's!" he cried. "You promised to take us to Lucas's ranch, Mama."

Rachel looked down at Sammy. "I know I did, and I am. Now scoot while I talk to your sister."

"Aw, Mom," Sammy grumbled but turned and loped off to find Neal.

"If you can't come now," Jae said as soon as her brother was out of earshot, "let's plan to go next weekend. Let me tell Daddy that we're—"

Shaking her head, Rachel interrupted, "No, Jae. You must understand that your father's house is no longer my home, and I don't want to go back."

"All passengers—" The recorded voice of the steward echoed through the departure area.

"Mom, I can't believe you really mean that," Jae whispered.

"We'll talk when you get home," Rachel promised.

"It's Lucas, isn't it?"

"Your father and I were through long before Lucas," Rachel returned.

"Be careful of Lucas, Mom." Jae embraced her mother. "Don't let him hurt you."

"I won't," Rachel answered.

When the second call for boarding rang through the terminal, Jae kissed her mother and pushed out of her arms. "I'll see you Sunday. Don't forget to pick me up."

"As if I would." Rachel laughed.

Jae picked up her suitcase and walked to the departure gate, turning to wave before she disappeared into the corridor.

The boys were eager to return to the parking garage so they could begin their day at the ranch, but Rachel was loath to leave until the plane was airborne. The three of them stood at the window and watched. Rachel's heart was heavy and her feelings were ambivalent. While she wanted Jae to have a good relationship with her father, she worried that Jared would totally destroy her influence with Jae. Yet she couldn't refuse to let Jae visit her father, nor would she allow herself to nurture fears and doubts about Jae's feelings for her.

As Rachel and the boys left the airport terminal, they were greeted by a gust of wind. The gray skies echoed her own sentiment. She looked forward to spending the day with Lucas; she didn't want to be by herself. Quite selfishly she wished that she and Lucas could have the day to themselves. She wanted to meet Cheryl, but she also wanted today... and Lucas for herself.

Chapter Eight

The den was comforting and soothing; the furniture expensive without being ostentatious. It was different from any other room in the house. Subconsciously Rachel had been aware of the difference the first time she had been at the Lucky Brand; today she understood. The rest of the house belonged to Debra, this room to Lucas. Glad that Dugan and Mrs. Molly had taken Neal and Sammy to the Children's Ranch for the afternoon, Rachel sat back on the sofa while she waited for Lucas to conclude a business call in his office. Leaning her head back against the cushion, she closed her eyes and totally relaxed to the soft music.

The door opened, and she heard Lucas say, "Sorry."

She inhaled deeply, opened her eyes and stretched. A soft smile contoured her mouth. "I suppose I should say it's okay, but it's not really. Since Dugan and Mandy are entertaining the boys and won't be home until tonight and since Cheryl is coming in later, I thought this would be our afternoon together." Rachel was surprised at her own temerity.

"Are you upset that Cheryl's coming?" Lucas asked.

Rachel shook her head. "No, I want to meet her. I just want us to have some time to ourselves."

"Me, too," Lucas murmured and sat down on the sofa. "It will be our afternoon," he promised, catching her hands and pulling her closer to him. "Yours and mine."

With a need far outweighing sexual gratification, Rachel melted into the embrace, lifting her lips for his kiss. His lips, covering hers, were warm and moist. She opened her mouth to receive his tongue. As the kiss deepened, she slid her hand up his chest to clasp the nape of his neck, splaying her fingers into the thick, black hair.

Lucas moved slightly, taking her more fully into his arms, taking her mouth more fully into his kiss. He felt the burning pressure of her breasts against his chest, the softness of her thighs against his. He wanted Rachel; he was hungry for more than mere kisses. His body was aflame with desire.

The kiss turned into a long deep one; it was warm and intoxicating. It was a kiss that both of them wanted, a kiss that began with restraint; but as they melded themselves to each other, fiery passion ignited to burn away all inhibitions and restraints. By mutual agreement the fire turned into an all-encompassing blaze. Both of them welcomed its searing heat. Both of them fanned the blaze until it was a wild inferno of desire.

Still Lucas knew he couldn't rush Rachel. He didn't want to. Reluctantly he raised his face from hers. A smile trembled on Rachel's lips as she stared at him for a moment before she dropped her head and laid her cheek against his chest and sighed contentedly. She moved her hand again, this time sliding it up the front of his shirt, letting her fingers play with the mother-of-pearl snaps.

Lucas laid his cheek on the top of her head. "Rachel, the other night you said I was a first for you in many ways."

"Mmm-hmm." Now she slipped a finger through the placket between the snaps to touch the warm, vibrant flesh.

"You're . . . a first for me, too."

Rachel opened a snap and slid her hand beneath the material, resting her palm on his chest. When she felt him inhale deeply, she laughed quietly. "I can't believe that," she said in a dreamy voice. "Every article I've read about you shows you with a different woman."

Desire burned through Lucas when he felt her soft fingers score the tip of his nipple. "True, I've dated," he admitted, maintaining control over his feelings, "but you're the first woman since Debra in whom I've had more than a casual interest."

His words—an honest confession, not designed to manipulate her emotions—set her atingle with excitement. But she wasn't sure what to do next. She'd forgotten all the rules of courtship.

"I want us to discover each other," Lucas continued. "To spend time together getting to know each other better. I want us to give ourselves the chance to fall in love."

Rachel listened to the steady beat of his heart and felt the steady rise and fall of his chest with his breathing. Then she pulled away from him and gazed into the sincere gray eyes.

"I'm so glad I met you," she whispered. "You're good for me, Lucas."

He caught her hands and raised them to his lips. He planted gentle kisses on each of her knuckles. The breathless strokes caused her to shiver. For the first time in almost two years Rachel felt the stirring of desire; she truly wanted to make love with Lucas...to have him make love with her.

His hands moved to her face, and she felt the gentle brush of his fingers on her cheeks. Her hands rose to catch his. She brought them down and turned them palm up. Cradling one, she traced the work-hardened flesh with the tip of her finger.

"A palm reader?" Lucas teased, watching the blond hair wisp against her cheeks as she stared into his hand.

"A little," Rachel replied and lapsed into silence.

Eventually he asked, "What do you see?"

Rachel raised her head, green eyes locking to gray ones. "A man who loves the land and works hard. Who is kind and gentle. Who loves children and the simple way of life." Her tongue darted out to moisten her dry lips, the innocent gesture totally evocative. "You're so different from what I first imagined."

"Different in a good way or bad way?" He lifted his hand from hers and traced the contour of her mouth with his fingertip.

"Good," Rachel whispered, trembling beneath his touch.

He dropped his hand, moved his head closer, and brushed his lips against hers, lightly at first, then more firmly as the tentative strokes deepened into a kiss. Rachel slipped her arms around Lucas, digging her fingers into his shoulders. She moved to press herself more fully against him. Her mouth opened willingly to receive his tongue, and she moaned softly.

Soon they were lying on the sofa. He slipped his hand down, his fingers massaging softly as they traveled the length of her spine, stopping at her hips, where they fanned out. Just the feel of those hot fingers drew her closer to the desire that surged through him. Their touch left Rachel in no doubt as to the urgency of his needs. Not consciously aware of what she was doing but instinctively reacting to what her body desired, Rachel rubbed her hips against Lucas, thrusting her softness against his hardness.

His deep gasp of pleasure sent the heated blood rushing through her veins. She matched his kiss in ardor, her hands touched him in equal measure, her legs pressed into the flexed muscles of his. She couldn't taste or touch enough of him.

Lucas unbuttoned her blouse and kissed the satiny swell of her breasts above her bra. His mouth moved over the frothy lace, his lips circling the distended nipple. Rachel sighed and arched her lower body against him.

His firm, full lips pilfered, invaded, conquered and explored. When he pulled back and unfastened her bra, the lace fell to either side to reveal the creamy whiteness of her breasts.

"You're beautiful," he murmured. He cupped her breast, stroking his thumb back and forth over the sensitive tip. "So very beautiful." The gray eyes traveled to her face. "When you're ready, Rachel, I want to make love to you."

"I know."

His hands continued to send shivers of desire through her body as his fingers caressed her breasts. His eyes were dark with passion, his voice husky. "When will you be ready?"

"I don't know," she whispered. "Soon."

"When can I see you?"

Rachel blinked in surprise. "You're...seeing me now. And we're planning to come to your Halloween party next weekend, or have you forgotten?"

"I haven't forgotten," he answered. "But I'm asking when you and I can go out together. Our prime time with no children, no disturbances. An evening for Lucas and Rachel."

"I don't know," she mumbled, pushing up on the couch to pull her bra together and button her blouse. She held her head down, her hair brushing against her cheeks.

"How about the Friday night afterward? I have tickets to attend the Majestic Theater. That'll give you time enough to get a baby-sitter for the children." He waited a moment, and when she didn't answer or even raise her head, he tucked his fingers beneath her chin and lifted her face.

"I'm scared, Lucas," she confessed.

"Don't be," he reassured her. "I won't go any further than you want me to."

"Friday night, two weeks," she said.

Lucas leaned forward and took her lips in a sweet, gentle kiss to seal her promise. Then he said, "Would you like to see the ranch on horseback?"

"I'd love to," Rachel answered. "It's been a long time since I've gone riding."

Within the hour, Lucas and Rachel were riding across the range. The storm had blown over, and now the Texas wilderness enjoyed a beautiful Indian summer day. The blue sky was dotted with large white clouds, and the sun shone brightly.

"I'm glad Elaine accepted my offer," Lucas said. "I've thought about nothing but the lodge and preserve for months. You're going to take the contract over to her Monday morning?''

"Bright and early," Rachel answered. "I offered to bring it tomorrow, but that was inconvenient for her. Make sure you've signed the contract and made your check out to the Alamo City Title Company."

Lucas grinned. "As if I would forget."

"I'm eager to get this deal closed," she answered, not minding the teasing at all.

"Me too," Lucas agreed. "I've already contacted Schwartz and Neger in Austin about restoring and renovating the buildings."

As they rode Rachel listened while he talked in detail about his plans for building the lodge and preserve at the Halston Ranch. As she identified with nature, she could understand Lucas's desire to progress with civilization and at the same time to preserve the land.

"I love the land and feel like it's always been mine," he confessed when they pulled to a stop on top of one of the hills and looked at the stone buildings in the valley below. "I think in another life I must have been a pioneer."

"In many ways you're an enigma," Rachel said. "You're one of the wealthiest men in Texas, yet you're not all caught up in money. You're probably one of the most unmaterialistic people I've ever met."

Lucas tugged his hat a little lower on his forehead. "I like money," he said. "I always intended to have plenty of it. But I've never liked slavery, and I determined never to become a slave to a financial empire. Money has its place, and I keep it there. I've seen too many people become addicted to it and their lives ruined."

"I know."

Lucas reached out to lay his hand on Rachel's lower arm. "I moved back here because I loved the land and the people who go with the land. I like simplicity, Rachel."

She covered his hand with hers. "I do, too."

"I'm happiest when I'm here. Do you mind?"

"No."

Suddenly he grinned, transforming his rugged features into sheer handsomeness. Spurring the bay, he called over his shoulder, "Follow me. I want to show you the Lucky Brand Children's Ranch."

They galloped down the hill and under the gate with the horseshoe and shamrock insignia. When they pulled up in front of the house, Mandy came running out.

"Lucas. Ms. March." She skipped down the steps to throw herself into Lucas's arms. "We didn't know you were coming."

Lucas picked her up and swung her around several times. "We were out riding and thought we'd stop by. Where's Arney?"

"Right here, Lucas." The screen door opened and a small, wiry man stepped out. He was cleaning his horn-rimmed glasses with a white handkerchief.

"Arnold Lagustrum," Lucas said, "I'd like for you to meet Ms. Rachel March, mother of Sammy and Neal."

"Ah yes." Arney shoved the handkerchief into his back pocket and put his glasses on again; walking up to Rachel, he extended his hand. "I've heard a lot about you, Ms. March."

"Call me Rachel, please."

The grayish-brown eyes twinkled. "Call me Arney."

After they'd exchanged the social amenities, Rachel asked, "Where are the boys, Arney?"

"They rode out with Dugan and Molly to check on the stock. They should be back soon."

As they walked into the building, Arney said, "Lucas, I'm glad you dropped by. I need to talk to you about Steve. You know, he's going to be graduating this year, and—"

Rachel listened to the discussion for a while, then excused herself to walk onto the front porch. She was sitting in the swing when Mandy came running.

"How come you're out here by yourself?" the child asked, flopping into a nearby chair.

Rachel grinned. "Lucas and Arney are talking business."

Mandy took off her hat and brushed strands of hair out of her eyes. "They always are. Always grown-up talk. Would you like to see my room?"

"Yes, I would."

"Follow me." Mandy leaped to her feet and ran into the house, holding the door open for Rachel. "I have one all to myself. All of us do. That's why we love living at the Lucky Brand."

"How many of you are here?"

"Only eight of us," she answered. "Us four girls live here in the big house with Arney and his wife, Susie. The four guys live with Mr. and Mrs. Stempleton in that building over there."

As Rachel followed Mandy through the house and heard the child talking about life at the ranch, she was inundated with old memories. At one time she had been very active in charity work. The Marches had insisted she do it because of her social standing; she had done it because she loved to give of herself to others. After the divorce that had changed, and she had promised herself that she would avoid such involvement in the future because it brought nothing but pain.

"This is my room," she heard Mandy say when they reached the second story.

She stepped into the bedroom. White muslin curtains hung over the windows. The blinds were drawn and sunshine poured into the room, spilling onto the red-and-white-checked bedspread. The dark hardwood floor was a perfect foil for a white oval throw rug. Oak furniture completed the furnishings: a single bed, dresser and desk. In the corner was a reproduction of an antique slipper rocker.

Mandy walked to the chair. "Mrs. Molly gives each of us a piece of furniture that goes with us when we leave. I chose this chair because my feet touch the floor when I sit in it. Would you like to try it out?"

"Yes, I would," Rachel murmured and crossed the room to sit down. She rocked back and forth several times.

"Guess what it's called?"

Rachel grinned and bent over to slip off one of her shoes, which she waved in the air.

"How'd you know it was a slipper chair?" Mandy exclaimed, and both of them laughed together.

"Rachel. Mandy." Lucas called from the bottom of the stairs. "Where are you?"

"Up here," Mandy yelled back. "I'm showing Ms. March my bedroom."

Rachel heard the light thud as Lucas came up the stairs and walked down the hall. He poked his head around the door frame.

"Susie tells me you're doing very well in school, Mandy. Straight A's this six weeks?"

Mandy flushed with pleasure and nodded.

"That's wonderful," Rachel said.

"Almost didn't make it in math, Lucas."

"But you did," Lucas said and walked to where she stood. "I'm real proud of you."

"Thanks, Lucas."

"Now I'm going to show Ms. March the rest of the ranch."

"Want to come with us?" Rachel asked.

"Can't. Tonight's my night to help Susie with supper." Mandy slid her hands into her back hip pockets and grinned. "'Sides, you and Lucas probably want to be by yourself without any kids."

"How about coming up to the house later with Neal and Sammy? You can join us for supper," Lucas suggested.

"Yes," Rachel agreed, "why don't you?"

"Great!" Mandy's face was one broad smile and two glowing eyes. Then she sobered and said, "I'll have to ask Susie."

"I already have," Lucas answered. "She said it was fine. Toadie wants tomorrow night free because she has a date with Chuck Allen." He winked at Mandy. "So Miss Susie said the two of you can switch chores."

Several hours later when the ride was over and the horses stabled, Rachel and Lucas returned to the main house. As they skirted the black Mercedes in the drive, Lucas said, "Cheryl's arrived."

Entering through the front door, Rachel followed Lucas through the living room into the den.

"Daddy." A tall, willowy beauty flew across the room to throw herself into Lucas's arms.

"Cheryl, baby."

"Oh, Daddy, I'm so glad to be home."

Lucas pulled out of the embrace and turned to Rachel. Catching her hand in his, he tugged her closer. "Cheryl, I'd like for you to meet Rachel March. You know, the woman I've been telling you about."

Cheryl dropped her arms, and her dark brown eyes centered on Rachel in a disapproving stare. "The real estate woman," she said sarcastically.

Rachel smiled and said, "The real estate woman." She wasn't ashamed of her occupation. "I'm glad to meet you, Cheryl. Your father has told me a lot about you."

Cheryl reached up and carelessly tossed thick black hair over her shoulder. "Yes," she said, stepping closer to Lucas and possessively wrapping her arm around him. "Yes, I'm sure he has. We're *extremely* close, Ms. March."

"Let's sit down and get better acquainted," Lucas said. He had never been quite so nervous when he'd introduced Cheryl to his female acquaintances before. And he'd never noticed her being so cool and aloof. He couldn't understand why she didn't seem to like Rachel.

"By all means, Daddy," Cheryl said, gracefully moving to the sofa. "Why don't you join me over here, Ms. March? I was just looking through some photograph albums. I'd like you to see what a happy family we were...when my mother was alive. You don't mind, do you?"

"Cheryl—" Lucas said.

"No, I don't mind," Rachel answered.

Cheryl lifted her head and smiled brightly. "Contrary to statistics for the eighties, Ms. March, my parents were married to each other for twenty-five years. They loved each other very much. Such a love doesn't diminish even in the face of death."

"Cheryl," Lucas barked, "that's enough."

"I think not," Cheryl exclaimed. "But I'm disinclined to sit here and discuss it at present. I think, *with your permission, Daddy*, I'll go over to Rhonda's."

"I think the least you could do is apologize to Rachel."

"Lucas, no—" Rachel began.

"Since my father thinks I owe you an apology, Ms. March, I shall give you one. Please forgive me." Her head aloft, Cheryl walked out of the room.

"Cheryl," Lucas called, but Rachel caught his arm.

"Let her go, Lucas."

"I won't tolerate such behavior," he said. "She had no right to embarrass you like this. I've never seen her behave this way before."

"It's all right," Rachel said. "I understand."

"No, it's not all right, and I don't understand."

"Lucas, she behaved like she did because she's protecting you. She's afraid of losing you."

Lucas refused to be convinced. "But it's not like you're the first woman I've dated since Debra died."

Rachel smiled gently. "I must be a first of some sort."

Lucas gazed into her eyes and finally said, "You're right."

EVENING SHADOWS LENGTHENED across the den; still Cheryl had not returned. Balancing an empty coffee cup on the arm of the recliner, Lucas sat and stared out the window. Every time he thought about Cheryl's behavior toward Rachel, he became angry all over again. This was the first time he had seen her act like a spoiled brat. Rachel had defended Cheryl, but he couldn't. Cheryl knew how much Rachel meant to him.

Even if Cheryl hadn't known, Lucas still couldn't excuse her actions. Rachel was a guest in their home, and

her visits warranted a better response than rudeness. In
hurting Rachel, Cheryl had hurt him, and he intended to
discuss the matter with her. He would not tolerate such
behavior from her. Absolutely not.

He heard the front door open and close. Soft foot-
steps whispered over the carpet.

"Hi, Daddy. I'm home." Cheryl paused in the doorway and peered into the room.

"It's about time." Lucas's voice was hard. He pushed
out of the recliner and set the empty coffee cup on the
reading table with a thud.

Cheryl switched on the overhead light, then moved
into the den. Making her way to the bar, she said, "I
really didn't think you'd care whether I came home or
not. You seemed to be fully occupied this evening with
Ms. March and the two little Marches. You didn't need
me."

"I've never needed you," Lucas returned. "But I've
always wanted you, and I wanted you to be here. You
knew that. I asked you to come so you could meet
Rachel. How do you think she felt when you bolted out
of here?"

"I'm sorry, Dad," Cheryl said. She opened the refrigerator and pulled out a can of Pepsi. "I just couldn't
stand it . . . the way the two of you were smiling at each
other when you walked into the room."

Lucas raked his fingers through his hair and moved to
the window. He was too angry to say a word.

Cheryl opened the soft drink but didn't lift it to her
mouth. She simply stood in front of the counter and
traced the rim with her finger. Softly she said, "I
couldn't bear to see the way you were looking at her. . . as
if you . . . as if you—"

Unable to complete her sentence, Cheryl picked up the cold drink and walked to the sofa where she flopped down. She set the can on the coffee table next to the opened photograph album.

"As if I what?" Lucas demanded.

Cheryl lifted her head. Her brown eyes were large and pleading. "Don't let's fight, Daddy."

"You behaved like a spoiled brat tonight. How do you think Rachel felt when you challenged her?"

"Challenged her?" Cheryl exclaimed.

"Yes, challenged her," Lucas said. "You brandished those old photographs of your mother as if they were weapons!"

"You don't want me to talk about Mother?"

"Don't try to twist up what I'm saying," Lucas snapped. "I was quite aware that you were telling Rachel to get lost by comparing her to your mother. And so was Rachel."

Cheryl leaned back on the sofa and folded her arms over her breasts. A tear trickled down her cheek, and her chin quivered.

His anger forgotten, Lucas's heart went out to his daughter. Beneath the defiance he saw his only child, grieving the loss of her parent. "I loved your mother," he explained on a softer note, "and if she were alive, I'd be married to her today. But she's dead, baby, and no amount of grieving is going to bring her back." He moved to stand behind the sofa, dropping his hand to her shoulders. He kneaded the tight muscles and ligaments. "I'm alive, Cheryl, and have the right to life and to happiness."

"Does that happiness include Rachel?" Her voice was thick with tears.

"I think so. I want the chance to find out."

Cheryl leaped to her feet, knocking the Pepsi to the floor. Unmindful of the caramel syrup that seeped into the carpet, she glared at her father. "How can you so easily fall out of love with Mother and in love with another woman? Do you think more of Rachel March than you do Mother?"

Lucas breathed in deeply. He walked to the bar and picked up a towel. Returning to the coffee table, he knelt and mopped up the spilt drink. When he stood up, he said, "I'm not devaluing or replacing your mother. No one can ever take Debra's place in my life or heart, but I have enough love and room in my heart to include another wife."

"And children?"

"And children." He walked back to the bar and dropped the towel into the sink.

"Rachel's in particular?"

Lucas turned on the spigot and rinsed out the towel. "I've only met the boys, but I like them."

"You promised Rachel that you'd go over to meet Jae on Monday evening?"

"Yes, I did."

"Daddy, don't you think you're getting too involved with Rachel? She's not the kind of woman you're accustomed to. How is she going to fit into your lifestyle?"

Lucas turned and leaned back against the bar. "Cheryl," he said quietly, "you requested that I butt out of your personal life when you decided to move in with Duanne. Now I'm asking for the same consideration. You're going to have to turn me loose and let me fend for myself."

Swallowing the knot in her throat, Cheryl managed a small smile. "What's the old saying, Dad, about having to eat crow?"

Lucas smiled. "Doesn't taste too good, does it?"

Two more tears slid down Cheryl's cheeks as she shook her head and ran into her father's arms to press herself against his shoulder. "I didn't mean to hurt Rachel, Daddy," she cried. "Honestly I didn't."

"I know." Holding her tightly, Lucas breathed a sigh of relief. His daughter was growing into a woman, and he was proud of her. In time she would apologize to Rachel, also.

"I can understand how you felt about Duanne now," she finally sniffed.

"And I know how you felt. So we've both learned a lesson. We'll give each other a little breathing space so our love can grow."

Chapter Nine

In the den Rachel kicked out of her pumps and tossed her purse and briefcase onto the sofa. Her blazer landed on the back of the platform rocker as she made her way to the cabinet. A glass of iced tea in hand, she returned to the den and sank into the cushioned softness of the sofa.

What a Monday! Sighing deeply, she stared blankly at the wall and wondered what else could go wrong. Her meeting with Elaine had been anything but auspicious. She had arrived at the house in time to see Elaine and her husband whisked away by an ambulance en route to the Methodist Hospital in San Antonio.

"Oh, Rachel," Elaine said, "I'm so sorry. Phil took a turn for the worse this morning. We're—we're taking him to the Methodist Hospital in San Antonio."

"I understand," Rachel said. "Is there anything I can do for you?"

"No," the harried woman replied, "Roberta's on her way from Austin. She'll meet me at the hospital."

"Shall I leave the contract with you?" Rachel asked.

"Yes...yes—" dazed, Elaine wasn't thinking straight "—just give it to me. I'll sign and send it to you as soon as possible."

Rachel gulped down the tea, returned the glass to the sink, and walked down the hall into her bedroom. The downhill slide had begun on Saturday with her meeting with Cheryl. Sunday hadn't been any better. On her return from Dallas, Jae had announced her desire to live with her father and proposed to move at the end of the fall semester. Rachel felt as if the world were crumbling in on her again. She had barely climbed through the emotional rubble of her divorce; now she must face Jae's leaving her.

She looked at the red, white and blue express envelope on the desk; it arrived just as she was leaving to go to meet with Elaine. She unfolded Jared's letter and re-read it for the umpteenth time—although she didn't have to. The words were indelibly printed on her mind. He was no longer asking for modifications to visiting rights; he was suing for them. He demanded more prime time with the children. But...he promised Rachel a large and contract-guaranteed alimony if she agreed to go to court voluntarily to reverse the provisions governing custodial rights. He also demanded that she fly the children to Dallas for the Halloween weekend.

She stripped off her clothes and moved into the bathroom. After a brisk shower and a change into slacks and blouse, she was reinvigorated and headed to the kitchen to prepare a snack. The kids would be home from school soon, and she'd surprise them.

"Cookies!" Sammy yelled later when he raced through the den, his bat and ball landing on the sofa. He skidded to a halt just inside the kitchen. "I smell cookies, Mom."

"You sure do," Rachel answered. "How about one or two with a glass of milk?"

Sammy's toothless grin was answer enough. He jumped onto a stool and propped up his face with his hands. "Did you cook enough, Mom?"

Rachel laughed. "Mmm-hmm."

The front door opened, and Neal called, "I'm home, Mom. Cookies!"

Before Rachel could turn around, he was sitting at the counter beside Sammy. "Gosh, Mom. You've saved my life. I'm starved."

By the time Jae arrived home, the boys were sitting around the kitchen table doing their homework, and Rachel was sitting at her desk in the bedroom.

"If you're hungry, Jae, Mom baked some cookies," Sammy shouted.

"No, thanks," she answered.

"Jae's on a diet," Neal said in a singsong voice. "Jae's on a diet."

"Neal," Rachel called out, "that's enough."

"Hi, Mom. I'm home. What's for dinner?"

"Lucas is taking us out to eat," Rachel replied.

"Oh, yeah—" the spirit went out of Jae's voice "—I'd forgotten about him coming."

Rachel hadn't. She was eagerly counting the seconds until she saw him again. She wanted to see him; she needed to talk to him. The phone rang.

"If that's for me, Mom," Jae called out, "take a number, and I'll call back."

Rachel nodded and picked up the receiver to answer. "Lucas," she exclaimed. "I was just thinking about you."

"Me, too."

"Am I glad you're coming over tonight. I need to see you, Lucas."

"That's what I called about," he said. "There's no way I can be there in time to take you and the kids out to dinner."

"Oh, Lucas," Rachel wailed, "not again!"

"I'll be over as soon as I can," he promised.

"Lucas, you know how Jae is going to take this."

"I know and I'm sorry, honey, but it can't be helped. I'm tied up in this meeting and can't get away right now. Please explain it to Jae."

Rachel sighed. "What kind of meeting?"

"Financial meeting for the Lucky Brand Senior Citizens Apartments. Did you get the papers to Elaine?"

"Yes," Rachel answered, and succinctly described what had happened. "She's going to sign and return the papers to me this week."

"Good," Lucas replied. "I want to get this signed, sealed and delivered, so I can start work."

After they rang off, Rachel leaned back in her chair and gazed at the new dress that was hanging in her closet—the dress she wouldn't get to wear for Lucas tonight, because he was going to be late.

"Who was that, Mom?" Jae called.

"Lucas."

"What's wrong this time?" Barefoot, toothbrush in mouth, Jae padded into her mother's room.

Although Rachel dreaded to answer, she smiled brightly and stood. "He's going to be a little late. He has a meeting."

Jae's hand dropped and she glared at Rachel. "So he's standing me up a second time!"

"Not really," Rachel answered. "He's going to come over as soon as he gets through with the meeting."

"What kind of meeting?" Jae asked.

"A financial meeting concerning the Lucky Brand apartments for senior citizens that he's sponsoring in New Braunfels."

On her way back to the bathroom, Jae yelled, "First time I'm stood up for work, now it's one of his pet projects. What next, Mom? A home for orphaned dogs and cats?"

"Don't speak so disparagingly, Jae. We'll simply change our plans. Instead of going out for dinner, we'll order—"

"Mexican food," Sammy shouted from the kitchen, where he was working on his lessons. "We haven't had any in a long time, Mama."

"Tell me what y'all want, and I'll go get it," Jae said.

Sammy raced down the hall, tugging his cap over his forehead. "I'll go with you."

"Have you finished your homework?" Rachel asked.

He frowned and shook his head. "Don't you think I need a break, Mom, so I don't wear my brain out?"

"Homework." Rachel pointed to the kitchen.

"Aw, Mom."

By the time Jae returned, Sammy and Neal were through with their lessons. After they ate, the boys watched television and Jae migrated to her bedroom and the phone. Rachel watched television with the boys for a while but soon tired of that and went to her bedroom, where she caught up on some of her paperwork.

At nine the boys said good-night and went to bed. As Rachel cleaned up her desk, she moved the express envelope, and Jared's check fluttered to the floor. She bent and retrieved it. Holding it over the wastepaper basket, she tore it into tiny pieces.

"I don't want your money, Jared March," she muttered angrily, "and I'll retain custody of the children, come hell or high water."

She extracted the letter from the envelope and dropped it into the file that held a copy of her answer to him.

Rachel wanted to be with Lucas now. She needed his strength and calmness; she needed to talk with him. Jared's letter had shaken her more than she cared to admit. While she wasn't affected by his money, she knew others could be. She also knew that Jared was accustomed to buying whatever he wanted—and that included people.

"Mom," Jae called from the doorway, "I don't think Lucas is coming, so I'm going to bed. So much for that!"

"He has to earn a living," Rachel said without conviction and wished Jae would stop harping on it.

"At a home for the elderly?" Jae asked skeptically.

"Jae, there are some things you don't understand," Rachel began.

"But I do understand this, Mom," she interjected. "Lucas has stood you up on two occasions. He professes to want to meet me, yet he never comes."

"He'll be here," Rachel answered. "If he weren't coming, he'd call."

"Sure—" Jae shrugged "—but I'm going to bed. I have to get up early in the morning. It's my week to drive."

Hours passed and Lucas didn't come or call. Finally Rachel went to bed, tossing and turning for a long time before dropping into a restless sleep. Much later she was awakened by the doorbell. Climbing out of bed, she slipped into her housecoat and raced down the hall. She called through the door, "Who's there?"

"Lucas."

"Lucas!"

Rachel turned the bolt and unhooked the chain to fling open the door. Lucas stood in the wedge of light that fell from the hall onto the porch. The collar of his shirt was opened; his tie hung loosely around his neck. He grinned.

"Hi! Am I too late?"

"No—" Rachel smiled and stepped aside "—come on in."

When the door closed behind him, he took Rachel into his arms and kissed her hungrily. Finally lifting his lips from hers, he murmured, "It seems like an eternity since I last saw you."

"Me, too," Rachel answered.

His hands swept down the length of her back to hold her close. "Wearing hardly any clothes!" he exclaimed in a low whisper. "You don't know how much you tempt me, woman."

"Maybe you need to take a cold shower," Rachel teased. "I think that's what they do in books."

"If I take a shower," he told her, tweaking her nose with tiny kisses, "it'll be with you."

Rachel laughed and shook her head, her golden hair swirling around her face. "Not tonight. I've already bathed."

"Totally inhospitable."

"Not quite," Rachel countered, pulling out of his arms. "I can offer you something to drink. Coffee. Tea. Hot chocolate. Soft drinks. Wine."

"A glass of wine." He followed her into the den and sat on the sofa, watching the gentle sway of her hips as she walked into the kitchen and rummaged through the cabinet for a tray and glasses. "I'm sorry about tonight."

"I am, too." She turned from the counter to the refrigerator.

"Jae was disappointed?" Lucas asked.

"Quite." Closing the door, Rachel set the wine bottle and glasses on the tray and moved into the den. "She thinks you don't want to meet her."

Lucas sighed and pushed his hand through his hair. "We're not getting off to a good start with the girls, are we?"

Rachel smiled tightly as she set the tray on the coffee table. "You haven't got a start, period, and I bombed out first try."

Lucas caught her hands and pulled her into his lap. Putting his arms around her, he said, "You haven't bombed out with me, and I promise to show Jae the time of her life this coming Friday night at the Halloween Party. I'll make up for all the false starts. Just give Lucas Brand a little time, and he'll—"

Rachel laid her head against his chest. "I'm afraid time is running out. At the end of the semester Jae's going to live with Jared."

Lucas held her tightly. "I'm sorry."

"Oh, Lucas," Rachel whispered, "I don't think I can stand it. I love her so much. I'm so afraid of losing her."

"You're not going to lose her," he murmured. "This is just a phase she's going through. By the time the semester ends, she'll have changed her mind."

"Maybe she will have, but Jared won't." Rachel moved out of Lucas's lap and snuggled up to him on the sofa. Quietly she told him about Jared's letter. "I'm going to fight him all the way," she declared. "I mean it, Lucas. I won't let him have the children. He didn't want them when we divorced, and he's not going to get them now.''

"He's bluffing," Lucas told her. "There's nothing he can do."

"I know," Rachel sighed. "He just wants to keep my life in a turmoil."

"He can't if you don't allow him to," Lucas answered. "Don't worry about Jae. She'll come to her senses."

"Now that I've unloaded on you," Rachel said, "tell me about your meeting."

For the next hour Lucas talked to Rachel about the obstacles he was having in getting funding for the proposed apartment complex for senior citizens. Sipping her wine, Rachel listened as he talked and realized that Jae, although young and immature, was farsighted when it came to her observation of Lucas. He was totally immersed in helping underprivileged children and the elderly. While this was commendable, Lucas was making it his first priority. All his time and energy went into it. Unlike the Marches, Lucas didn't do it because it was expected of him, but because he believed in it. As Jared made success and work his life, Lucas made crusades his.

"Am I boring you?" he asked when she stifled a yawn with the back of her hand.

"No, I'm just relaxing for the first time in days." She smiled. "You're good for me, Lucas Brand."

"And you're good for me, Rachel March." He took the empty glass out of her hands and set it on the table. "Have you given any more thought to our spending weekend after next together?"

Rachel's smile turned into a teasing grin. "A little."

"How much?" Lucas playfully lunged at her, tickling her under the arms.

"Don't, Lucas!" Rachel giggled and squirmed. "I've really thought about it a lot. The children are spending weekend after next with Jared."

"That's more like it," Lucas said and ceased tickling her.

"Do you always use such tactics to get confessions, Counselor?"

"Only from those I really care about."

Rachel smiled and snuggled into his arms, the two of them sitting quietly on the couch. Finally the clock chimed the hour.

"Morning is going to come mighty early," Lucas said.

"I wish you could stay," Rachel murmured.

"So do I."

Long after Lucas had gone, Rachel lay in bed thinking. She and Lucas were on their way to being in love, but she didn't want to be wedged in between meetings, no matter how worthy. She wanted a total commitment from the man whom she loved. She also wanted a man who would be a good parent for her children. She knew that before long she and Lucas would have to have a serious discussion.

The week passed quickly for Rachel. Reassured by Lucas that Jared could do nothing to gain custody of the children, she pushed his threats aside. She didn't realize how much self-confidence she had gained until she called Jared on Thursday morning to tell him the children weren't coming for Halloween; they had other plans. She would send them the following weekend. When Jared went into a cursing tirade, she laughed softly and hung up the phone. Normally his shouting and vilification would have haunted her for days; not so now. Jared March didn't have the power to hurt her any longer.

Saturday afternoon when Rachel arrived home from work, Sammy and Neal were running around the house, screaming and yelling as they donned their costumes and made up their faces for the party.

"Sammy, I don't think a vampire would wear a baseball cap," Rachel said.

"That's what I've been telling him, but he'll give up his fangs quicker than the hat," Neal yelled. "But at least he's going in costume. Jae isn't."

"Where is she?" Rachel asked, setting her briefcase on the hall table and shucking her yellow blazer.

"On the bed, sulking," Neal replied.

"Not anymore," Sammy said. "She's talking with Donna now about Allen Parker, the new guy who just transferred to Roosevelt from Madison."

"Mom," Neal said, "will you help me paint my face and neck?"

"Give me a few minutes," Rachel answered and walked down the hall to Jae's room.

When Jae saw her, she said into the receiver, "Donna, I've got to go now. I'll call you tomorrow. Okay?"

After she hung up the phone, Rachel asked, "Don't you think you ought to get ready? We'll be leaving in about an hour."

"Mom, I don't want to wear a costume. I'm not a child."

"I'm wearing a costume and I'm not a child," Rachel pointed out.

"That's different," Jae said. "You want to impress Lucas. I couldn't care less. He's not very high on my list of priorities. I'd much rather be in Dallas with Daddy.

You're not letting me go because you're still angry over the gown."

"Yes, I am," Rachel admitted, "but that's not the reason why I'm not letting you go to Dallas. One, you have two tests on Monday, which you need to study for, and I want you rested. Second, you accepted Lucas's invitation to the party, and you're keeping to it. You'll get to spend next weekend with your father."

"Just remember I'm going under duress," Jae grumbled. "I'm not going to have a good time."

"We'll see," Rachel said and turned to walk into her room, closing the door behind herself. She grinned when she looked at her costume—a golden-yellow gown, all satin and lace and chiffon—laid out on the bed. Tonight she would be the Good Witch of the East, wand and all. She quickly slipped out of her skirt and blouse. Before she could put on her gown, the telephone rang and she answered. "Hello."

"Rachel, this is Elaine."

"I'm so glad you called," Rachel said. "I've been worried. How's Phillip?"

"As good as can be expected," Elaine answered wearily. "He came home day before yesterday. I've just been so busy I haven't had time to call you."

"I understand," Rachel said.

"Rachel," Elaine began anxiously, "I—I don't know how to tell you this. You've been so wonderful to work with, but—"

"What's wrong, Elaine?" Rachel asked, unconsciously tightening her hold on the receiver.

"I've changed my mind about selling the property to Lucas."

Rachel sat down. "What happened to change your mind?" she asked.

"Raymond Gordon of Kline Industries came to see me yesterday and made me an offer I can't refuse. He's offering me more than I originally asked."

"But you verbally accepted Lucas's offer," Rachel said. "You were happy with it."

"I know I did," Elaine answered, "but that was before... before... Rachel, please understand, I do need the money."

At that moment Rachel was only concerned about Lucas. "Elaine, you know Kline's reputation. They have a total lack of regard for the environment. Their only thought is money. Can you imagine what they're going to do to your ranch?"

"Rachel, I'm sorry," Elaine said, "but I must do what I must."

Rachel couldn't persuade Elaine to talk with Lucas first or to change her mind; she was resolute in her decision to accept Kline's offer. When Rachel replaced the receiver, she was stunned, then depressed, then angry. How dare Elaine do this to Lucas!

"SHE CAN'T DO THIS!" Lucas exclaimed, pacing back and forth in his den, his black cape swirling around him. He wore a black tuxedo with a red cummerbund; his shirt was frilled with rows of lace ruffles. His warlock costume combined with his anger to make him look sinister. "She can't do this to me, Rachel. I've already hired the architect to draw up the plans. I've already started to work on this."

"If only I had insisted she sign the contract the day I was out there," Rachel said, then added, "But I couldn't, Lucas. She was taking her husband to the hospital and didn't know if he was going to live."

"It's not your fault," he said. "No one would have expected you to do differently."

"Kline was willing to go above what she originally asked, and—" Rachel's voice softened "—she does need the money, Lucas."

"There's not many of us who don't," he answered. "I'm going to call her, Rachel. Maybe we can strike a deal that'll be satisfactory to her."

Walking to where he stood, Rachel laid her hand on his arm. "I have other listings, Lucas. Wouldn't one of them do just as well?"

"The others might do, but the Storch-Halston Ranch is what I want, Rachel."

"Then we'll fight for it." She picked up the phone and dialed.

"Hello," Elaine said.

"Elaine, this is Rachel. I'm calling for Lucas Brand."

"Rachel, I've already—"

"I know what you've said, Elaine," Rachel interrupted, "but Lucas wants an opportunity to make a counteroffer." She listened, then said, "Yes, he understands. When can we meet? Tuesday morning. Ten o'clock." Rachel looked at Lucas, and he nodded. "Fine. We'll meet at your home." When she hung up the phone, she grinned. "Well, at least she hasn't signed with Kline yet and is willing to talk with us."

"Now, it's time for me to meet Jae." Lucas caught her hands in a warm clasp and pulled her close to him. "I still have to prove to Jae that I'm not an ogre."

"While you're not in her best graces," Rachel said, "I don't think you rank quite that low."

"Must," he replied, "or she would have come into the house when you got here instead of going directly to the barn with Dugan and the kids. Courting kids is hard, Rachel."

Rachel laughed quietly. "For you, it shouldn't be such a hard task. You're quite a persuasive man. *Quite a charmer,* if I remember the quote from *Texas Monthly* correctly."

"I am," he admitted quietly, the gray eyes penetrating and honest. "As an attorney I must be. That's what people pay me for. There's only one person in my life whom I wish to charm...and that's you, Rachel."

"Lucas," Rachel whispered, unconsciously moving nearer to him, lifting her face for his kiss.

Their fingers were intertwined, but their bodies scarcely touched. He brushed his lips lightly over hers in a sweet, tentative kiss that held no sexual overtones, yet Rachel yearned to be totally possessed by Lucas. She craved fulfillment. Desire, hot and molten, coursed through her veins; passion turned her eyes a deep, forest green.

She lowered her lids and swayed toward Lucas, lost in a world of her own making. Of its own volition, her body melded perfectly with his. She realized at this moment that the little girl in her had loved and needed Jared, but the woman in her loved Lucas Brand. Never had she known such emotions as she now experienced.

"Mom!" Jae's cry thundered through the room.

Rachel jumped away from Lucas, her face suffused with soft color. Her hand flew to her cheek in embarrassment as she looked into the scowling countenance of her daughter.

Without the least embarrassment, Lucas smiled and moved toward Jae. "At last we get to meet."

Jae didn't return the smile. Slowly her gaze shifted from Rachel to Lucas. Her green eyes were glacial; her lips curled into a petulant snarl. "At last we meet, Mr. Brand. I rather wondered if at the last moment you would have to cancel the Halloween party because of... business. You are a busy man, so Mother says."

"Yes," Lucas drawled, "I must admit that I am, and I do apologize for having to break two dates with you." The gray eyes twinkled and his lips twitched into a beguiling smile. "I didn't do it intentionally."

"That's what Mother says," Jae returned icily. Her gaze swept from Lucas to Rachel, then back to Lucas.

"Had you been so eager to meet me, you could have come into the house when you and your mother first arrived," he added.

"I wanted to go with the boys to the barn," she said.

"Lucas, where did I put that basket of apples?" Molly called out, her voice growing louder as she neared the den. "I thought I left them on the kitchen table, but evidently I didn't. We can't have the apple bobbing without them."

"They're in the back of the pickup. I was going to bring them when I came."

"Good. If I had known that, I wouldn't have insisted that Jae make the trip to the house with me." Molly stood in the den now, her hands resting on her ample hips. Her white hair was covered with a bright blue poke bonnet that matched her turn-of-the-century calico dress. With a wink in Lucas's direction, she said, "I brought her to help me carry things. Lord only knows, we have a lot to do before the rest of the guests start arriving. Well, Jae, I see you've finally met the mystery man."

"Yes," Jae mumbled, "I have, Mrs. MacAdams."

"When you know him as well as we do, you'll love him."

"Perhaps my mother and brothers will get to know him that well, Mrs. MacAdams, but I don't think I will." Jae walked across the room, deliberately putting distance between Lucas and herself. "I'm returning to Dallas at the end of the semester to live with my father."

"Jae—" Rachel called out and started to go after her daughter.

Lucas caught her hand and shook his head. After Jae had disappeared into another part of the house, he said, "Give her some space, Rachel. She's got to work her way through this."

"He's right," Molly agreed, nodding her head vigorously, the bib of her bonnet waving through the air. "She'll come around. Don't underestimate the girl. I'll take her back to the barn with me."

"No," Rachel said, more sharply than she meant to. "I want her to ride with Lucas and me. Right now she doesn't feel wanted."

Molly's blue eyes rested on Rachel; quietly she said, "I don't mean to stick my nose in your business, Rachel, but from experience I know that right now Jae is playing a little game with you. It's called emotional blackmail. If you let her, she'll start pulling strings and you'll find yourself a puppet to her whims."

"She's never seen me with another man before," Rachel murmured. "It's hurting her."

"I grant that," Molly answered, "but she'll have to get used to it, Rachel. She'll have to learn that you can be her mother and live your life, too. Jae is your daughter, but I wouldn't push Lucas on her. Give her some time."

Rachel lifted her head and rubbed her temple. "You're right," she muttered. "I—I—"

"No one said it was easy being a single parent," Molly said softly. "You're doing an excellent job, Rachel. Right now, Jae is making the transition from little girl into young adulthood. You've taught her right from wrong; you've taught her to make decisions. Now you've got to release her and let her apply the lessons she's learned. Give her a chance to experience life."

Rachel smiled gratefully at the older woman. "You're right," she acknowledged. "I just get frustrated at times."

"Don't we all." Molly laughed and raised a hand, splaying her fingers in the air. "Dugan and I raised five. Every one was different, yet each one was easier to raise. Our two older kids vow and declare that they were guinea pigs, and in a way I guess they were. We learned off them and didn't make some of the same mistakes on the younger ones."

Rachel laughed tightly. "Good for Sammy, but tough on Jae."

"Well, now—" Molly pursed her lips, returning her hands to her hips "—I don't reckon none of my kids suffered too much, and as far as I can see Jae's enjoying martyrdom right now. When she finds that it's easier to carry the cross than hang on it, she'll get off. Don't worry none. Everything's gonna work out okay. Since no one else seems to be concerned with getting things ready, I guess Jae and I will go back to the barn and set up the rest of the games. Guess y'all are gonna come sometime tonight with the prizes and the piñatas?" Her grin took the rancor out of her words.

"Is that a hint or is it a hint?" Lucas said with a laugh. "Subtlety isn't one of your strongest points, Molly."

"Don't need to be," she answered and turned, moving toward the door. "Now I'll be seeing you in a little while."

Reassuring Rachel that all would be well between them and their daughters, Lucas drove behind Molly to the barn.

"Oh, Lucas," Rachel exclaimed when they parked the truck, "it's just right for a Halloween party."

Lanterns were suspended from the interior beams, their light glowing through the opened doors. A rainbow of light glittered on the outside from the Chinese lanterns that were strung through the trees. Jack-o'-lanterns, their smiling faces illuminated with candles, lined the walkway. Others without their candles sat inside on bales of hay. Among the foods garnering the long serving table was pumpkin pie with whipped cream topping.

"Hi, Mom." In hot pursuit of another youngster, Sammy skidded to a halt in front of Lucas and Rachel. He pulled the peak of his cap lower over his face. "We're having fun. Neal and Mandy's helping Dugan blow up the balloons for the dart throwing. I'm gonna win me a prize. Just wait and see." Then he was gone.

Jae helped Molly unload the car, but soon migrated to a far corner of the barn where she sat and pouted. Nothing anyone could say would entice her to join the festivities. Lucas pushed all else out of mind as he set out to make this the best Halloween party the children had ever experienced.

Rachel thoroughly enjoyed the old-fashioned games they played with relish and vigor. Gunnysack racing. Bobbing for apples. Ringing the bottles. Later in the evening she looked around for Sammy and Neal, only to see them sitting on a bale of hay beside Jae in the corner.

Walking up to them, she asked, "What's wrong? I thought you were enjoying the party."

Jae shrugged her shoulders disdainfully. "This is child's play, Mom. We're too old and sophisticated for this."

Sammy swiped a shock of brown hair out of his eyes. "I'm not," he declared, jumping off the hay and scooting to the center of the barn where the children were getting in line to swing at the piñata. "I'm just a little boy, so this is fun. Hey, Dugan, I want to hit that donkey."

Dugan laughed. "Then git in line, Sammy. First come, first served."

"Rachel," Molly called from the other side of the building, "will you help me, please? I can't get these knots untied, and Dugan needs me to be a team captain."

"Coming," Rachel answered but continued to look at Neal and Jae, wondering what she should do.

Lucas walked up to her, catching her shoulders and spinning her in Molly's direction. "Go on and help, Molly. I'll see if I can persuade Jae and Neal to join the party."

Lucas sat down on the bale next to Neal, but before he could speak, Dugan called, "Neal, come be one of our team captains. I need to be the referee."

A grin split Neal's face and he leaped from the hay to the floor, running to the center of the barn. When Dugan flipped the nickel, Neal got first choice. "Mandy." He pointed.

"Hey," Sammy yelled, swinging his arms through the air, "that's no fair. Let's make it boys against girls."

Neal laughed. "Can't do that, Sammy. It's discrimination."

"Sammy," Molly called out. "Why don't you be on my team? I need a co-captain to help me."

Sammy grinned and pulled himself up, tucking his thumbs under his arms. He strutted around like a little bantam rooster. "Hey, everybody," he crowed, "just call me Mr. Samuel Joseph March from now on."

Lucas chuckled softly, then looked at the pouting girl sitting next to him. "Whether you enjoy the party or not, Jae, is your prerogative, but you shouldn't discourage the boys from having fun."

Jae's hand swept around the barn. "You call this fun?"

"Yes," Lucas answered, "I do, and most of the children do, too."

"This stuff went out of style years ago," she exclaimed.

"Your brothers seem to enjoy it, and so could you if you were willing. If you cared about your mother and brothers like they care about you, you wouldn't be trying to make them suffer through the evening with you."

Guilty because Lucas had seen through her ruse, Jae jumped to her feet. "You're not my father, Lucas Brand, and you're not going to tell me what I can or can't do. You may have my mother wrapped around your little finger, but not me."

"I don't want either you or your mother wrapped around my finger," Lucas said, suppressing his anger. "Neither do I have any intention of passing myself off as your father. You have one already and that's enough."

"You don't fool me," Jae sneered. "I know what you want from my mother."

Inwardly Lucas recoiled from her bitter accusation.
Gray eyes coolly assessed the girl standing in front of
him. "I'm glad you do," he finally said, "but just so
there can be no misunderstanding, let me tell you how I
feel about your mother. I respect her and want to be
around her, because she's a lovely and intelligent
woman. I want to get to know her better. I want her to
learn to know me better."

"Well, Mr. Brand," Jae said, "you'll probably get the
chance to know my mother very well. She seems to be in
agreement with you."

"Let me be your friend," Lucas said as he eased off
the bale of hay and moved closer to Jae.

Jae backed away. "I have enough friends in my life,"
she snapped.

Lucas sighed and dropped his glance to stare at the toe
of his shoes, the shine long since camouflaged by a coat
of dust. Rather than making headway with Jae, he had
pushed her further away.

"I don't need or want your friendship." Saying this,
she turned to run from the barn but bumped into someone.

"Sorry." Cheryl laughed and caught Jae by the
shoulders to keep her from falling. "I didn't know you
were going to dart out like that."

Jae relaxed and smiled at the older girl. "Me neither.
Sorry."

"Cheryl," Lucas exclaimed, "I didn't expect you."

Cheryl grinned at her father. "Did you think I was
going to let you have this Halloween party without me?
You may get Rachel to be your Good Witch of the East,
but the party's still not the same without me."

"No," Lucas murmured, his eyes glowing, "it's not.
I'm glad to see you." He turned to Jae. "Let me intro-

duce Rachel's daughter to you. Jae, this is my daughter Cheryl.''

"Hello, Jae," Cheryl said, dropping her arm over Jae's shoulder in a friendly gesture. "I'm glad to know you. Your mother told me quite a bit about you."

"Yeah, I bet." Jae grimaced, then grinned. "She told me a lot about you, too."

"I guess we better stick together then," Cheryl said. "We need to compare notes, to see if they told the truth about us." She turned to Lucas. "Have we had the Worst Dressed contest yet, Dad?"

He shook his head. "In another hour. Let them finish with the massacre of the piñatas and the square dance."

"Come on, Jae," Cheryl said. "Let's go inside and see if we can get ourselves a costume. We wouldn't want to miss out on anything, would we?" Over Jae's head, Cheryl smiled and winked at her father. "We'll be seeing you and Rachel later. Have fun."

"I will," Lucas promised and added softly under his breath, "I will." As soon as the girls moved away, he saw Rachel looking at him anxiously from across the barn. He waved and crossed over to her.

"I saw you talking to Jae," she said. "Is she still angry?"

"Yes, but at least she's talking." Quietly he repeated his conversation with Jae. "Don't worry," he reassured her. "Now that she's said all that's on her heart, she's going to be better."

"I don't know, Lucas. Rather than getting better, it seems to get worse." She looked around. "Where is she?"

"With Cheryl."

"Cheryl's here?" Rachel felt as if her heart had dropped to her feet.

Lucas laughed. "Everything is fine. She and Cheryl are going to the house to find a costume."

"Jae is going to wear a costume?" Rachel exclaimed.

He nodded. "She and Cheryl are getting along fine. I told you, everything is going to be all right."

"Oh, Lucas—" her eyes brimmed with tears of happiness; her lips lifted in a tremulous smile "—this may turn out to be one of the best Halloweens I've ever had."

Looking deeply into the beautiful green eyes, he said, "I'm working to make it your best, Rachel."

STANDING IN THE SHADOWS away from the doors of the barn, away from the buzz of activity, Rachel leaned against the building and stared into the sky. For a day that had begun so hectically, the evening was truly beautiful. The children were having a wonderful time; so was she.

"Hello, Rachel."

Rachel turned her head to see Cheryl approaching.

"I came tonight because I wanted to see you. I wanted to apologize for my behavior last Saturday. I was acting the part of the spoiled brat."

Rachel smiled and said, "Apology accepted. And for the record, I can understand your behavior. You were defending your father."

Cheryl shrugged her shoulders and grinned through the clown makeup. "Whatever, I was rude." Suddenly she caught Rachel in a hug. "I want us to be friends."

"So do I," Rachel said.

"And don't worry about Jae." Cheryl pulled back. "Give her time. She'll love my dad as much as I do."

"I know," Rachel whispered.

"I'm going to go now," Cheryl said. "I promised Jae that I'd teach her how to do the square dance. Are you going to join us?"

"After a while."

Minutes later music poured out of the barn, and Dugan called out the reels. Rachel moved a little farther away from the building. She had to have time to herself. For the moment she was too overcome with feelings to return to the barn. She looked up at the beautiful, star-studded night and remembered the Ferris wheel ride. How beautiful her life had been since the day Lucas came into it.

Two hands settled gently on her shoulders. "Stargazing?"

Rachel turned into his embrace, nestling her face against the soft, lace ruffles of his shirt. "Mmm-hmm."

"Did you make a wish?"

"That I could always be as happy as I am right this minute."

"You shall be," he whispered, his lips covering hers as a seal to his promise.

Chapter Ten

Tuesday was a gorgeous autumn day. The sky was clear and sunshine bathed the hill country in warm brightness. A little after noon, Lucas backed the Mercedes out of Elaine Halston's driveway and headed for San Antonio. She had agreed to give him a little more time to come up with the cash she wanted, because she was having second thoughts about the offer from Kline Industries.

"Are you satisfied?" Rachel asked as they drove through town.

He shrugged. "As much as I can be. I understand that Elaine wants more money and wants it immediately, but as I told her, if she'll just give me time, I'll match whatever Kline gives her."

"Do you think the property is worth it?"

Lucas negotiated a turn before he grinned at her. "You're supposed to be fighting for this sale, woman. This is your livelihood."

"I'm not about to give up on the sale, Mr. Brand," she declared, also grinning. "I just don't know that the Storch-Halston property is worth what you're going to be paying for it."

"It's worth it," Lucas reassured her, "because it's what I want."

"Then go for it," Rachel said.

"I am. I hope we have the deal closed before Thanksgiving. And speaking of Thanksgiving, what do you and the children usually do for the holidays?"

"I have the children at Thanksgiving. On Christmas they go to Jared."

"Don't you get lonely without the children at Christmas?" Lucas asked.

"Since Jared walked out on me two years ago at Christmas, I haven't been able to muster up any Christmas spirit. I thought it was best for the children to spend the holidays with their daddy and his family. At least they will have a good holiday."

"This year, Rachel—" Lucas reached across the seat and laid his hand over hers "—let the children spend Thanksgiving with Jared and Christmas with you."

Rachel turned her head and looked at him in surprise.

"Share Christmas with me and the Christmas Elves."

"I don't mind sharing Christmas with you, but I'm not sure about the elves. Who... what are they?"

"It's a program the directors and I have begun at the ranch. By allowing the children to help others, they are experiencing firsthand the true meaning of Christmas. They're learning to give as well as to receive."

Rachel grinned. "Another one of your charity programs?"

Warming to his subject, Lucas nodded his head and said, "Truly a work of love. From Thanksgiving on Dugan, Molly and the kids will convert the Lucky Brand barn into a workshop. They'll collect toys and food to be distributed to needy families on Christmas Eve." He grinned. "I'm Mr. Christmas. Dugan is Holly Jolly, the workshop director, and this year Mandy is Misty Mistletoe, elf in charge of production."

As old memories flooded in, Rachel remembered again her own work with such organizations—and her promise to herself that in future she would avoid the pain it had brought her.

"I believe this would be a good year to introduce Mrs. Christmas," Rachel heard Lucas say, and he gently squeezed her hand, then twined their fingers together. "Please."

"I'll have to think about it," she murmured.

"Then I must persuade you," he said, and launched into a description of Christmas Elves programs in the past. Rachel listened, and for the first time in two years found herself excited about the coming Yuletide season. Gently Lucas pushed her reservations aside and reintroduced her to the wonder of interaction with people.

"What do you say?" he asked when they pulled onto I-10.

"I'd love to," she answered, "but I can't answer for the children. I think the boys would have fun, but I'm not sure about Jae. She—"

She left the sentence unfinished; both of them knew that Jae liked Cheryl, but her feelings toward Lucas hadn't changed. If anything her dislike of him had intensified.

"The children are going to Dallas this weekend?" he asked.

"Yes."

"Friday is still our night?"

"Yes," she murmured, her stomach fluttering with anticipation.

LUCAS COULDN'T BELIEVE his eyes as he stepped into Rachel's house on Friday evening. Rachel was a vision of loveliness. Her hair was swept into an elegant chignon, soft curls wisping about her face. She was dressed simply but elegantly. She wore a black sheath dress with a high mandarin collar and long sleeves. Totally covered, she created a uniquely sensual illusion. Her accessories were pearls. High-heeled pumps enhanced long, slender legs.

When his gaze finally returned to her face, he handed her a bottle of champagne. "Would you like to have a drink before we leave?" she asked.

Lucas shook his head. His lips twitched into a smile, and his gray eyes glinted devilishly. "Put it in the refrigerator. It's for us when we come home tonight. If I come inside for a drink now, I don't know that we'll be going out again. And it's a shame to waste such beauty."

"Thank you." Pleasure delicately stained Rachel's cheeks. Accepting compliments was difficult for her. Life with Jared had conditioned her to criticism. "Let me put this away and get my purse and stole."

She turned, and Lucas sucked in his breath. Her back was bare, revealing a wealth of creamy, satin flesh. He was fascinated by the pull of the silk material over her hips as she walked. When she returned, he took the stole from her but didn't immediately cover her shoulders. He leaned down and pressed his lips against the nape of her neck, just below the collar, just below the diamond clasp on her pearls. When Rachel felt the whisper-soft touch of his lips, she shivered with anticipation.

"Just a hint of what's to come, my darling," he murmured and stepped back, letting the soft white cashmere fall about her shoulders.

When they walked out of the house, Rachel saw the sleek, black limousine parked next to the curb, a uniformed young man standing next it. She looked up at Lucas in surprise.

"I thought we might be doing a lot of celebrating tonight," he murmured. "And I wanted to concentrate solely on you, Rachel March. Is that all right with you?"

"Perfectly."

The chauffeur smiled and opened the door for them. "Where to, Mr. Brand?"

"La Louisiane," Lucas answered.

Sliding into the Lincoln, Rachel was enveloped in sheer luxury, leather and soft music and champagne...and she and Lucas were alone, cut off from their driver Kenny by the tinted window. Her evening was spectacular. After they dined, they saw *The King and I* at the Majestic Theater. Rachel had been there many times, but never before had the historic theater seemed so romantic.

Lucas put his arm around her. "Having a good time?"

"Yes," she whispered. "Even though I miss Yul Brynner, the play has never been as captivating."

Rachel laid her head on Lucas's shoulder, feeling a oneness with him that she'd never sensed with another individual. She felt as if she had been waiting for him all her life.

After the performance, she and Lucas walked out of the theater into the chilled night. He held her close as they waited for the street to clear and Kenny to drive up. She looked up at Lucas and smiled dreamily; he lowered his head and kissed the tip of her nose.

"You're a beautiful woman, Rachel March."

"And you're a handsome man."

By the time they stood inside the house, the door locked behind them, Rachel was nervous. She laid her purse on the entry table; Lucas removed her stole, but fearing he would kiss her on the back once more, she quickly stepped away. She felt gauche and clumsy.

"A—a drink," she said. "Would you like to have a glass of champagne?"

"Perhaps more than a glass," he answered, an enigmatic smile touching his lips.

While Rachel poured the wine, Lucas walked into the living room and turned on the stereo. As soft classical music wafted through the house, he shed his tie, jacket and cummerbund. When Rachel entered with the drinks, she found him going through a photograph album on the coffee table.

His hair was tousled, a recalcitrant lock falling across his forehead. Several buttons at the top of his shirt were undone. He looked up, smiled and reached for his glass. Rachel moved to go past him and sit in the chair opposite the sofa, but he caught her hand.

"Sit with me."

Rachel's heart leaped to her throat when she sat down and his hand slipped to her back. His fingers felt like five tongues of pure fire.

"A toast," he said. "To us."

"To us," Rachel murmured.

Their glasses touched. The enigmatic smile moved from his lips to his eyes, as gray eyes stared into bright green ones. "And to love."

"To love," she whispered.

Rachel slowly raised her glass and sipped the effervescent liquid, the bubbles tickling her nose. Then Lucas reached out, took the glass from her fingers, and touched his lips to the spot where hers had rested. He handed his glass to her and watched.

Hypnotized by the sheer intimacy of this act, Rachel did not have the will to deny him. Without taking her eyes from his face, she lifted the glass and put her lips where his had been. She felt the warmth of his mouth on hers; she felt his lips on hers.

Lucas took the glass from her again and leaned over to set it on the table beside the other one. "Rachel," he murmured, enveloping her in his arms, "I love you."

Such a small phrase, yet one of the most important that Rachel had ever heard. These were the words she had prayed that Lucas would say to her. Although they included desire, their meaning extended beyond the physical. The words promised friendship, honesty and communication; they promised a solid foundation for a relationship.

"I love you," she said, her voice low and caressing.

As their lips met, her declaration of love became the essence of their kiss. She melded herself to him, becoming altogether malleable and pliant in his arms. She kissed him with all her heart, entrusting herself utterly to him and his passion. The kiss deepened. His lips moved on hers, opening wider, his tongue entering her mouth, drinking the honey-sweet nectar.

Rachel delighted in the feel of his hands as they gently kneaded the base of her neck, in the fingers as they enveloped her waist to move up and down her spine, sending thrills throughout her body in a thousand places at once.

"I want to make love to you . . . now," Lucas said, his voice thick with desire.

"Yes," Rachel whispered.

He picked her up and carried her down the hall. Her face was cradled against his chest, her cheek nuzzling the soft fabric of his shirt. Soft murmurs escaped her parted lips. He laid her down on her bed but didn't lie down himself. Standing in the spill of light from the hallway, he unbuttoned his shirt and shrugged out of it. He unfastened his slacks. Mesmerized, Rachel pushed herself up on her elbows and watched him kick his way out of the slacks, letting them fall over the shirt. In tight briefs he stood with his legs straddled, his hands resting on his hips.

His hands, palms sliding down his torso, slid beneath the elastic of his shorts, and he pushed them over his hips and down his thighs, kicking out of them, also. Rachel watched him move across the carpet until he was standing beside the bed.

Unashamedly her eyes feasted on the naked torso that was darkened with a mat of hair that swirled over flexed muscles and around flat nipples. It narrowed down the stomach and lower. Her eyes roved over his taut thighs.

For the first time in nearly two years Rachel wanted to make love with a man. She wanted to relieve the growing ache within her. She wanted to fill her emptiness. Unbeknownst to herself, her desire flashed in her eyes, and she licked her lips, the moisture forming a filmy sheen on them that captivated Lucas.

Rachel couldn't read his face in the muted light, but she could see the rigidity of his body. She could sense his ardent desire. Caught up in the same tide of passion as Lucas, she raised her hand to lightly touch his leg, running her fingers from the knee up to the thigh, gradually moving higher and higher.

The slow caress was beginning to set off an avalanche of passion in him. He could stand no more and collapsed on the bed beside her, clasping her hand in his.

"We're in no hurry, sweetheart," he admonished softly. "This night is ours, and I want to enjoy it at a leisurely pace."

Rachel's husky laugh wafted through the room. He caught the loop of pearls, lifted them from around her neck and dropped them to the floor. He turned her around and unfastened the collar of her dress, pushing the material off her shoulders. He ran his finger lightly down the indentation of her back. Soon she lay naked, her dress and panty hose on the carpet on top of her necklace.

Propped on an elbow, leaning over Rachel, Lucas pushed a curl out of her face and planted small kisses from her ears down the side of her neck and across her collarbone to the tip of her breasts. He nipped the delicate skin and felt the nipple grow firm in his mouth.

He drew away, and Rachel felt as if a path had been burned into her skin. Then those same burning lips captured hers in a soul-searching kiss, designed to discover her most secret self.

Her hands tangled in his thick hair, and she pulled his face closer to hers. She wanted more; she was hungry for the feel and taste of his body. The kisses were prolonged and became more intoxicating and at the same time kindled a fire in her. She was excruciatingly aware of her two-year-long celibacy, and his probing tongue only helped to make the awareness more acute.

"Lucas," she begged, "I can't wait. Please make love to me."

"Yes, my darling." He arched his body above hers. "I love you," he whispered and lowered himself into her welcoming softness. "Dear God, I love you with all my heart."

Afterward they lay together in bed, enjoying the aftermath of their love, basking in the glory of the moment. Eventually Rachel jumped up from the bed, and, quite naked, ran out of the bedroom.

"Where are you going?" Lucas called.

Rachel didn't answer until she returned to the bedroom, wine bottle and glasses in hand. She smiled. "I didn't want this to go to waste. Since my divorce I've learned to be quite frugal." She set the glasses on the nightstand and filled them up.

She and Lucas fluffed the pillows against the headboard and sat in bed, drinking their champagne and talking and laughing and making love again. In the wee hours of the morning, they lay close together, Lucas on his back, Rachel on her side, her face resting on his chest.

"Have I made you happy?" he asked.

"More so than I have ever been in my entire life," she confessed.

"The photographs on the coffee table," Lucas said. "Are they of him?"

"I don't love him," Rachel confessed.

"I know." He pushed his hand through her hair and felt her cheek nestled against his chest.

"I have them there because of the children. My being divorced from him doesn't keep him from being their father. I don't think they will ever understand how cruel their father has been to me...and to them. With you and Cheryl it was different."

"Different—" he agreed so far "—but tragic." Now Rachel listened as Lucas poured out the anguish of his heart. Some she'd heard before. They had married when they were extremely young, and Debra had worked to send him through college. She had continued to work until his law practice was established.

"Then she quit and stayed home, in time getting pregnant. After Cheryl was born, Debra swore she'd never get pregnant again. She didn't like anything that went with pregnancy."

Lucas pushed himself up on the bed and poured himself another glass of wine. "But even with contraceptives, she did get pregnant." He put the glass to his mouth and drank the wine in one swallow.

"She lost the baby?" Rachel questioned.

"Yes," Lucas said and softly added, "It was a boy."

Rachel pulled Lucas into her arms, and for a long time they held each other tightly.

"Debra never got pregnant again and didn't want to adopt, so we had only the one child."

THE NEXT MORNING Rachel awakened to find Lucas gone. She bolted upright in bed and sniffed. The aroma of bacon and coffee and biscuits permeated the air. She crawled out of bed and brushed her teeth, then lay down again to snooze a little longer.

"Time to get up, sleepyhead," Lucas called minutes later. Barefoot, he wore only his trousers and unbuttoned shirt. Rachel opened her eyes and sat up as he set the breakfast tray on the bed beside her. He pushed the bud vase to the front of the tray. "A rose for madam."

Rachel giggled. "A rose picked from my bouquet of artificial flowers on the dining table."

Lucas grinned and shrugged. "It's the thought that counts. Next time I'll have one sent from the florist. Let's hurry up and eat and get going."

"Where are we going?" Rachel asked as she watched him pour coffee into their cups.

"I thought we'd go hiking in the hill country," he said.

"Hiking!" Rachel exclaimed. "Is this where you took those society women you've been dating?"

"Jealous?" Lucas teased.

"Not really."

"Good," he said, leaning down to plant a light kiss on her cheek, "you don't need to be. I only took them to stuffy, boring places. We never had any fun like you and I do. Now let's eat and get dressed. We have an action-packed day ahead of us."

"The kids will be home at six," Rachel said, munching on a slice of bacon.

"Leave it to Lucas Brand. I've already thought about driving to New Braunfels to pick Mandy up and bring her back in time for us to get the kids at the airport. Then we'll come home to barbecue and *Star Trek* movies."

"Just like that?" Rachel snapped her fingers. "Voilà. Barbecue and *Star Trek* movies."

"Well—" Lucas grinned "—I figured you could barbecue while the kids and I watched the VCR."

"You just figured wrong, Mr. Brand." Rachel laughed. "I'll VCR with the kids while you do the barbecuing."

"You like your man to wear the apron?" Lucas teased.

"I like my man wearing nothing," she whispered, her eyes smoldering.

"Then, madam, your wish is my command." Lucas picked up the breakfast tray and swung it through the air to set it on the floor. Leaning across the bed, he hugged

Rachel. "I think maybe we've had a slight change in plans."

"What's that, Mr. Brand?"

"This," he murmured, lowering his lips to hers, "before we head for New Braunfels." His mouth closed over hers in a thorough kiss.

"Before last night," Rachel murmured when he lifted his lips once more, "I might have been satisfied with only this, but now I want more."

"More you shall have," Lucas promised.

Later—much later—after they'd eaten their cold breakfast and dressed, they headed for New Braunfels. At the ranch Lucas hurriedly changed clothes and drove Rachel over to the Children's Ranch. He, Rachel and Arney spent the better part of the afternoon organizing the Christmas Elf program.

"This black book is for the toys," Arney pointed out. "The blue one over there is for the food. We'll be moving all our operations over to the barn right after Thanksgiving."

Mandy sauntered into the office and leaned on the edge of the desk in front of Rachel. "Dugan and the boys are over there right now getting everything ready," she announced. "The week before Thanksgiving the telephones will be connected, and we'll start working."

The chair creaked as Rachel leaned back. "You like the Christmas Elf program, Mandy?"

Mandy grinned and nodded her head. "Sure do. I'm going to be Misty Mistletoe, and that means I get to have a special costume. Cheryl's gonna design it for me. She'll bring it home Thanksgiving weekend. Lucas says you're going to be Mrs. Christmas," Mandy said.

"He's asked me," Rachel said. "What do you think about it?"

Lowering her head so Rachel couldn't see her face, Mandy picked up a pencil and studied it. "We haven't had a Mrs. Christmas before."

"That's true," Rachel agreed, understanding Mandy's concern. The child was afraid she was going to come between Lucas and herself. "Maybe it's not such a good idea."

"I don't know," Mandy drawled. "I don't reckon it's much fun for Mr. Christmas to be by himself."

"No," Rachel answered, "I don't reckon so."

Mandy's head raised, and two solemn blue eyes pierced Rachel's. "Do you like Lucas, Ms. March?"

"Yes," Rachel answered, "I like him very much."

"I love him," Mandy said simply. "I wish he was my father."

"He couldn't ask for a better daughter," Rachel said. For a moment she gazed at Mandy who again dropped her head and played with the pencil. Eventually Rachel added, "Would you like to go to San Antonio with Lucas and me to pick the boys and Jae up at the airport?"

Mandy's head jerked up; her eyes rounded and a grin spanned her face.

"We're going to barbecue chicken for dinner and watch a *Star Trek* movie."

"Oh, yes, Ms. March," Mandy exclaimed. "I'd like to go. Are you sure you don't mind?"

"I'd love to have you," Rachel replied, "and I'm sure the kids would love to see you."

"Mandy," Lucas called from the front porch, "we've got to get everything boxed up so we can start moving it."

"Lucas—" Mandy jumped off the table and raced out of the house "—Ms. March invited me to come to the airport to pick up Neal and Sammy and Jae. We're going to barbecue chicken for dinner and watch *Star Trek* movies.''

''Just maybe, Miss Mandy, you and I can recruit the three of them to work with the Christmas Elves.''

Mandy grinned and nodded her head. ''I'll just bet maybe we can, Lucas.'' She skipped back into the office where Rachel sat. ''Since we'll be doing most of our work on Saturday, will Sammy and Neal and Jae be able to come?''

''If they want to, I'm sure we can arrange something,'' Rachel answered. Hearing the booted steps coming down the hallway, she looked up to see Lucas in the doorway. He reached up and pushed his hat off his forehead. ''Well, Rachel and Mandy, it's about four o'clock. Time for us to be shoving off if we're going to greet all the little Marches at six at the airport.''

''Give me just a minute to tell Mr. Worthmore where I'm going,'' Mandy cried, rushing out of the house, the screen door banging behind her.

Lucas walked into the room and sat on the edge of the desk. ''I'm glad the kids are coming home, but I'm sorry our weekend is over.''

''Me, too,'' Rachel murmured, ''but we'll have many more.''

''That's a promise, ladylove.'' He caught her hands and tugged her to her feet to place a chaste kiss on her forehead.

''I'M GLAD you're spending Thanksgiving with us.'' Cheryl lounged on the bed in the guest bedroom.

''I am, too. Thank you for inviting me,'' Rachel said as she unpacked her suitcase and hung her clothes in the closet. ''I would have been quite lonely without the children.''

"I wish they could have come with you, but they were excited about spending Thanksgiving with the Marches, weren't they?"

"As Neal said," Rachel replied, "it was a new and novel experience for them."

"Do you find this Thanksgiving weekend a new and novel experience?" Cheryl asked. "One that you'd like to repeat in the future?"

"Yes to both questions," Rachel answered, glad that she and Cheryl were getting an opportunity to know each other better.

"I'm really sorry I behaved so rudely to you the other day," Cheryl said, apologizing for a second time. "I don't ordinarily behave like a spoiled brat."

Her clothes hung, Rachel sat on the foot of the bed. "You don't have to keep apologizing," she said. "I know how you felt. Jae has been upset about my seeing Lucas, too. All of us are quite protective of those whom we love."

"You're nice, Rachel." Cheryl laid her hand over Rachel's. "I'm glad Daddy met you. You're good...for both of us."

"Thank you," Rachel murmured.

"We're going to have fun together this weekend. And later with Jae."

"Yes," Rachel said, her heart swelling with happiness. "We are."

A knock on the door was followed by Lucas's call. "Aren't you girls about ready to come out? I could use some help in the kitchen. If I had known you two were going to hole up like this, I wouldn't have taken so kindly to Molly's suggestion that she and Dugan spend Thanksgiving in Austin with her sister."

"Well," Cheryl drawled, winking at Rachel, "we're not ready to help with the cooking, but you can come in here with us."

Without a second bidding, Lucas opened the door and walked into the bedroom. Hands on hips, he glared teasingly at the women. "Both of you are lying down on the job. Leave me to man the kitchen while you're up here gossiping." He advanced into the room. "I suppose it's left up to me to take matters into hand."

"Well," Cheryl said again, gracefully rising from the bed and moving to the door, "I guess this is my cue to leave. I'll be in the kitchen. I'll let the two of you settle this."

"You don't have to go," Rachel said absently, her attention now fully focused on Lucas.

"No," Lucas said, "you don't."

Cheryl grinned and walked out, throwing her parting words over her shoulder. "Don't have to, but want to. The two of you need some time to yourselves."

The words fell on deaf ears. Lucas caught Rachel's hands in his and tugged. She rose to move into his embrace. "Thank you for spending Thanksgiving with us," he said.

"The pleasure is all mine," she whispered.

"I must disagree." His hands slipped down to the small of her back, splaying his fingers across her hips. "This is a great pleasure for me, too."

"On second thought," Cheryl yelled from the foot of the stairs, "don't take too much time to yourselves. I don't want to have to cook Thanksgiving dinner by myself."

Lucas grinned at Rachel. "If we're planning on eating tomorrow, I don't think we want that, either."

Chapter Eleven

Rachel arrived at the Lucky Brand late Saturday night. The days following the Thanksgiving weekend had been demanding, the hours long, busy and totally unproductive. She was exhausted but excited about the Christmas Elf program...about the holiday season, period. Providence had smiled on her when she met Lucas; he had brought so much joy back into her life. He soothed and nursed back to health her inner spirit, and she found that she had more to give. Moreover, she discovered that once again she desired to give of herself...freely, unconditionally.

Before she left San Antonio, she stopped at Wolfe's Nursery and bought a tree. She had actually enjoyed moving shoulder to shoulder with the crowds up and down the rows of trees. Standing them upright to see if they stood straight. Twirling them around to see how full they were. Her hands were slightly red where the needles from the trees had lightly grazed and pricked them. Even now she hummed a popular Christmas jingle she'd heard on the radio on her way to the ranch. She was thoroughly caught up in the Christmas spirit, and was looking forward to Lucas coming over later tonight and helping the children and herself decorate the tree.

For a few minutes she sat shuffling her papers into their respective folders and dropping them into her briefcase. She picked up a white plastic shopping bag and smiled. She had really splurged today: first the tree, then the pattern and material for her Mrs. Christmas costume.

Opening the car door, she slid out and moved to the barn, so different from the one where she had first met Lucas. This was one of the newest and most expensive ranch structures, Lucas had told her proudly, and it was ablaze with light and activity.

Lucas and several older boys were unloading boxes and stacking them in neat piles in front of the opened doors. With clipboard in hand, Dugan was checking off food items as Sammy went through the donations and sorted the canned goods. Inside the barn, Jae and Mandy cataloged the toys, and Neal separated them into two stacks: those that were ready for delivery and those that needed to be mended.

Rachel moved through the maze of cars and trucks. When she reached the barn, Sammy waved but didn't stop his inventory.

"One can of sweet potatoes," he said to Dugan. "Two cans of cream style corn. One of pumpkin. Two cans of green beans. What are French beans, Dugan?"

"Could be a foreign kind, but I don't rightly know," he answered, "but guess I better figure it out 'cause we don't have a column for French beans."

Sammy screwed up his face as he looked at the picture. Then he held the can for Dugan to see. "They look just like the other green beans, 'cept they aren't short and fat; they're long and stringy."

"Maybe your mama has an answer to that one," Dugan mumbled and leaned down to peer at the label.

"All of them are green beans," Rachel answered. "They're just cut different."

Dugan grinned and straightened up. "Well, Sammy, reckon we'll just classify them all as green beans."

"But they're different," Sammy exclaimed. "We can't put all of them in the same box."

"Reckon you're right about that." Dugan shoved his hat back and scratched his brow with the pencil eraser. "Reckon if we're gonna give everybody two cans of green beans, we'd like 'em to be cut the same way, don't you think?"

"Reckon so," Sammy said, unconsciously mimicking Dugan and accepting him as a new role model. He scooted around and dragged up another box. "Reckon we'll have to label this one French green beans and that one American."

Dugan chuckled. "Sounds pretty good to me, Sammy."

"Rachel—" Lucas set several boxes on the ground near the door; his face brightened "—I'm glad to see you. I was beginning to worry about you." He straightened and walked to where she stood. Lowering his head, he gave her a brief welcome kiss.

"Long day," she said, a feeling of warmth and contentment permeating her when Lucas draped his arm around her and gently kneaded her shoulder.

"Good day?"

Sighing, she shook her head. "Not so good."

Lucas hunched a shoulder and wiped the perspiration from his forehead. "I'm going to get something to drink. How about you?"

"A diet soda, please."

Moving into the barn, he called over his shoulder, "Be back in a second."

"Did you get the new decoration for the Christmas tree, Mom?" Sammy asked. "Are we going to decorate the tree tonight like you promised?"

"Yes to both questions," Rachel replied.

Sammy leaped to his feet and tugged on the peak of his cap. "You really got the tree?"

Rachel grinned. "I did. I stopped at Wolfe's Nursery before I came up here."

"How big is it?" he said, throwing his arms out. "This big?"

"Bigger than that and taller than your daddy."

"Wow!" Sammy exclaimed. "It's big, Mom!"

"It sure is," Rachel agreed and searched through the barn for Lucas.

"What's in the bag?" Sammy demanded. "Something for me?"

"Nope. It's mine. My material for my Christmas dress."

"What about me?" Sammy asked. "I'm supposed to have one."

"A dress?" Rachel teased.

"Nope," Sammy replied, "An elf suit. Lucas promised."

"And you'll get one. Cheryl's in charge of the elf costumes." Rachel grinned and lifted Sammy's cap to brush his hair out of his eyes. Replacing it, she added, "You'll just have to wait your turn."

"Okay, Sammy," Dugan said, grinning, "Break's over. If we're gonna get this food organized tonight, we better get moving."

"Yes, sir," Sammy said, dropping onto his knees to fish through another box of canned goods. "See you later, Mom."

Unable to locate Lucas, Rachel meandered through the barn, finally stopping at the table where Jae and Mandy were working. Molly, hands on hips, peered disapprovingly over the rim of her glasses at both girls.

"Your job, girls, is to sort through the toys. We discard the junk."

"We can't throw it away," Mandy cried, her pigtails flying through the air as she whirled around to look at Jae. "Can we?"

"We can't, Mrs. Molly. I already love him," Jae sighed and crushed a worn-out teddy bear against her cheek. "I can't *bear* to give it away."

"He's an orphan, Mrs. Molly," Mandy said. "He needs a home more than all these other toys do."

"Hmm!" Molly snorted good-naturedly. "Looks like it should have been thrown away instead of given away."

"We can't," Jae and Mandy cried simultaneously. "He needs a home."

"Better yours than mine," Molly said dismissively. "What's that pile over there?"

"The toys that need paint. I'm going to wait to catalog them until they're finished. We can set them on the shelf over there." Jae pointed across the room. Then she saw Rachel and grinned. "Hi, Mom! I didn't know it was time for you to be here. Look! I'm going to take him home."

"Don't you have enough junk in your room without adding more?" Rachel said dryly.

"Junk!" Jae exclaimed, clutching the bear to her heart. "How can you call this adorable little orphan junk?"

"It's quite simple really," Molly said and pulled off her glass to rub her temples. "Your mother is an extremely smart woman, Jae. Howdy, Rachel. It's good to see you out here tonight. The kids have really been working. I'm glad they decided to join us.''

"Me, too." Rachel emptied the contents of her shopping bag on the table. A dress pattern. Red velvet. Yards of white lace. "Well, Molly, here it is. You said if I bought the material and pattern, you'd make the dress."

"Yes, I did." Molly slipped her glasses back on and rubbed her hand over the delicate fabric. Then she picked up the pattern and studied it. "Good style for you. Won't take me long to whip this up." She lifted her head, running her eyes over Rachel's slim frame. "One fitting ought to do. I'd say you're pretty true to size."

"Name the time and place, and I'll be there," Rachel said.

"I'll give you a call when I see how my schedule is going. I'll just take this with me," Molly said, shoving the goods back into the bag. "Guess I'm about to call it a night. Been on my feet most of the day, and they're killing me. Jae tells me that y'all are gonna spend the rest of the evening decorating your tree."

"We are if I can gather them all up," Rachel said. "We need to be on our way. They can sleep in in the morning, but I have to work."

"Lucas still planning on coming?" Jae asked. She hadn't forgiven him for Halloween night and held him responsible for the change of plans regarding the holidays. But because Lucas and Cheryl had spent the Sunday following Thanksgiving with them in San Antonio, Jae had relented and was on speaking terms with him.

"As far as I know," Rachel answered. "Where is he? He left a few minutes ago to find me a cold drink, and I haven't seen him since."

"He had a phone call. I guess he took it in the office," Molly said and pointed to a door at the rear of the barn. "We're using that storage area over there for the main office. Go right on in."

Rachel turned and walked to the office. She knocked softly and heard Lucas call, "Come in." When she entered, he was sitting behind a desk, holding the receiver against his ear with one hand and writing figures on a desk pad with the other.

He clapped his hand over the mouthpiece. "Sorry," he said. "Had to take a call. Bob Granger, a general contractor who works for me."

Rachel nodded her head in acknowledgement and walked to the small refrigerator. Opening the door, she took out a can of diet drink. "You want one?" she mouthed.

"Sure, Bob—" Lucas nodded his head at Rachel "—I understand, but I don't see how that affects us." He listened for a while, then said, "Damn! Okay. I'll see what I can do about it. Yeah. How about first thing in the morning?"

When he finally dropped the receiver onto the cradle, Rachel said, "Bad news?"

"Problems at the site." Air whooshed through the room when he twisted the tab and opened the can.

"One of your grocery stores?" Rachel asked.

He shook his head and swallowed the Pepsi. "Senior citizens' apartment complex I told you about."

"Mom. Lucas," Neal called and knocked at the same time. "Dugan says it's about time for us to go."

Lucas looked at his watch. "You're right," he said and stood to move from behind the desk. "Come on in."

Neal rushed into the room, his usually solemn face covered with a smile. "Sammy said you've already bought the tree, Mom."

"I did." Rachel's gaze swept to Lucas. "You might say this was one of the most important purchases for me since the divorce."

"We're going to decorate it tonight?"

"We are," Rachel answered, her eyes never leaving Lucas's face. In the expressive gray eyes she saw admiration and pride. Although he didn't move, he touched her soul in that one glance. He didn't speak, yet they communicated.

"Well, Lucas," Neal said, breaking the fragile moment between them, "if you don't mind, I'll ride back with you. We'll let the girls and Sammy ride together."

"I am not going to ride with the women!" Sammy shoved his way into the room. Easing his little hand into Lucas's, he planted his feet firmly on the floor and threw back his chest as if to stake his claim. "I'm going to ride with you. And can Mandy come with us? She wants to decorate the tree, too. She can ride with the women."

Rachel grinned at her youngest. Her heart melted within as she watched Lucas kneel in front of him and clasp both his shoulders. The hands were large and powerful, yet they were so gentle.

"You and Neal are going to have to ride home with your mother," Lucas said. "I just received an emergency phone call and can't come with you. I'll be over later."

The sparkle went out of the blue eyes; the smile drooped. "Why, Lucas?" he asked. "You said you would."

Yes, Rachel thought, *why can't you, Lucas? You said you would.* Disappointment coupled with exhaustion completely overwhelmed Rachel. She was tired of Lucas doing this to her; she was tired of making excuses for him to Jae. And he was the one who'd insisted that she get into the Christmas spirit. He had promised such great things for the holidays. Yet he was backing out of decorating the tree—the one event she had planned for and was looking forward to.

Too tired to cry, she said, "Let's go, Sammy. I'm sure Lucas thinks he has a good reason for not coming." Smiling brightly at Lucas, she pulled the strap of her purse over her shoulder and said, "Come on, boys, we have a tree to decorate tonight, and I have to be up early in the morning."

"Sammy," Lucas said, "I can't come because I have an important meeting I must attend tonight."

"It's more important than decorating our tree?" Sammy asked with childlike simplicity.

"It's very important." Lucas sighed and straightened up.

"Okay," Sammy said, "if it's that important."

"Scoot," Rachel ordered, not as easily mollified as Sammy, "and get Jae on the way out."

Neal and Sammy ran out of the room, Rachel following, but Lucas caught her arm and pulled her back. "Rachel, it's imperative that I meet with Bob tonight. If we don't get this resolved, we'll lose about fifteen thousand dollars and two weeks of work."

"I wouldn't want you to lose your precious money," Rachel snapped.

"You're angry," Lucas said.

"More disappointed. I've had a hard day, and I'd looked forward to us having some time together after we'd decorated the tree."

"I didn't plan this, Rachel."

"Do you realize how much time you and I have spent together during the past few weeks?" she asked. Once the dam had broken, her emotions were running at flood tide. She was beyond reason. "Every time I see you I'm sandwiched in between the Christmas Elf program or the senior citizens' complex or the Lucky Brand Supermarkets. You're the one who talked about prime time, Lucas. I've given to you, but you haven't given to me."

"Rachel, this isn't the time or place to be discussing this," Lucas said. "I'll be over later. Okay?" When she didn't answer, he repeated, "Okay?" He caught her shoulders in his hands and pulled her to him. Lowering his head, he pressed his lips against hers. When she didn't respond, he said, "Rachel, I promise I'll be there."

"Right now, Lucas, your promises are tentative at best."

"We'll talk about this later."

Lucas's promise didn't appease Rachel's hurt and disappointment. It didn't soothe her bruised ego. It seemed as if Lucas was always putting somebody or something else before her. Alone with her thoughts, the ride from New Braunfels to San Antonio was long and uncomfortable. Neal and Sammy were behind her in the back seat, talking in low tones; Jae sat up front with Rachel.

"Mom," Jae finally ventured, "I told you Lucas was more interested in work than in you."

"He does have to earn a living." Rachel defended him quietly, unwilling to hear criticism of him.

"And he's gonna come to the house as soon as he can, Jae," Sammy interjected.

"Yeah. I'll bet."

"Will, too. He said so, Jae. Lucas said so."

Ignoring Sammy's impassioned defense of Lucas, Jae spoke to Rachel: "This meeting he's attending tonight has nothing to do with his earning a living, Mom. It's one of his pet projects." Jae picked up the crushed bear and held it against her cheek. "Like some people collect animals and things, Lucas collects projects."

"I'd say that was more worthwhile than collecting torn-up stuffed animals," Neal said.

"You don't know everything, Neal Jared March," Jae exclaimed.

"I know a lot," he retorted.

Lost in her own thoughts, oblivious to the children's bickering, Rachel exited from the expressway and turned left onto Walzem Road.

"Mom," Sammy called, "can we get a pizza? I'm starving."

"Did you have supper?" Rachel asked.

"Mmm-hmm," Jae answered. "We had baked chicken and noodles, green salad and broccoli."

"But we didn't have dessert, Mom," Sammy yelled. "And the pizza could be our dessert."

Looking into the rearview mirror, Rachel grinned at her six-year-old. "Okay," she agreed, "I think one pizza is in order."

"Pepperoni," Sammy called out.

"Canadian bacon," Neal chimed in.

"Only one," Rachel said. "So you better have your mind made up by the time we get home. We'll call our order in and let Jae go pick it up while we're working on the tree."

"Gee, thanks," Jae said dryly. "Any other chores you want good ole Jae to run for you?"

Laughing quietly, Rachel reached over and patted Jae's hand. "I'll tell you if I do."

When they arrived at the house, Jae ordered the pizza, then walked into the living room to watch Rachel and the boys put the tree into its stand. Finally after about thirty minutes of grunting and squabbling, the Douglas fir stood firm and straight, its point almost touching the ceiling. Christmas music wafted through the room.

"Now for the decorations," Rachel said with more enthusiasm than she felt. She walked to the sofa and began to sort through the bags, handing one box of lights to Jae, another to Neal. "All new and just for us."

Jae laid down her box. "I have to get the pizza, Mom. I'll help you when I get back."

Neal sat down on the floor and began to unwind the electrical cord. Sammy deserted both Rachel and the cause. He sat cross-legged in front of the television set in the den and cupped his chin in his hands.

"Hey, Neal," he called minutes later, "here's a monster movie you'll like. It's real good. I've seen it a million times already."

"What monster?" Neal called, tossing the lights aside and disappearing into the den, too.

Rachel stood alone in the living room, listening to the last stanza of "I'm Dreaming of a White Christmas." Tears coursed down her cheeks. She knew she shouldn't cry; she didn't want to but couldn't stop herself. She understood why Lucas had to postpone his visit. But she wanted him here. Tonight of all nights she needed him. Headlights flashed through the curtains to announce Jae's arrival. Rachel dropped the string of lights onto the sofa and rushed to her bathroom. Still she couldn't stop the tears.

Jae knocked on the door and called, "Mom, I'm home with the pizza."

A tissue pressed against her eyes, Rachel said, "I'll be out in a minute."

"Is something wrong?" Jae asked.

"No." Rachel didn't want to burden Jae with her troubles and disappointments, nor did she want Jae to see how unhappy she was, because that would only increase her resentment toward Lucas.

"You sound like you're crying." Jae jiggled the knob. "Tell me what's wrong."

"I'm—I'm not crying. I'm—I'm just having an allergic reaction to the tree." After splashing cold water on her eyes, she opened the door. Blotting her face on the towel, she forced herself to laugh. "It's been two years since I've had a real tree in the house with me."

Jae peered intently into her mother's face. "You're sure you're not crying?"

Rachel slung the towel over the rack and reached out to muss Jae's hair. "Absolutely not. I'm looking forward to our Christmas together. Now, let's get into the kitchen and eat our pizza before it gets cold."

"Or eaten by the Two March Glutton Monsters," Jae added.

Munching on a slice of pizza, Rachel joined the boys in the den to watch television. The movie was one she had seen several times; she was sure Sammy was telling the truth when he said he'd seen it a million. When it ended, she stood and pointed to the living room. "Now, let's get the tree decorated."

The four of them filed into the living room and soon wound strings of tiny lights around the tree. The overhead lights off, only those on the tree glowing like little candles, Rachel stepped into the foyer to see if they had been evenly distributed over the branches. When the doorbell rang, her heart seemed to leap within her breast. *Lucas,* she thought, a smile automatically curling her lips. *He's here in time, after all.*

She unlocked and opened the door. She stared in astonishment at her ex-husband. "Jared!" she whispered, unable to believe her eyes.

"Hello, Rachel." His deep, resonant voice echoed through the house.

"Daddy!" Jae screeched and flew through the hall to throw herself into Jared's arms. "Oh, Daddy!"

Yelling, "Daddy! Daddy!" the boys were right behind Jae.

After the boisterous greetings were over and the boys had returned to the tree, Rachel said, "This is quite a surprise, Jared. Why didn't you let me know you were coming?"

"I didn't know until the last minute," he answered. "I just had to see you again, Rachel. I've missed you."

A satisfied smile touching her lips, Jae melted into the background, leaving her parents alone. She hadn't planned her father's visit, but she would do all she could to encourage a reconciliation.

"I'm in town on business. I planned to call you tonight and ask if I could come over. But you've . . . you seemed to have changed . . . so much, I was afraid that you'd refuse to see me."

"I might have," Rachel returned honestly, "but I wouldn't have refused to let you see the children."

"I didn't come only to see the children," he confessed. "I came to see you."

In the muted glow of the tree lights, Rachel studied him. He was as immaculate, as fastidious and as handsome as ever. He wore a dark business suit with a pastel-colored silk shirt and coordinating tie. His brown hair, now silvered at the temples, was a mass of thick waves. Tonight his eyes were soft and warm and beautiful. For a moment she was caught up in Jared's charm.

His gaze flicked past Rachel to the living room. He was instantly aware of its warmth. Boxes and ornaments were scattered about; the tree was partially decorated.

"May I stay, Rachel?"

"Please, Mama," Jae called from the living room. "Let him help us?"

Recalled to the present, Rachel was furious. Jae knew Lucas was planning to come over later.

"Yeah," Sammy chimed in. "Lucas can't, so why don't you? We need someone tall to put the angel on the top."

"Lucas?" Jared asked, his gaze swinging from the children to Rachel.

"Yep," Sammy answered as he fastened the hooks onto the colored balls, "he's the man Mama's been dating. He was gonna come over and help us with the tree, but he had a business meeting and couldn't come."

"I didn't know you were dating." Jared's lips automatically thinned; he clenched his teeth together and a muscle twitched in his temple.

"I didn't know I had to ask permission," she countered.

"You don't," he said softly, his features relaxing. "May I stay for a while?"

Jae silently pleaded with Rachel.

"I'm expecting Lucas to come over later," she said.

"This works out swell," Sammy shouted. "Then you can stay here and baby-sit us, Daddy."

Rachel laughed. "Sounds good to me."

A frown on his face, Jared followed her into the living room, slipping out of his jacket and laying it over the back of the sofa. Soon the room was filled with laughter as Jared entertained the children with humorous stories. Rachel curled up in a chair, laid her head on the cushioned back and just watched Jared.

How different he was. She could count on one hand the times that Jared had spent with the children. In fact, she found herself listening with rapt attention to the tall tales he was spinning. She'd never heard them before herself.

She had been angry that he'd come without asking her, but now she was glad. His presence alleviated her last lingering fear and assured her that she had made peace with herself. She accepted the divorce and was no longer bitter. Moving beyond pain and anguish, she had triumphed and made a new life for herself. She was ready for love and a new commitment . . . with Lucas.

"How about a cup of coffee?" Jared called out, his eyes clouding when he saw the dreamy look on Rachel's face.

Rachel grinned, rolled her head on the cushion to look at him but didn't move. "I don't drink it this late. If you want a cup, you'll find the coffee maker in the kitchen. The coffee is in the cabinet above. I don't have any de-caffeinated. I drank the last cup last night and haven't been to the store yet."

"Mom," Jae said, "that's no fair. You fix coffee for Lucas."

Refusing to feel guilty, Rachel laughed softly and un-curled her long limbs to stand. Her green eyes, sparkling pure devilment, focused on Jared. "Lucas is an invited guest, your father is not. However, I'll take into consideration that he's working on our tree, and I'll make a pot of coffee."

Frowning, Jared tossed an empty carton onto the sofa. "How about our going out for a cup?" he said. "I'd like to talk to you, Rachel. Privately."

"Sure, Mom," Jae hastily interjected. "I'll be here with the boys. You and Daddy need privacy."

"I don't know," Rachel said. "Lucas said he was coming over tonight."

"This late?" Jared asked, looking at his watch.

"I asked him to," Rachel explained. "He had a meeting and couldn't come earlier."

"We won't be gone long." Jared sighed and unconsciously raked a hand through his hair. "Jae'll be here if he comes."

"If he comes," Jae repeated.

Rachel was reluctant to go with Jared but knew they had to talk sometime. It might as well be now as later. The sooner she cut this last tie that bound her to Jared, the quicker she could build a foundation for her future...her future with Lucas.

"All right," she said. "If Lucas comes, have him wait for me, Jae. We'll be right back."

"Okay, Mom."

Fifteen minutes later, Rachel and Jared were seated in a booth at Jim's Coffee Shop. Jared stirred sugar and cream into his coffee. Only answering his questions, never initiating discussion herself, Rachel watched. Finally he dropped the spoon onto the saucer and reached out to lay his hand over Rachel's.

"You're beautiful," he murmured. "You're one of the most beautiful women I've ever seen, Rachel. I'd forgotten how your eyes sparkle. They're such an unusual shade of green."

"If I remember correctly," Rachel said, pulling her hand from beneath his, "they're clinging-vine green. Wasn't that the way you described me, Jared?"

Jared shoved his hand through his hair again. "You've changed, Rachel."

"Yes," she admitted, pleased because Jared was having no effect on her whatsoever. "I have. I'm independent now, Jared. I've discovered myself and trust my own judgment. On this knowledge, I've built a new life for me and the children."

"I didn't think you could do it. In a way, Rachel, I almost wished you hadn't. I fully expected you to come begging for help."

"That's part of your problem," she said. "You never thought about anyone but yourself, Jared."

"Rachel, come back to me. Come home."

"After all these years, Jared, I am home. Surely you can see that."

He stared at her for a while, then asked, "Are you happy living the way you are, Rachel? Really happy?"

"I'm happier than I have ever been in my entire life, Jared."

"Is Lucas the reason why you're happy?"

"One of them. Probably the most important reason."

"MAMA TOLD ME to tell you that she went out with Daddy and doesn't know what time she'll be home." Holding the front door open, Jae talked with Lucas who stood in the spill of porch light. "I know it's not my place to tell you this, but they're thinking about reconciling."

Although Lucas knew that Jae was getting back at him and was possibly exaggerating, he still reeled from the blow. He had thought of Rachel as being exclusively his, and her being with another man hurt. Particularly since that other man was her ex-husband. Lucas was most disconcerted when he remembered the unhappy note on which he and Rachel had parted earlier in the evening. He hadn't realized how much he loved her until now, until he thought of the possibility of her not being an integral and permanent part of his life.

"Tell your mother that I came by and will call later."

"I'll probably be in bed," Jae said. "I don't expect them back until real late. But I'll leave a note on her desk. Good night, Lucas."

He heard the door softly thud behind him; he heard the night chain slip into place but didn't look back. He walked to the street and climbed into the blue and white pickup. He turned the key and the engine purred. The lights flickered to life, he pulled away from the curb and made his way through the housing development. He turned onto the interstate and headed for New Braunfels.

Not trusting Jae to give Rachel his message, he was determined to call her first thing in the morning. He had to talk with her to find out if Jae had been telling the truth. Perhaps he had read too much into their relationship...taken too much for granted...assumed she felt about him the same way he felt about her. His fingers tightened around the steering wheel. Perhaps she didn't love him as much as he loved her.

Chapter Twelve

Rachel and Jared stood in the living room in the rainbow glow of Christmas lights. "This is the first time I've observed the holiday since the divorce," she murmured, her eyes settling on the angel atop the tree. "I'd forgotten how wonderful it was. I didn't know how much I missed it."

"Rachel—" Jared reached for her, but she quickly skirted away from him; he brushed the back of his hand across his forehead. "All of this is my fault. Please forgive me for divorcing you. It was a mistake I want to rectify."

"No, Jared." Rachel slipped out of her jacket and laid it on the back of the chair nearest her. "While it may have seemed like a mistake at the time, it really wasn't. It was the best thing that you've ever done for me."

"Maybe I deserve this, but I sure as hell don't like it." A pained expression on his face, he took a step toward her and held out his hand. "Rachel, I'm lonely. I don't like being divorced. Let's try again."

"No." Again Rachel moved away from him; she couldn't stand the thought of him touching her. She stood in front of the tree, straightening some of the decorations. She wasn't fooled by Jared. He was a professional when it came to getting what he wanted, and he always wanted what he couldn't get. At that moment he wanted her.

"I've changed, Rachel," Jared said. "I'm not the man I was two years ago."

"I'm glad." She picked up a wad of icicles and one by one hung them over the tips of the branches; she grinned, thinking about her impatient six-year-old who had gotten tired and tossed them on the tree by fistfuls. "Because I'm a different woman, Jared. I've made a new life for myself."

"I love you, Rachel."

His declaration startled her. She draped the last bit of tinsel on a limb and stood there, staring but not seeing the brightly decorated tree. Without turning around, she said, "Two years ago that confession would have thrilled my soul, Jared. It would have meant something to me, but not now."

Cursing under his breath, Jared crossed the room in long, angry strides. He clamped his hands on Rachel's shoulders and whirled her around. "Look at me, for God's sake! I'm telling you I love you, and you're playing with the ornaments on that damn Christmas tree."

Rachel shrugged out of Jared's grasp and stepped back to say quietly, "Don't ever touch me again, Jared, in passion or in anger. For seventeen years I let you emotionally abuse and intimidate me. Never again. And I refuse to be physically abused."

He balled his hand into a fist. This new Rachel was a woman he didn't comprehend; he wasn't prepared for her reactions. "Rachel, I'm sorry," he murmured. "I didn't mean to do that."

Rachel's expression didn't change. "Please understand, Jared. You're here this week because of the children. I don't love you, and I'm not sure that I ever did. You and I shall always share a relationship because we lived together for so many years and because we share three children, but I want nothing more from you than friendship."

"I don't believe you're saying that!" he exclaimed. "We had a wonderful marriage, Rachel."

"We had a marriage," Rachel stressed, "but we have it no longer, and I don't want it again."

Jared shoved a hand through his hair yet again. "What about the children?" he countered angrily. "Have you given any thought to them?"

"More than you gave when you announced you wanted a divorce." No longer was Rachel shaking; her fear was gone. She enjoyed telling Jared exactly what she wanted and demanded from life. She felt power surging through her body.

As if he could visibly see the change in Rachel, Jared backed away and peered at her. "You're right," he said. "I've brought this all on myself. I have no one else to blame."

The anger seemed to drain out of him to be replaced with resignation, but he gained no sympathy from Rachel. She wasn't fooled; she knew Jared Jaeson March only too well. He had just begun to attack her defenses. When one tactic failed, he switched to another. He walked to the sofa and picked up his jacket.

At the door, his hand on the knob, he turned and asked, "Please reconsider."

"No."

"I know you have a right to feel the way you do, but I'm begging you, Rachel." His voice thickened and grew husky. "Begging you! Give us some time together. A week, Rachel. One small week out of your life."

This was a new experience for Rachel. She had never heard Jared beg before; she had never seen him so near tears. It took her off guard and left her nonplussed.

"We can be a family again, Rachel."

"It's . . . it's," Rachel faltered, at odds with this side of Jared, "no good, Jared. It's over."

Seeing he'd scored a point, Jared pressed his advantage. His voice softened. "You don't mean that, Rachel. I'll call you in the morning."

"My answer won't be any different."

"I'll call anyway," he answered.

Her emotions a chaotic mess, Rachel closed and locked the door behind Jared. In a daze she walked back to the living room and curled up in the chair to look at the Christmas tree. Although she hadn't been pleased to see Jared, she was glad that he'd come. His visit had been illuminating. She entertained no doubts about her future. Although she and Jared had been separated for nearly two years, she had still been emotionally bound to him. Not anymore. She was free. She no longer harbored bitterness about the divorce.

Reconciliation was out of the question; she felt no attraction between the two of them. Yet a part of her was flattered to find that he wanted her so much that he was willing to beg—a tactic he'd never used with her during their years together. But Rachel was smart enough to know this was only a ploy, a means to get her back into his clutch. Jared March hadn't changed. She wondered if he ever would.

A soft knock on the door disturbed Rachel. *Jared,* she thought and grimaced, wanting to ignore him, but the knocking, though light, was persistent. Finally heaving a sigh, Rachel stood to walk to the window and peer out through a slit in the blinds. She saw Lucas standing on the porch.

His hair was disheveled as if he'd been running his fingers through it. His lightweight jacket was unzipped, pulled open by the hands that rested on his hips. His head was lowered.

She rushed into the foyer and opened the door. "I didn't think you were coming."

"I was here a lot earlier—" the gray eyes were shadowed with concern "—but you were out...with Jared."

Her eyes grazed his face anxiously. "He dropped by unexpectedly." Lucas said nothing. "He...uh...he wanted to talk privately to me about the children," she stammered. "He...uh... We thought it best to... We only went to Jim's Coffee Shop."

Lucas didn't care where they'd been; he only cared that she'd been with Jared at all, no matter what the reason. "Why did you go out with him when you knew I was coming?"

He was tormented by an emotion that was totally foreign to him, one he didn't understand. He was jealous...jealous of Jared March. Because jealously was so unfamiliar to Lucas, he didn't know how to handle it. He knew he didn't like it. He was a man who was always in charge and didn't like losing control of his own emotions.

Haunted by thoughts of Rachel with Jared, Lucas wanted to pull her into his arms and to make love to her. But he didn't. That wasn't his way. He wanted Rachel to come to him because she loved him, not because she was caught up in a web of desire, not because of emotional blackmail. Lucas was a farsighted man. He had learned

long ago that passion wore thin; love was enduring, and
he wanted love.

"I didn't know if you'd get through with the meeting
in time to come or not," Rachel said. "But in case you
did, I told Jae to have you wait for me. She knew we
were coming right back." When she saw the surprised
look on his countenance, she said, "Jae did tell you,
didn't she?"

Not wanting to implicate Jae in a lie and further
alienate her, he shrugged and smiled warily. "I guess I
was so jealous, I really wasn't listening to what she said.
I only heard what I wanted to hear. That you were with
Jared."

"Not as a woman," Rachel confessed. "Only as an
ex-wife interested in the welfare of her children. Come
in," she invited. "I wanted to talk to you."

Lucas closed and locked the door, then followed her
into the living room. She sat on the sofa, he in the opposite chair. Because of her love for Lucas and for what
they had shared together, Rachel told him that Jared
professed to have changed and wanted a reconciliation.
Lucas listened, his face immobile and expressionless. He
was angry with Jared and suspected that he hadn't
changed anything but his tactics. He also knew that now
was not the proper time to press his own cause. Rachel
needed time and space to think. But something inside
compelled him to tell her what was in his heart.

"Damn him," Lucas whispered. "I hate him for
doing this to you, Rachel." He moved to sit beside her
on the sofa and took her hands into his. "I love you,"
he said, the gray eyes staring steadily into hers, "and I
want to marry you."

"Oh, Lucas!" Rachel cried, her emotions flickering
across her face for him to read: surprise, amazement,

then sheer delight. Her heart overflowed with love. This was truly the happiest moment in her life.

"Do I presume the answer is yes?" he asked.

Rachel slowly shook her head. "If I had just myself to consider, Lucas, my answer would be so simple and so quick. But I have the children."

Remembering Jae's words, he said, "You're not thinking about going back to Jared, are you?"

"No."

Lucas stood and angrily paced the room, every once in a while rubbing his hand down the back of his head. "Damn it, Rachel! Why did he have to come back now and ruin Christmas for us?"

"Lucas, even though I don't love Jared and don't want to live with him, he'll always be a part of my life because he's my children's father. If you're going to be a part of my life too, you'll have to accept that."

"It's more easily said than done," he replied. "Are you going to see him again?"

She nodded. "He's in town for a business convention this week and has asked to spend his free time with the children."

"He really wanted to see you," Lucas exclaimed bitterly.

"Probably," she agreed, "but I wasn't going to be selfish and refuse his request. The children have a right to be with him."

"You're right," Lucas conceded tightly, then added, "I wanted to remind you that I'd be in Houston next week for the grand opening of my new stores."

Rachel nodded. "I remember."

"I'll call you every night. Rachel, I can't bear to leave, knowing that Jared is trying to persuade you to return to him."

"I love you, Lucas. Now believe in me."

Rachel freed her hands from his clasp and threw her arms around him. Holding him tightly, she pressed her cheek against his chest. His arms went around her, his hand moving in soothing circles on her back. He bent down and dropped sweet kisses on the top of her head.

Life hadn't been easy on Lucas Brand, and he'd had to make some grave decisions during the years. To leave Rachel tonight was by far the hardest one he'd ever made. He knew at this moment that to lose her would be to lose a part of himself. He was fighting for her love the only way he knew how: by giving her space, by allowing her to make up her own mind without emotional persuasion.

At the same time, Jared wasn't going to do the same. Without having met him, Lucas knew Jared's type. He'd dealt with people like Jared all his adult life. So in love with themselves that they couldn't love someone else. They had to possess a person body and soul. When they had drained it of life and vitality, they tired of it. When they no longer wanted the person, they didn't want anyone else to have them, either.

"I've got to go," Lucas said and Rachel pulled back to look at him with haunted eyes.

She lifted her hands to cradle his face. "I wish you didn't have to. I don't want you to," she whispered and guided his lips to hers.

With a low groan Lucas pulled her into his arms again, his lips claiming hers in a soft kiss that quickly deepened as passion in all its beautiful savagery raged through both of them. She opened her mouth for the fullness of his kiss. As his tongue gently greeted her lips, slipping into the velvety warmth of her mouth, Rachel moaned and pressed herself into his hard, rugged frame.

Her arms rounded his body; her fingers clutched his shoulders. Lucas finally lifted his mouth and held her in his arms.

"Good night," he whispered, hoping it was only good-night and not goodbye.

RACHEL AND JAE LAUGHED until they cried as Jared and Sammy battled each other in a video game of *Star Wars*. There was absolutely no competition. Sammy won hands down every time.

"Little boys must be better at this than grown-ups," Sammy consoled his father, taking time to twist his cap on his head so the bill was lowered over one ear. "Our hands fit on the controls better." He was quiet for a minute, then added, "But Lucas beats me sometimes."

"You sure do talk about Lucas a lot," Jared said stiffly. "He must spend a lot of time with you."

"Yeah," Sammy answered innocently, "he does. He likes *Star Trek*, too, Daddy. He rents the movies and he and Mama watch with us while they cook barbecue. We have a lot of fun with Lucas, don't we, Neal?"

"Mmm-hmm," Neal answered, never looking up from the science fantasy he was reading.

"Well, it's about time for me to be leaving. I have one last meeting to attend."

"Oh, Daddy," Jae cried, leaping to her feet and running across the room to him. "You don't have to leave so early, do you?"

"Got to." He dropped his arm about her shoulders but looked at Rachel. "Will you join me for a drink afterward?"

"No—" the telephone rang and Rachel stood "—I'm really too tired, Jared. I think I'll go to bed early tonight."

His eyes narrowed and the mouth thinned; otherwise he concealed his displeasure. "If you were to come home with me," he said, the blue eyes warm and persuasive, "you wouldn't have to work. We could be a family again, and you could stay home and take care of the children...like a mother ought to."

"We are a family, Jared," Rachel said, "and don't try to make me feel guilty because I'm a working mother." In the background she heard Neal answer the phone. "Just because a woman stays home every day doesn't make her a *good* mother. Good parents are those who work at being good and give their children prime time. I refuse to accept guilt, Jared. That's one of the yokes I threw off when you and I divorced."

"Mom, telephone. A Mrs. Halston in Kerrville."

Rachel moved into the kitchen, taking the receiver from Neal.

"Hello Rachel. This is Elaine Halston. I'm sorry to call so late in the afternoon, but I've been thinking about Lucas's counteroffer and wanted to talk to you about it."

"Just a minute, Elaine," Rachel said, "let me change phones. I'm not sure I want to compete with *Star Wars*." Returning the receiver to Neal, she said, "Hang this up as soon as I take the call in my office."

When Rachel answered on an extension, Elaine said, "I've really been thinking about this, Rachel, and it's one of the hardest decisions I've ever made in my life. In fact, Phillip is the one who helped me see what I must do. I want the money Kline can pay me, but I want Lucas to have the property."

"You can't have both, Elaine."

"My opinion exactly." Elaine paused a second, then said, "While Lucas can't pay me as much up front as

Kline Industries can, I'm willing to work something out with him. I've seen some of the commercial areas that Kline has developed and I don't want that for my ranch.''

"Thank you, Elaine," Rachel said. "I know Lucas is going to be thrilled. He really wants that land."

"I know," Elaine answered, "that's what made up my mind. I knew he would love the land like I did and would put it to good use. I'd like to get this settled as quickly as possible. When can you come over with the papers?''

"I'm not sure," Rachel answered. "Lucas is out of town. I'll call to set up an appointment as soon as I contact him."

"Fine," Elaine said.

Rachel was walking on clouds when she hung up the receiver. As she neared the den, she overheard Jared talking. She stopped to listen.

"It's up to you guys," he said. "You've got to convince your mother to come back home. Don't you want to come home, Sammy?''

Furious with Jared for using the children like that, Rachel stormed into the room.

"Not before Christmas," Sammy said. "I want to win that ten-speed bicycle."

"I'll buy you a bicycle. Ten of them if you want," Jared answered sharply. "You don't have to win one."

"It's not only the bicycle, Dad," Neal said quietly, laying his book aside to come to the defense of his little brother. "We enjoy working with Lucas. He's a lot of fun to be around, and we like doing things for people."

"Who is this Lucas?" Jared exploded. "He sounds like some sort of god, the way you talk about him."

Sammy turned to look at his father. His face was solemn, his eyes rounded. Almost reverently he said, "He's a cowboy, Daddy, who baby-sits with old people."

"He doesn't baby-sit old people," Neal said.

"Does, too. That's what Jae told me." Sammy shrugged. "Anyway, I'm going to be just like him when I grow up."

"Damn it!" Jared shouted and threw his hands into the air. "I'm sick to hell, hearing about this Lucas Brand. I wish to God you'd never met him. He's turning you against me." Dramatically he thumped his chest with his index finger and walked toward Sammy. "I'm your father. Don't you want to be like me?"

Thinking his father was yelling at him, Sammy dropped the controls to the television game and shrank into the corner. Large tears swam in his eyes.

"Don't shout at him like that, Jared!" Rachel planted herself between father and son. "You're scaring him. Now get out."

Two tears ran down Sammy's cheeks, and he caught his mother's hand. "Lucas doesn't shout at me when he gets mad," he sniffed.

"All of you go to your rooms," Rachel said with a calmness she was far from feeling. "I want to talk privately with your father before he leaves."

"Mom—" Jae caught Rachel's lower arm "—Daddy didn't mean to hurt Sammy. He just overreacted to what Sammy said. Please think about going home with Daddy. Remember how Lucas hurt your feelings last Saturday night. Remember all the times he's stood you up because of business or his charity functions. Can't you see Daddy's changed?"

"I see," Rachel answered dryly. She wouldn't say so to Jae, but Jared March hadn't changed at all. "Now go to your room, Jae."

"Please, Mom," Jae begged as she backed away down the hall.

Rachel hardened her heart to Jae's pleading. When the children were gone and the doors to their bedrooms shut, she turned to Jared. She didn't know a time when she'd been as angry as she was now. She was determined to make it clear to Jared once and for all that he was out of her life.

"Our divorce was the best thing that could have happened to me," she said, "and not one time during this past week have I considered our getting back together. I don't want to be married to you. I refuse to be married to a man who stoops to emotional blackmail with his own children."

"Rachel, I'm sorry," he apologized and moved to where she stood. Rachel backed away from him. She couldn't tolerate his touch. "Can't you see I'm jealous of you and this man? I can't stand the thought of his becoming a stepfather to my children."

Rachel believed Jared, but his pleading fell on deaf ears. He didn't love her; he had simply possessed her. Now he was jealous because she was no longer his possession. He was also jealous because she had learned to stand on her own two feet, because another man was interested in her. His ego was shattered, and he couldn't bear that.

"You weren't overly concerned about the children when you wanted the divorce, Jared. Why now? Well, I'll tell you why. You want to use them to manipulate me, and I don't intend to be manipulated."

"No, Rachel, you've got it all wrong. I want you to come home and be my wife. We'll be happy again...the perfect couple...just like we were."

How well Rachel remembered when they were the *perfect couple*...as if they had ever been! "If anything during these past two years, I've learned there is no such thing as the perfect couple, Jared, only a couple who loves...who loves unconditionally. The perfect couple goes with a playhouse. I had that once, I don't want it again. This time I want love and a real marriage. Not for you or anyone will I give up my independence, Jared. I love being free. I don't want you planning my life and treating me like I was a mannequin without thoughts and emotions."

"Tell me you're happy living in this cracker box that looks like every fourth house on this street," Jared said. "Tell me you like going to work every day at a real estate agency. Tell me you don't miss the affluent life I provided for you."

Ordinarily Rachel would have been reduced to tears after such an ordeal with Jared, but today she wasn't. Her fury had turned into resolve. She walked farther into the den to stand beside the recliner.

"I'm not ashamed of my home," she answered quietly, "that looks like every fifth house on this street. I love and am proud of it. I love my job at the agency, and I don't miss the affluent life that you afforded me. Success isn't the amount of money you make or possess, Jared. It's what you accomplish with your life. And I am doing something constructive with mine. Now get out and don't ever come back unless I issue you a personal invitation."

"You can't mean this." Jared was stunned at her outburst; never had he figured on this. He wilted in the face of her determination. "Haven't you thought about the children at all?"

"Constantly," she answered, smiling at his confusion. "They'll come to accept the wisdom of my decision. They wouldn't be happy living in a home where the parents don't love each other."

"You think you're really smart, standing there so cool and calm!" Jared shouted, a balled fist flying through the air. "Well, you're not. When I get through dragging your name through the mud and besmirching your reputation, Rachel March, these kids are going to hate you. They'll never want to have anything to do with you."

Rachel listened as Jared ranted and raved and cited the ways he could alienate the children from her. She didn't know if he was serious or just bluffing in a last and desperate effort to get his own way, but she didn't care. She had finally come to the conclusion that she was not going to allow him to control her by always threatening to take the children.

When he finally stopped for a breath of air, she calmly rubbed her hands over the back of the recliner. "There was a day when you could have frightened me, Jared, and possibly could have forced me to come back to you, but not now. No matter which one of us they should choose to live with, I have no fear of losing their love. Nothing you can do will separate them from me."

Rachel realized at that moment that she had matured. The frightened little girl who had married Jared March was no more; a woman now took her place.

"I'll tie you up in court with custodial modifications," he threatened.

"Please leave," Rachel said. "We've said all there is to say to each other."

"By the time I get through with you—" his first tactic having failed, Jared started another line of attack "—Lucas Brand won't have you."

Rachel laughed Jared's threat away. "Lucas loves me," she said. "Nothing you can say or do will change that." She walked to the phone. "Leave peacefully, Jared, or I'll call the police. Whichever you prefer."

"I'm leaving," Jared shouted, "but don't think this is over because it's not. I'm not finished by a long shot."

A door opened and Jae came darting down the hall. "Daddy," she cried, "don't go back to Dallas without me."

"Pack your clothes," he said.

"She can't go without my permission," Rachel said. "Furthermore, she has to withdraw from school."

"And you would deny it to get even with me," he taunted.

Rachel looked from Jared's smug face to Jae's.

"Please, Mom," she begged. "Let me go with him. I can withdraw from school tomorrow. It's just a few weeks until the semester ends. What's a few days?"

"All right," Rachel sighed, although her heart was breaking. If she didn't allow Jae to go, she could see a big rift developing between them, something Jared would like to see and would make every effort to widen into a chasm.

"What about the boys, Rachel?" Jared asked. "Maybe they'd rather spend their holidays with me, too? Shall we ask them or do you think you can stand to hear their answer?"

Emotionally pushed to the edge by Jared, Rachel called both boys. When they returned to the den, she said, "Your father wants to know if you'd like to spend Christmas with him."

Neither boy answered immediately. Both looked at their father, then their mother, and finally at the floor. Sammy kept readjusting his hat on his head. Finally he lifted his head and said, "Don't reckon I can go to Dallas for Christmas, Daddy. Dugan's counting on me to help him with the food we're gonna give out to poor people. Besides—" he inched closer to Rachel and slipped his hand into hers "—I want to stay with Mama and our Christmas tree. She'll be lonely if I don't."

"What about you, Neal?"

"I like it here, Dad," he answered. "I want to stay with Mom."

"All right. That's that," Jared said quietly, almost ominously. He turned to Jae. "I'll be by tomorrow afternoon at three to pick you up. Be ready."

Long after Jared had gone, the house was dark, and the children were asleep, Rachel lay in bed thinking. Her heart was heavier than it had been since the divorce. She couldn't imagine life without Jae. Yet she wouldn't force her to remain in San Antonio; she couldn't alienate her daughter like that.

She turned over and saw the luminous dial of the digital. Eleven o'clock. She sat up and switched on the lamp. Picking up the receiver, she dialed. "This is the Brand residence," the answering machine announced, and she hung up the phone but didn't immediately lie down again.

It was just as Jae had said. Lucas was always gone when she needed him.

EARLY THE NEXT MORNING Rachel called Craig to let him know that she wouldn't be coming in to work. She was withdrawing Jae from school, so she could return to

Dallas to live with her father. As soon as the boys were off, she made a second call.

"Brand residence. Molly MacAdams speaking."

"Hello, this is Rachel. Is Lucas home?"

"Nope," Molly answered. "He's still in Houston. Don't rightly know when to expect him. Can I take a message?"

Wanting to tell him herself about her decision not to return to Jared and about Elaine's wanting to accept his offer on the land, she said, "No message. Just tell him I called."

"I'll tell him, Rachel," the housekeeper promised.

Rachel returned the receiver to the cradle and picked up her briefcase to shuffle through some papers. "Let's go, Jae," she called.

Jae poked her head around the door frame. "Mom, I've been doing some thinking."

Rachel's heart turned somersaults. Perhaps Jae had reconsidered her decision to go with Jared.

"I want you to know that I'm not going to live with Daddy because I don't love you."

Rachel's heart sank again. Dropping the papers into the case, she turned and caught Jae in a tight embrace. "I know you love me," she whispered. "I've never doubted that for a minute."

"I just love Daddy, too," Jae cried. "I want to be with both of you."

"That's not possible."

"It is—" Jae lifted a tear-stained face "—if you'd go back to Daddy. We could be happy again, Mom. Just like Daddy said, we could be a family."

"Things wouldn't be the same, Jae. They never are when you go back. I know the divorce is hard on you, and I wish it were different. Really I do."

"Then make it different," Jae pleaded. "It's all in your hands, Mama."

Rachel guided Jae to the bed, where they sat down. She grieved for Jae and wished she could make things easier for her. The divorce had been hard on all of them. But she wouldn't allow herself to be coerced into going back to Jared.

"My marriage to your father is over."

"Do you love me?" Jae asked.

"More than life," Rachel returned.

"Yet you won't go back to Daddy for me?"

"No, Jae, I won't be manipulated by love into doing something that won't be good for me. If it's not good for me, it won't be good for you or the boys." She stroked Jae's hair out of her face. "I know you love me. You don't have to prove it to me. I love you, but I'm not going to prove it by returning to your father."

"Daddy said you were selfish." Jae pulled out of her mother's arms and reached for a tissue.

"I wouldn't call it selfishness," Rachel replied, refusing to let Jae anger her. "I call it self-interest and self-love, both of which are virtues. If I am interested in my own welfare, I can be interested in others'. Only if I love myself can I love others."

Jae walked to the mirror and delicately blotted her eyes so as not to smear her makeup. "You're in love with Lucas?"

"Yes," Rachel answered, "I love Lucas."

"You're going to marry him?"

"We're talking about it."

Jae spun around and leaned back against the dresser. "That's why you won't go back to Daddy?"

Rachel stood and straightened her yellow blazer. "No," she replied, "I wouldn't go back to your daddy whether or not I loved Lucas. I simply don't want your father in my life." She smiled. "We'd better get going."

"Mom—" The green eyes flooded with tears again.

They moved simultaneously into each other's arms. "It's okay," Rachel consoled her daughter. "I understand." At the same time her own heart broke into a million pieces. Turning loose those whom you love was no easy task.

EARLY SATURDAY MORNING, Rachel drove the boys to New Braunfels and returned to San Antonio to work. Dugan promised that he and Molly would bring the boys home that evening. Rachel protested, but Dugan explained they were coming in to town to do some Christmas shopping, anyway. Rachel agreed to meet them at North Star Mall at six that evening.

As soon as Rachel and the boys completed their shopping and returned home, Rachel checked her answering machine but had no messages from Lucas. Every time the phone rang, she jumped up and ran. Still Lucas didn't call.

After dinner, she helped each of the boys wrap their gifts. Then they set them beneath the tree; the pile was growing by the day. Eventually the three of them migrated into the den and watched an adventure movie. Later they spread out on the floor and played a board game.

When the phone rang, Rachel was tempted not to answer. It was her turn, and she knew she would win the game. But the idea that she might miss a call from Lucas prompted her to forfeit the game point. Jumping to her feet, she raced across the room and lifted the receiver—to hear his deep voice at last. It settled warmly over Rachel.

"Lucas," she murmured.

"Lucas," Sammy mimicked in the background; then he and Neal giggled.

"Mrs. Molly said you called but didn't leave a message."

Rachel heard his anxiety and rushed to say, "I did. I called to tell you that I'm not going back to Jared."

"Rachel, I love you," Lucas said gently. "I only wish I were there to show you just how much."

"I wish you were, too," Rachel replied, unconsciously turning her back so the boys couldn't hear her.

"I'm coming in tomorrow afternoon at three," he told her. "Will you be able to pick me up at the airport?"

"Yes." Her heart was beating so fast that Rachel was breathless. She couldn't remember when she'd been so excited and happy before.

"And Rachel . . . will it be possible for you to get a baby-sitter for the boys, so we can have the evening to ourselves?"

"What about the Christmas Elves?" she asked.

"I think Dugan and Molly can handle it for one evening, don't you?"

"Yes," Rachel agreed.

"I have something special planned for us."

"Oh, Lucas."

Lucas laughed. "You're certainly talkative tonight. Is there anything else you want to tell me, or are you going to save it for tomorrow?"

Rachel thought about Jae, but decided she didn't want to discuss it in front of the boys. That would keep until tomorrow. "Elaine Halston called me."

When she said no more, Lucas said, "Well?"

Rachel laughed softly. "She's ready to go to contract with you and wants to do it as soon as possible."

"Me too," Lucas said. "Call her up and make an appointment for one day next week. I'm free, so it's at your convenience. As far as I'm concerned, the sooner the better."

They talked a little longer about the property, then Rachel asked, "Lucas, has Mandy's cousin decided?"

Lucas sighed. "It's evident he's not going to give me custody voluntarily. I'm going to have to take it to court. That's why I haven't returned your call any sooner. I've been in Woodville, talking with them, trying to persuade them."

Through the phone Rachel heard a masculine voice in the background. "Lucas, I want you to look this bid over. I can't get these figures to jibe, and we're gonna need them for the investors."

"Look, honey," Lucas said, "I've got to go. I have some work to do before my morning meeting."

"I can hardly wait for you to come home," she whispered, then asked with childlike anticipation, "What do you have planned for us, Lucas?"

He laughed. "If I tell you, it won't be a surprise. I'll see you tomorrow, darling."

Never had an endearment sounded so rich and warm. "Tomorrow, darling."

Chapter Thirteen

Riverwalk was costumed for Christmas. Millions of tiny lights twinkled in the huge cypress trees that lined the banks. Christmas music floated through the air: carolers stood atop one of the stone bridges singing. Farther down at the Arneson River Theater the Mexican Folk Dancers were presenting a Christmas pageant. The cafés and shops were full to overflowing. Throngs of people—locals as well as tourists—plodded up and down on either side of the river. San Antonio was in the midst of one of its most festive seasons—Christmas on the river.

Lucas sat across from Rachel at a small sidewalk café. "I'm sorry," he said. "I know it must have hurt you when Jae decided to go live with her father."

"It hurt," Rachel agreed, "but I think we'll have a much better relationship in the long run. If she's around Jared long enough, she's going to discover for herself what kind of person he is."

Lucas smiled. "I have a feeling that she's going to be coming home fairly quick."

"I hope so," Rachel said, a catch in her voice.

"One glass of wine and one margarita," a young waitress announced, setting the drinks on the table. "Anything else?"

"Not right now." Lucas laid several bills on the tray.

Rachel picked up her glass and sipped her wine. When the waitress left, she said, "I'm sorry I missed the Riverwalk last Christmas, but I'm glad I'm seeing it for the first time with you, Lucas. It's truly one of the most beautiful sights I've ever seen."

"I told you it was."

"Isn't it amazing that a river this small could leave such a mark on Texas history?" she asked.

"Yes," he replied and reached across the small table to clasp Rachel's left hand. Those sensuous lips lifted into a wondrous smile. "But no matter how beautiful the Riverwalk is, you're what I came home to see, and I would love to have my mark on you."

Rachel tingled with excitement. "Getting rather primeval, are we not?"

"I think I am," he returned, his voice low and serious. "I knew I loved you, Rachel, but I didn't know how much until that night Jared came to see you. The thought of your preferring him to me . . . of your going back to him drove me out of my mind. I'll admit that was one of the few times in my life when I wanted to become downright primitive." He tightened the clasp of his hand on hers. "I was ready to fight for you, darling, whether you wanted me to or not."

"But you didn't."

"No, I didn't because in the long run that wouldn't have been good for you. I wanted you to come to me of your own free will, no strings attached. I wanted to know that you love me as much as I love you."

"I do love you," Rachel murmured, "but I know of no way to measure if it's as great as yours."

"Rachel, will you marry me?"

She wasn't surprised by the proposal. She had known it was coming, but she was surprised to hear herself say, "I want to marry you, Lucas."

"That's not quite the answer I'd hoped for." He looked at her curiously. "Nor the enthusiasm."

"I can't agree to marry you without our talking first," she replied. "I've been doing some serious thinking since Jared left."

Lucas's eyes narrowed. "What has Jared got to do with your decision to marry me?"

Rachel ran her fingertip around the base of the wine-glass. "Everything. Our confrontation forced me to come face-to-face with myself, Lucas." She raised her head and looked directly into his eyes. "I was able to tell myself exactly what I wanted and expected from life. Jae told me that Jared said I was selfish. Perhaps I am, but I spent seventeen years of my life being emotionally abused by another person and I don't intend to ever do that again."

"Rachel!" Lucas was shocked. "How can you accuse me of wanting that?"

"I'm not." Rachel held her hand up for silence. "Just give me time to explain. I'm not going to relinquish my newly found freedom for anyone. Nor am I going to settle for less than a total commitment of love and time from the man whom I marry the second time."

Lucas leaned back in the small chair. Rachel could tell just by looking at him that he was angry. His face was hard, even implacable, the eyes were pure flint. His voice was dangerously soft. "Get to the point."

"I understand your love of charity work, and I commend you wholeheartedly for it. But I don't want to be sandwiched in between work and charity. I want a man who is totally committed to me—Rachel. I want to come first."

Lucas breathed in deeply and took several swallows of his drink. He admired Rachel's independence and respected her for having matured and for having broken the emotional bonding to Jared, but he was irritated by her accusations. "I don't think you realize it, Rachel, but I've spent years working on these organizations and bringing them to where they are today. Right now I have sponsors all over the Southwest who are interested in establishing small children's ranches like ours."

"I know," Rachel said, not backing down. "I'm proud of you, Lucas. I know how much it means to you. But I still must come first."

"You *are* first," Lucas declared. "I wouldn't ask you to marry me if you weren't. Right now you're acting like a child," he accused. "Instead of being jealous of people, you're jealous of my work."

Stung by his accusation, Rachel didn't immediately answer, but sipped her wine. Setting the glass down, she said, "Jared accused me of being selfish, you of being childish and jealous. Probably I'm all three, but I call it self-interest. And when it comes to the bottom line, Lucas, I am the one who must look after myself."

"What do you want me to do?" he asked, then answered himself. "Drop them? Or maybe you're jealous of Mandy? Do you want me to drop my plans to adopt her, too?"

Rachel blanched. "Of course not," she snapped. "I love Mandy. I feel as if she's one of my own children. You're blowing this out of proportion, Lucas."

"*I* am?" he countered. "What about you?"

"I just want you to put things in proper perspective."

"Proper perspective or your perspective?"

Rachel sighed. "You could delegate the authority and spread the work load. That would give you more free time to spend with those whom you love."

"Rachel, when we get married you won't have to work," Lucas said. "You can travel with me. We'll be together and work together."

Rachel visibly started. That was exactly what Jared had suggested. "That sounds wonderful," she replied, "but I don't want anyone planning my life for me again, Lucas. I want to make the decision about whether I work or not. I want to choose where I work. I spent the majority of my life with a man who equated work with success and who had no time for me or our children. I won't do that a second time."

"Do you realize what you're asking of me, Rachel? You're asking me to prove my love to you by giving up the Lucky Brand Children's Ranch and the Lucky Brand Senior Citizens Apartments."

"No, I'm asking you to make time for me."

"When haven't I had time for you?" he countered.

"Jae's homecoming game. The night you promised to take us out to dinner." Rachel counted on her fingers. "The night you were going to decorate the Christmas tree with us."

"I only stood you up on one occasion," he said, catching her hand in his. "I came on the other two. I was just late, and my reasons were legitimate. I think maybe you're making a mountain out of a—"

"Don't say it!" Rachel couldn't bear to hear him accuse her with Jared's worn-out cliché.

Lucas grinned. "Maybe I've hit the nail on the head."

Rachel smiled grudgingly. "Please take me seriously, Lucas, because I am serious. You're first in my life, and I want to be first in yours."

"I promise you're first in my life," he said, lifting her fingers to his mouth and brushing kisses across the tips, "and always will be. And you're right. I do have my priorities mixed up."

"What are you going to do about it?"

After a lengthy silence, he said, "It'll be tough, Rachel, but I'll try to change. As you've suggested, I'll delegate more responsibility so I'll have more time for me and . . . my growing family."

"Thank you," Rachel murmured, "that's all I can ask."

"Shall we walk awhile?"

"Yes."

Hand in hand they strolled down the river. When they reached the bridge in front of the Palacio del Río, they stopped to listen to a group of high school carolers as they sang medieval Christmas carols.

"Neal's choir will be singing here tomorrow night," Rachel said.

"What time?" Lucas asked.

"Seven o'clock."

"May I join you?"

"I'd love it. Sammy's been fussing ever since he learned that he's got to come with me.

"How about my bringing Mandy with me? We'll pick you and the boys up at . . . say . . . five forty-five."

Lucas and Rachel wandered farther down the walk, up the stairs at the outdoor theater and into La Villita.

"Have you set up an appointment with Elaine?"

"In the morning at ten. Her place."

"Good."

"And this time we won't leave until she's signed the papers."

Lucas smiled. "I thought I'd take my plans with me and let her see them. I know she'll approve of what I'm going to do."

By now Lucas and Rachel were standing in front of a white frame structure, the Church of La Villita. Candlelight filtered through the windows, and soft organ music playing traditional Christmas carols wafted through the air. Lucas caught Rachel's hand and they walked up the steps into the sanctuary to sit in the back pew. When the service ended, the congregation filed out of the building. Rachel and Lucas remained where they were for just a moment. In the candlelight she was beautiful, almost ethereal, her hair a golden halo around her face.

"Rachel," Lucas murmured when the church was empty, "I love you."

"I love you," she whispered.

Hand in hand they walked out of the church and down the stairs. Lucas lowered his head and lightly kissed Rachel on the mouth. "I guess we'd better go. Dugan will have the boys home pretty soon."

Rachel nodded, and they returned to the Riverwalk. "Thank you for tonight, Lucas," she said, gazing at the trees. "I had no idea the river was this beautiful at Christmas. The lights look like millions of stars twinkling in the sky, don't they?"

"Mmm-hmm," Lucas said, content to look at her.

"Gosh, Lucas, with you here, it's not so bad when Mama has to work late."

"Thanks." Arms crossed over his chest, Lucas lounged in the opened door.

"This cowboy hat is great!" Sammy posed in front of the mirror in his bedroom, cocking his head from side to side. "Guess I'm gonna hafto get me some boots like you and Dugan wear."

"Wouldn't be a bad idea. What about going to Shepler's to do some shopping tomorrow?"

"Wow, do you mean it?" Sammy exclaimed, his blue eyes dancing with excitement.

"I sure do." Lucas looked over his shoulder at Neal who was strolling down the hall. "How about you? Are you in the market for cowboy boots?"

"I don't think so," Neal drawled. After he tied the white sash around his waist, he spread his arms and asked, "How do I look?"

Pushing through the doorway past Lucas, Sammy cast him a quick glance. "Silly. I don't like those choir uniforms."

"You look just fine, Neal," Lucas said.

"Looks silly." Sammy giggled.

"Lucas, when are we going?" Mandy's head poked around the corner of the den. "I'm getting tired."

"In just a minute. We have to wait for Rachel."

"Why don't we go on?" Neal suggested, looking at his wristwatch. "Mom can meet us down there."

"Yeah," Sammy chimed. "That's a great idea, Neal. Don't you think so, Lucas?"

"I'd like to wait for your mother," Lucas answered. "We'll have more fun if we all go together."

"We'll all be crowded in the car," Sammy grumbled. "And Mandy's gonna get her clothes all wrinkled. You wouldn't want that, would you, Lucas?"

In the den by now, Lucas smiled at the little girl who sat in the large platform rocker. Instead of jeans and T-shirt, she wore a beautiful blue cotton dress with white tennis shoes and blue socks.

"We're just about ready." The phone rang, and being the closest to it, he answered. "March residence. Yes, this is Lucas." He listened for a long time, then said, "Of course, I'll come. What time do you want me to meet you?" When he hung up, he said to Neal, "Go next door and see if you can stay with Cindy until your mother gets home."

"Why?" Sammy demanded.

"I have to leave on some business."

"What about Neal's concert?" demanded Sammy.

"Tell your mother I'll meet her at the concert. I have something I must do first."

Sammy peered at Lucas from beneath the broad brim of the hat. "Are you going to baby-sit with those old people again, Lucas?"

"No, it's something more important than that," he said. "I'll tell you all about it later."

"What about me?" Mandy said.

"You come with me," he said.

About twenty minutes later, Rachel walked into the house, setting her briefcase on the hall table. "Anybody home?" she called. When no one answered, she walked into the kitchen, switched on the light and checked the bulletin board. She read Neal's scribbled note:

We're next door with Cody and Ethan.

Not long after Rachel had called to let Cindy know she was home, she heard the door to the utility room open, and both boys trekked into the kitchen in single file.

"Where's Lucas?" she asked.

"He got a telephone call and had to go somewhere important," Sammy said.

"He said for us to go on to the Riverwalk, Mom. He's going to join us later," Neal added.

"Where did he go?" Rachel repeated.

Neal shrugged. "Didn't say. Just said it was important."

Disappointed, Rachel walked into her bedroom and quickly changed from her blazer and skirt into slacks and sweater. Around her neck she tied a brightly colored silk scarf. She wondered if this would be the pattern of her life if she married Lucas. Would he always be running away to important business meetings?

Picking up the phone, she dialed. When Cindy answered, she said, "How would you and the boys like to go to Neal's concert with me?"

"What about you and Lucas?"

"He had a business meeting. I don't know what time he'll be joining us." *I don't know that he is joining us.*

"Sure," Cindy replied. "We'd love to go."

An hour later Rachel and Cindy were strolling down the river. The three boys raced ahead. Rachel was so disappointed that she could hardly enjoy the Christmas festivities. She wondered if a needy person or charitable organization would always come between Lucas and herself.

Bundled up against the brisk night, she and Cindy finally came to the arched bridge where the Middle School Choir was performing its annual Christmas on the River show. Sammy and Cody played nearby. As the choir sang, Rachel gazed up at the heavens.

"Star light, star bright," she whispered. "First star I see tonight. I wish I may, I wish I might—" *have Lucas here with me tonight.*

A hand closed over each of her shoulders and she heard a husky, masculine voice inquire, "Stargazing again?"

"Lucas." She turned into his arms. "You did make it."

"I did."

She laid her face against his chest and hugged him tightly, blinking back the tears of joy. "I'm so glad you came. I didn't think you would. I couldn't think what could have been more important than me."

"Only this," he said and gently pushed her away.

Looking beyond him, she saw Cheryl, Jae and Mandy, standing there grinning at her. "Oh, Lucas," she cried, "why didn't you tell the boys?"

"I knew Jae was here," Sammy announced proudly. "I was going to tell you, but Lucas shook his head, and I didn't."

"I wanted to surprise you," Jae said softly, running to her mother's outstretched arms. "I asked him not to let you know."

"What happened?" Rachel asked. "What are you doing here?"

"I want to come home, Mom," she said. "I don't want to live with Daddy."

Rachel walked Jae away from the others to a quiet spot. Sammy would have followed, but Lucas caught his hand. "How about an ice cream?"

"Cookies and cream," Sammy yelled.

"Cookies and cream," Cody seconded.

When they were alone, Rachel said, "We're not going to play this game, Jae. You're not going to run back and forth just because you get angry at one or the other of us."

"I don't blame you if you don't let me stay," Jae said, "but you were right, Mama. Daddy hasn't changed. When we got home, I found out that he's been dating a whole bunch of women. The one he's going with now is Bea Taylor, a model."

"And you're jealous of this woman?" Rachel asked softly. That Jared was dating didn't surprise her; in fact, she would have been more surprised if he had not been seeing anyone. But she grieved for Jae.

"A little," Jae confessed, "but not nearly as much as I was of Lucas. I thought Lucas was going to push me out, but I realized I care more about you, Mama, than I do about Daddy."

Rachel pulled Jae into her arms and hugged her tightly. "No one can take your place in my heart. You're my daughter, my only daughter."

"Bea hates me, Mama. When I found out she and Daddy were going to Europe for Christmas and were planning on leaving me at Grandmother's, we had an argument."

Rachel had never disliked Jared more than she did at that moment. She despised him for mistreating Jae. His only reason for wanting her was to get back at Rachel.

"She called me a brat," Jae continued, "and told me I wasn't going to keep her from having a good time. Then she locked me in my room."

"Jared allowed her to lock you in your room?" Rachel exclaimed. *How dare he allow a strange woman to mistreat Jae!*

"He didn't know until later, Mama, but she lied to him and he believed her. He wouldn't even listen to my side of the story."

While Rachel was upset by Jared's behavior, she was grateful that Jae was seeing her father's true nature herself. "Did he send you home?"

"No, he doesn't even know I'm gone. I told him I was spending the night with a friend. You remember Nan Griffin?" When Rachel nodded, Jae continued, "I had her drop me off at the airport."

"You shouldn't have left without telling your father," Rachel said.

"I was afraid he wouldn't let me come home." Jae's eyes sparkled with tears. "Please don't send me back, Mama."

"I'm not about to," Rachel promised me. "I never wanted you to leave in the first place, but we do have to call and let him know you're okay. He loves you and will be worried."

"Maybe," Jae mumbled.

"For all his faults," Rachel said, giving Jared his due, "he does love you. Now, I think we'd better join the others."

"Mom—" Neal came running "—what did you think of my choir?"

"You were wonderful," Rachel replied.

"Jae!" Neal's face broke into a smile. "What are you doing here? I thought you were in Dallas with Daddy. Did you get here in time to hear us sing?"

Jae nodded her head and laughed. "I came home, and I heard you sing." She mussed his hair with her hand. "You were great."

"Thanks," he said and looked around. "Where are the others? Did Lucas come?"

"He came," Rachel answered. "He's the one who went to the airport to pick up Jae."

"Where is he?"

"At the ice-cream parlor."

"Well, come on." Neal laughed. "Let's go get us one."

Three abreast, Rachel, Jae and Neal walked up the river to the second-story ice-cream parlor, where they joined the others.

"What do you want?" Lucas asked, his gray eyes resting on Rachel.

I have what I want. "Vanilla."

"Plain old vanilla?" Lucas asked softly.

"Just plain old vanilla."

"Strawberry for me," Jae said.

"Caramel turtle fudge for me," Neal added.

"Neal, your choir did a good job," Lucas said. "And your solo was excellent."

"You really think so?" Neal asked, his eyes shining.

"You sing okay," Sammy conceded, his chin covered in melted cookies and cream "but your pants look silly. Don't see why you can't wear your jeans."

"And you got a scarf on your waist." Cody giggled.

"It's not a scarf," Cheryl said, coming to Neal's rescue. "It's his sash and part of his uniform. I think it looks swell, Neal. I can hardly wait to see you in your elf costume."

"I'm gonna wear one, too," Sammy yelled. "Lucas, am I gonna get to wear a costume, too?"

"I think so," Lucas answered, reaching down to swing him, then Cody onto a stool. "Now settle down and finish your ice cream. See if you can get as much in your stomach as you're getting on your clothes."

"Rachel," Cheryl said, "why don't you let the children ride back to New Braunfels with me and Mandy tonight? We have plenty of room."

"Yeah, Mom," Sammy exclaimed.

When Rachel turned to Jae, she said, "I'd like to, Mom."

"And it's time for me and the boys to be going," Cindy said, a twinkle in her eyes. "How about giving me the keys to your car, and I'll drive it home."

Soon only Rachel and Lucas were left. He guided her down the Riverwalk, and they boarded one of the boats, where a group of carolers in the stern was singing. Cuddled together, they listened to the Christmas carols and gazed at the wonder of the river. For the first time since her divorce Rachel felt the warm glow of Christmas spirit.

His mouth close to her ear, Lucas said, "Tomorrow we'll go shopping for your engagement ring. I'll give it to you Christmas Eve when you're standing underneath the mistletoe." He took her into his arms and sealed his promise with a kiss.

Above them the stars twinkled brightly.

Epilogue

"Golly, Lucas," Sammy shouted, opening the door and jumping out of the pickup, "this is the first time we've ever had a real Christmas tree."

"No, it isn't." Neal leaped from the bed of the truck, zipping up his jacket and tugging his cap a little lower over his face as a cold gust of wind whipped around him. "Remember last year?"

"Yeah, but that one doesn't count, 'cause Mama bought it. We cut this one down ourselves, Neal."

Lucas lowered the tailgate. "Okay, fellows, let's get it to the garage."

Heavy gloves on his hands, Neal reached down and caught the cedar tree by its trunk and heaved it up.

"Let me carry it," Sammy shouted, jumping up and down, but Neal didn't stop walking. "Make him let me, Lucas."

"Tell you what," Lucas suggested, turning his jacket collar up against the bitter north wind and following Neal, "let's figure out how we're going to build a stand for a tree this big."

"That's right," Sammy exclaimed. "I know where Dugan put the nails when he used them last week."

"Go get them," Lucas said, "and I'll rustle us up something warm to drink. How about you guys? Would you like a cup of hot chocolate?"

"You bet," Neal replied, and Sammy echoed.

"To the kitchen then," Lucas said, opening the back door. "We'll fix the tree stand later."

"Make mine real creamy, Lucas, and put lots of marshmallow on top. Okay?" Sammy stripped off his jacket and cap and hung them on the rack in the utility room. Then he darted into the den to turn on the television set. "When's Mama gonna be home?" he yelled, kicking off his shoes.

"She ought to be here any minute," Lucas answered as he opened the cabinet and set three mugs on the counter. Glancing over his shoulder at the clock, he added, "It's already three-thirty."

"Don't count on it." Neal slid onto a stool in front of the breakfast counter. He grimaced and said dryly, "You know how women are when they get to shopping. They forget all about time."

"I think we can forgive them this time," Lucas said with a grin and a wink at his stepson. "After all, they're buying our Christmas gifts."

Sammy came barreling into the kitchen, sliding to a halt on the tiled floor. His blue eyes big with excitement, he said, "Mama won't guess in a million years that I bought her a sweat suit, will she, Lucas?"

"She will if you don't hush," Neal said sharply. "They just pulled into the driveway."

Giggling, Sammy clamped his hand over his mouth and rolled his eyes. Then he headed toward the den. Lucas reached for more mugs. Filling the kettle with milk, he set it on the stove.

Minutes later, the back door opened and Rachel called out, "Oh, Lucas, the tree is lovely!" All bundled up against the cold, her arms were laden with packages. "What fun we're going to have decorating it."

Lucas moved toward her. "Here, let me help you."

Grinning, Rachel turned away from him and moved to the bedroom. "No way you're going to see your presents before Christmas Day, Mr. Brand."

Skipping in after Rachel, her arms also full, Mandy giggled. "Guess she told you, Lucas."

Neal grinned. "Lucas, I'll bet when you asked Mama to marry you, you never thought what life would be like living with four women, did you?"

"Well," Lucas drawled, measuring the cocoa mix into the mugs, "they may outnumber us, Neal, but we'll just have to outdo them."

"Unlikely," Cheryl yelled from the garage.

"Are you women ganging up on me?" Lucas teased.

Her packages put away, Rachel returned to the kitchen. She had taken off her coat and was wearing a blue sweater and navy slacks. "Not if that's hot chocolate you're making."

"Mmm," Cheryl said, sniffing the air as she walked into the den. "Fix me a big mug of it, Daddy, with lots of marshmallow. Neal, come on in here. Mandy and I bought a new video game. Thought we'd try it out before we challenged Sammy, the Video Whiz Kid."

"Wow!" Neal slid off the stool and joined the others in the family room. "Which one?"

"Where's Jae?" Lucas asked.

"She'll be here in a minute," Rachel answered. "She and Molly are doing some last-minute work at the barn."

"She's turned out to be one of the best workshop directors the Christmas Elf program has ever had," Lucas said.

"She's enjoyed it. She's grown up so much in the past year, Lucas."

He nodded and leaned down to kiss her softly on the mouth. "Tell me, Mrs. Brand," he said, taking her fully into his arms, "how did your day go?"

"Lovely." She straightened his collar, then laid her palms against his chest. "We have all the shopping done, and tonight, you and I and all the little Brand Elves will help deliver the last of our Christmas boxes to the needy."

"And tomorrow night we celebrate our first Christmas Eve as a family," Lucas said, then added, "Well, not quite. Mandy's adoption isn't final yet."

"With or without the papers she's a part of our family."

"I agree," Lucas said, "and I'm glad you do."

"I was later getting back than I anticipated, or did you notice?" she said.

"Thirty-five minutes and six seconds, to be exact," Lucas said.

"I stopped by the office to talk with Craig."

"And?" Lucas asked softly.

"I gave him a four-week notice. My last day is January 15."

"Are you sure this is what you want?" Lucas asked.

Rachel grinned. "Are you having second thoughts about my staying home?"

"No, and I don't want you to."

"When I was married to Jared," she confessed, "I was caught up in charity works and organizations because it was expected of me. Now I'm caught up in them because it's an integral part of your life, a part that I want to share with you."

"Oh, Rachel." Lucas embraced her tightly, laying his cheek on the top of her head. "I didn't think it was possible to care for you any more than I already do, but every day I find that I love you more and more."

"So do I, my darling," she murmured.

Just as his lips touched hers in a sweet, warm kiss, Cheryl called from the den, "Hey, somebody, how about the hot chocolate!" Giggling followed the call.

Lucas and Rachel laughed, and Rachel gently pushed out of his arms to lift the kettle from the burner. As she poured the warmed milk, Lucas opened a bag of miniature marshmallows and dropped them into the steaming chocolate. When she set the mugs on the tray, Lucas caught her left hand in his and rubbed her wedding band with his thumb.

"Merry Christmas, Mrs. Brand."

"And a very Happy New Year, Mr. Brand."

Harlequin American Romance

If you can't decide what to make for that all-important Christmas dinner, we've got a solution. This month's American Romance authors have put together their favorite recipes. Toast the new year with a cup of *Mulled Cider*. Then serve the refreshing *Cranberry Citrus Salad*, along with old-fashioned American turkey with *Bread Stuffing*. Top this off with a seasonal *Snowball Delight* dessert.

Emma Merritt's Snowball Delight

This cool dessert is a favorite in the Merritt household on those balmy San Antonio Christmases.

    1 angel food cake, homemade or store-bought
    1 medium can drained, crushed pineapple
    ½ tsp. salt   1 cup boiling water
    1 cup sugar   3 packages Dream Whip
    1 tbsp. lemon juice   Shredded coconut
    2 packages unflavored gelatin   Maraschino cherries

Pull apart the angel food cake in pieces the size of half-dollars. Set aside. Mix the pineapple, salt, sugar and lemon juice in large bowl and refrigerate. Dissolve the gelatin in ¼ cup tap water. Add boiling water. Stir into pineapple mixture and return bowl to refrigerator. Mix *2* packages of Dream Whip and add to pineapple mixture. Return to refrigerator. Line 2 ½-quart bowls with wax paper. Layer pineapple mixture and cake pieces, beginning and ending with pineapple mixture. Refrigerate until firm. Invert onto a serving platter. Mix 1 package of Dream Whip and frost cake. Top with shredded coconut and maraschino cherries for color. Refrigerate until serving.

For the remaining three recipes, see the other December American Romances. Happy Holidays!

AR276-1

TEARS IN THE RAIN

STARRING
CHRISTOPHER CAVZENOVE AND
SHARON STONE

BASED ON A NOVEL BY
PAMELA WALLACE

PREMIERING IN NOVEMBER

TITR-1

Exclusively on
SHOWTIME®